Killing Me Softly

By

Kathryn R. Biel

Heather —
Happy Reading!

KILLING ME SOFTLY

ISBN-10: 0-9913917-8-0

ISBN-13: 978-0-9913917-8-3

Cover design by Becky Monson.

Cover image via depositphotos.com by sheftsoff.

DEDICATION

To Cahren:

I'm not sure how I managed to survive all those years
without the other half of my brain. But I'm sure you already
knew that.

CHAPTER ONE

The first person I ever killed was a has-been comedian. I didn't mean to kill him, of course. The tabloid websites said it was drugs and alcohol, but I knew the truth. It was all my fault. My friends and I had been out drinking, and I quoted a line from this guy's most popular movie. The movie was still relatively obscure, and I had to explain it. Someone asked, "Whatever happened to that guy?" and my answer was, "Oh, he's probably drinking himself to death right now."

Guess what? He was.

This sort of thing happens to me more often than I'd like to admit. I don't even know what to call it—psychic ability, premonitions, a sixth sense? It's not creepy, not really. Just enough to send a small chill up my spine. It never bothered me—until death got involved. Most of the time, it's pretty innocuous. Like someone from my past will pop into my head, and the next day I run into them. Or I think about a song that I haven't heard in years and then suddenly it comes on the radio. Nothing big, just coincidences. A lot of coincidences.

Until the day it started turning fatal.

Rob, my boyfriend of almost two years, doesn't believe me. When something happens and I tell him, "Oh, I had a dream about that," or "I was just thinking about this," he says I'm trying to be dramatic and seek attention. (which wouldn't really be such a big stretch, considering my family. We're the poster children for dysfunction). But I'm not like the rest of my family. I actually don't even tell many people about it because I don't want attention, certainly not for this. I want to be taken seriously. I teach high school American history. With kids these days being tougher and tougher, I need as much street cred as I can get. The last thing I need is for them to think I'm some kind of quack or whack job.

My best friend, Therese, knows all about it. She's one of the few people I can talk to about this topic. She doesn't judge me or think I'm weird. I think she thinks I can predict the future or something. Which would be cool, but it is not what I do. I think I'm just intuitive at times. Who knows?

Over the years, since the comedian episode, I think I've been "responsible" for at least four deaths. A couple celebrities, a distant relative, and a well-known local businessman. When I have the dreams or make the comments, I don't recognize them as premonitions. They're just random thoughts that pop into my brain and often fly out of my mouth without me even realizing what I'm saying. People are used to me doing that. It's only later, after the event, that I realize what happened. In each case, I made an unkind remark. It's not just a premonition—I say something mean and then someone's dead.

Some days I worry I'm obsessed with death. It would only make sense. I was born in the back of a hearse, next to a dead person. *True story.* Sometimes I wonder if there was some sort of cosmic energy transfer as a result of my odd entrance that has left me with a connection to the other world. Other than that, I feel like a relatively normal person until—WHAM—I have a clairvoyant episode. Then I start freaking out again. To deal with it, I've found that I have to compartmentalize the whole death-premonition thing. Otherwise, I'd probably go crazy.

So, when I'm sitting in the faculty lounge one day in mid-February, the week before winter recess, eating my lunch and not bothering anyone, the last thing I expect is to cause the death of a student. Looking back, I know I was responsible. I had to be. I didn't think so at the time, but there is no other logical explanation for the events that I unknowingly predicted. Not that my being responsible is logical either, but I don't know how else to rationalize it. I didn't have the student in class, but I knew the name. I'd taught his sister a few years before. So I'm sitting there, eating my ham sandwich and potato chips, flipping through the real estate listings, and Janet, the P.E. teacher, mentions something about the family. I'm not really paying attention at first. Then I realize who she's talking about. "Oh, the Austins? Yeah, I had Trinity a while back. She seemed lost. Those parents are a piece of work. I hear Tristan is no good. I'm due to have him next year."

"No, that family's no good at all. It's too bad, because he is actually pretty smart."

I circle a property that has potential. I won't even have time to drive by it until next week, so hopefully it will still be on the market. Rob's not ready to move in together, but I've been bitten by the real estate bug. Too many home improvement shows on HGTV. "He's probably too smart for his own good. But instead of making a better life for himself, he's probably gonna wind up getting himself killed one of these days doing something very stupid." The lunch period passes too quickly, as does the rest of the day.

The following day, Janet and I are back in the faculty room. Today, I'm looking at *People Magazine*. I don't know what it says about me that I find the classifieds more entertaining than the Kardashians. Too bad I read all the classifieds yesterday. Janet's reading a book. We're using our time to decompress today, rather than to talk about students whose lives are spiraling out of control.

The peaceful break ends quickly when Mrs. Peale, the secretary, comes racing into the faculty room. She's obviously upset. Mrs. Peale is about ninety years old and has been with the school since it opened. She knows everyone and everything. Personally, she terrifies me. It's like she can see right through you and can read your deepest, darkest thoughts.

"Mrs. Peale, what's wrong?" I stand up, and go over to her. I'm worried she might be having a stroke or something.

Mrs. Peale tries to spit out an answer or two but appears unable to form words. Janet, who has been at the school longer than I have and is on the verge of retirement, has no fear of Mrs. Peale. "Jesus Gwen. Spit it out. What's wrong?"

"Sadie, Janet, it's terrible. There ... there was an incident. An accident. Tristan Austin was just shot and killed by the police while he was trying to rob a convenience store. Why would he rob a store? What a stupid thing to do!"

I look at Janet, and she looks back at me. Her eyes are wide, as I'm sure mine are as well. "Didn't you say that yesterday?"

I'm unable to speak, so I just nod. Oh crap.

Janet goes back to Mrs. Peale, who has calmed herself down and pulled herself together. She's smoothing her white hair down, not that any of it could escape the hairspray helmet she wears. "Gwen, do you know what happened?"

"He was out today. I called the house, and of course, the dad answered. Like it would kill him to ever actually work for a living. But you know those Austins. No good. The whole lot of them. But I thought Tristan was different. I thought he was going to get out and make something of himself, if for no other reason than to prove his folks wrong. I guess he decided to boost the mini-mart over on Turnpike Road. The owner, Mr. Busmati, hit the silent alarm. The police were right down the street. I think Tristan had a gun and well ..." she breaks off, obviously too upset to continue.

My sandwich has turned to sawdust in my mouth. I do my best to swallow. The room is spinning, and my hands are shaking. I try to cover my downright visceral reaction.

"Poor kid. What are we going to do here?" I feel like I'm going to vomit.

"You know the policy. Carry on as best you can. Guidance is on alert. You can send anyone who is having a hard time to them. No early dismissals."

I would be sort of lucky, since I had juniors and seniors, who probably don't know Tristan. Rob taught senior and AP economics (snooze), so he probably isn't even really with the family either. Mrs. Peale goes on to spread the word to other teachers, and it's just Janet and me again.

Janet appears as shaken up as I feel. "I just get upset at the waste. I don't even know that he had much promise—Lord knows the family didn't, but he never even got the chance. He could have cured cancer. He could have made world peace. But now he's dead. And for what? What was worth stealing that it cost him his life?"

"I don't know, Janet. I wish I did. You know, some days, I feel like we make a difference with these kids. Other days, I feel like I'm banging my head against the wall. Maybe, just maybe, someone will learn a lesson from this and make a better decision. Maybe Tristan's death will save someone else."

"Maybe." Janet pauses and then gives me a strange look. "That was weird, you know that yesterday you said this would happen. Are you clairvoyant or something?"

"No." I'm defensive. Too defensive. I don't like anyone to notice. It makes it hard for me to squash down the unpleasant feeling of being responsible down and to ignore it.

Janet just can't leave it alone though. "It was like you knew what was going to happen."

"But I didn't. I couldn't have, could I?" I say defensively.

Janet's taken aback by the bite in my tone. "No, but it's too bad. Just think, Sadie, if you knew what was going to happen, you could have saved that poor boy."

CHAPTER TWO

The rest of the school day is interminably long. Janet's words weigh heavily on me. That if I knew, I could have prevented it. Wracking my brain, I try to figure out if there is any way I could have done that. Those thoughts ricochet and pound through my head and put me on edge. I'm sick to my stomach over the matter. There are tears and drama from the students, and I'm annoyed by it. I would not be annoyed if the tears were for Tristan or his parents, as sucky as they are. Those tears are well deserved. No, the tears and the drama are the normal high school stuff, amplified to maximum volume. Girls who you know never gave Tristan the time of day are weeping, saying how "deep" he was and how he was "misunderstood." I heard from more than one girl that she could have rehabilitated him and put him on the straight and narrow.

Blech.

I couldn't wait to get to the nursing home after school. I go almost every day to see my dad. He has been there for over three years now—actually almost four—and I hardly ever miss a weekday. I take the weekends off, generally, as that's when other family flock in there. I try to avoid them as much as possible. I'm the one who is there for my dad day in and day out. Today is no different and totally different all at the same time. My dad was the one person who I really, really talked to about the whole premonition, death prediction thing. He knew about it, before the stroke stole his ability to walk and talk. No one was sure of how much he even understood now. I didn't know either, but I always felt better just talking to him.

How I wish that one day, just once, he would answer me. I know it won't ever happen but a girl can wish, can't she?

Dad had the same sort of clairvoyance about things. Not about people dying, but about mentioning the obscure only to have it surface. I am the only one with the death connection, I think. Maybe it's because he never said mean things about people like I do. Nonetheless, I wish we could talk about it. He would understand how I feel about the whole Tristan situation. I just wish I could hear his voice, telling me that I'm overreacting about it. That's probably what I miss the most. His voice.

Dad was my ally in the family. He buffered me from my siblings, and then from Mom, who inevitably took their side against me. He balanced things out. Not totally even, but at least it wasn't me against everyone else. Like it is now. So every day, I go in and tell Dad about my day. I complain about Mom and Brady and Jenna. I tell him about Rob, and Therese's escapades with her three-year-old tyrant twins. I talk to him about news stories and goings on in the town. I check in with the nurses who report any changes to me, not that there ever are any.

"Dad," I say, flopping down in the blue Barcalounger next to his bed. "You would not believe what happened today. I'm getting really freaked out about it. No, check that. I'm already really freaked out about it. Janet, the PE teacher, mentioned a kid yesterday. I don't really—didn't really—know the kid, but I'd had his older sister a few years ago. I made an off-the-cuff comment about the kid getting himself killed, and today the school secretary comes in and tells us this kid was just shot by the police."

Dad, sitting up in his wheelchair, looks at me with that vacant stare that constitutes his predominant facial expression these days. My blue eyes are the same as his. I used to think that having the same feature connected us in some way. I can't tell if there is anything going on in his head. I choose to think there is. A little trail of drool runs out of the left corner of his mouth. His left side is totally paralyzed, although he doesn't move his right side much either. I've heard the word 'catatonic' batted around. Brady, my asshat brother, has referred to him as a vegetable. I wanted to punch him for that. I want to punch Brady a lot. He deserves a good ass kicking. Someday.

I wipe the corner of Dad's mouth and try not to let it bother me. Dad had always been larger than life. Boisterous and funny. His sense of humor was irreverent, and his laugh was infectious. Sort of a contradiction considering he was a funeral director. He could be very serious, but his humor usually surfaced and had a way of putting the bereaved at ease. The stroke stole that from him. From us. At least he's well cared for—the only thing about this situation that can be considered lucky. Dad had his stroke during a minor medical procedure. He has an abnormal clotting disorder, which means a filter needs to be used during any medical procedures. His doctor knew but didn't put the filter in. It was malpractice, clear and simple. So Dad was taken care of here in the nursing home, and Mom got to stay in her house. She was financially set while Dad could be looked after as well.

The money is part of the issue in our family. When is it not? When this first happened, Brady and Jenna hovered around Mom, flitting and floating, looking to gain her favor and hopefully her cash. I couldn't care less about money. I would give everything I own to have Dad back. Brady and Jenna, not so much. Although they know they have to wait for Dad to pass before any money is disbursed, they don't act much better now. Their behavior disgusts me and diminishes my already-low tolerance for them. Mom's caught in the middle, but for some reason, always seems to come out on their side. Especially Jenna's side. It's as if she can do no wrong in Mom's eyes.

"Dad, what if this kid's death is my fault? What if I thought it, and it came true? What if I could have—should have—done something to stop it? Can I channel this? Should I go to psychics or mediums or tarot card people and see if they can help? Are they all quacks? Am I a quack?"

Dad says nothing, of course.

Helga, a buxom nurse who represents her name well, bustles in, interrupting my plea for help. She has been at the nursing home for years and years and years. She's not my favorite nurse, but I know she takes good care of my dad, and that's all that matters.

"How're you doing today, Sadie?" Helga is not usually outgoing or friendly. I must look sufficiently distraught to garner kind words from her.

"Not great. One of our students died today. Hard day."

Helga shakes her head, muttering. "I heard about that. It's all over the news. Such a shame. What a waste. I'm so glad my son is grown up and past all that trouble. His biggest problem is finding time for all his work and finding someone to settle down with. I'm sure you know what he's going through."

Helga's looking at me with that expectant look. As a thirty-five-year-old single woman, I get that look a lot. These mothers want to set me up with their single sons. You know, the ones who can't hold down steady jobs and have set up permanent residence in their mothers' basements. They don't care what I want. I have Rob, anyway. I'm not in the market for anything—or anyone—new. I shift gears, stuffing all the bad feelings about Tristan down into a little box inside. It's better that way. For my sanity, at least. Onto another topic.

"Oh yeah, this is a hard time of year to be single. My boyfriend—we've been together almost two years—is taking me away for Valentine's weekend. I'm so glad I have him, and I don't have to try to find people to date anymore. I'd hate to still be out there."

"Well, you're lucky you found someone. I just hope he takes good care of you. You're good to your dad here. Most young people don't stick around like you do. I hope my son finds someone nurturing like you someday."

As she's turning to leave the room, I blurt out, "Well, if I suddenly find myself single, I'll let you know and you can introduce me to your son."

She looks over her shoulder and smiles. It's a rare occurrence and doesn't fit her face well. "Okay Sadie. I'll remember you said that."

When she exits, a chill runs over me. I have Rob, so I have nothing to be afraid of. Yet for some reason, I have a bad feeling about this.

CHAPTER THREE

"I really wish you could stop focusing on those kids and focus on me for once," I tease Therese.

Her voice, coming over the speaker of my car as I'm driving to the library, is dripping with sarcasm, as usual. "Oh sure. Let me just duct tape the kids to their chairs for a minute so I can address your crisis of the day."

"Who says I'm having a crisis? I just want your attention." I signal and wait to turn left. The dashboard clock tells me I have seven minutes before the tutoring session starts.

"Sadie, you can have my attention in fifteen years when these hellions move out."

"Deal. I'm holding you to that." Therese always makes me smile. It's probably why we've been friends since the second grade. We can talk three times a day or not talk for three months, and we pick right back up where we left off.

"Okay, they're playing with Play-Doh. You have about ninety seconds to talk. Go."

"Just coming from the nursing home. No change." I add in quickly, before she can ask. I know she's going to and I hate that she does. Because there's always no change and there never will be any change. "Just a rough day at school with that kid getting shot."

"Oh, that's right. Did you teach him?"

"No, I had the sister a few years ago. I would have had him next year. I guess he's the only one in the family who had any promise. Such a shame."

A roar erupts in the background, and I know my time is up. Therese shouts over the kids, "Gotta run. Call me after you go shopping tonight. I wanna know what you get for the weekend!" And with that the call ends, and my radio resumes blasting.

Today is a busy day. I want to just go home and curl up in bed and not think about what happened, but I can't. It's Thursday, which means I tutor. Seeing as how I'm unmarried and a teacher, I apparently have tons of free time. At least that's what people outside education, namely my mom and brother and sister, seem to think. I do get done with work early—two-thirty. On the other hand, I'm at work between six and six-thirty every morning. Not to mention the hours I put in after school and on weekends preparing and grading. When school lets out, I visit Dad. On Mondays, Wednesdays and Thursdays, I tutor from four-thirty on. I got suckered into tutoring because of all of my "free time." In reality, it's a cash cow and has helped tremendously. Fifty bucks an hour? Please and thank you.

Tonight I have to run to the mall after tutoring to get stuff for my weekend away with Rob. And when I say stuff, I mean sexy, romantic stuff. We're leaving tomorrow right after work, going to a romantic B&B for Valentine's weekend. I want to surprise him with something nice and risqué. Of course, finding the right things will be difficult considering I'm the one who will be wearing it. I'm average height, average build. I'm not fat by any means, but I'm soft. Yeah, that's a good way to describe it. I try to watch what I eat, but my schedule doesn't leave a lot of time for exercising. I try to do something active every weekend. Sometimes, being lazy just wins out, which doesn't always make me the best lingerie model.

I'm also terribly shy when it comes to this sort of thing. Like, I hate buying even regular bras and underwear.

God help me if I have to buy tampons and there's a male cashier. And condoms? Forget it. I have chosen not to have sex rather than to have to go to the store to buy them. Un uh, no way. Can't do it.

This weekend is different. It will be different. Rob and I have never been away together before, despite the length of our relationship. We've taken things slow, but at our ages, how slow can you really take them? After last fall, I think it's time that we move our relationship out of its holding pattern. Despite the fact that our classrooms are next to each other, we keep our relationship on the QT. Like, the waaaay QT. I'm not sure that even some of the faculty realize we're together. Since I go to the nursing home after school, and he moderates several clubs, we don't leave school with each other. Actually, I don't see him that much during the week. Tuesday nights, when I don't tutor, we usually try to hang out together. And weekends of course, when I'm not busy running inane errands for my mom. Rob doesn't really care for my family and makes every effort not to spend time with them.

I can't say I blame him.

It's not like our relationship is a secret—we just don't like to publicize it. The town is not that big, and with both of us being teachers, things could get messy. I feel like people are too up in my business as it is. I don't need them analyzing my romantic escapades. He's against PDAs of any sort, so even when we're on a date, we look more like friends than lovers. I kind of—not kind of—really hate that. Not that we need to be one of those gross couples or anything, but a little hand holding every now and again would be nice.

I finish up my last tutoring session at seven-thirty. Normally, if I'm going to go to the mall, especially on a mission like this, I'll go to the mall a few towns over. Less chance of running into people I know. Considering the time, I know that I need to go to the mall in town. They don't have a Victoria's Secret but I should be able to find something at the department store there. It is Valentine's Day after all. They should have something appropriately sexy. Something that will blow Rob out of the water.

Sliding into a front-row parking spot, I think the gods must be smiling on me for once. I can get in, get what I need, and get out. Making a beeline for the intimate apparel department, I am totally lost once I get there. I would love a corset and garters but realize that I would have absolutely no idea how to go about putting them on. And in all reality, Rob wouldn't know how to take them off. He has enough trouble with undoing my bra hooks. He's pretty clumsy in that department. Then I see it—the perfect thing. It's a red, sheer baby doll with a built-in push-up bra and G-string. I could certainly do without the butt floss, but I guess my sensible cotton granny panties might just spoil the look. I yank it off the rack and head into the dressing room.

Damn, I look good, if I do say so myself.

Even in the dressing room mirror, with that horrendous lighting, I look pretty hot. Well, except for my gray roots, that is. When did they grow back in? I just colored my hair. Oh wait, that was around Christmas. I guess I am due again. I look at my watch and hurry to get dressed. Now I have to stop by the Target to pick up a box of hair color. It's after eight and I still haven't eaten dinner. I left my house fourteen hours ago. At least I'll have this very sexy, very flattering negligee for the weekend. Rob is going to love it.

I pull my shirt back on and walk out of the dressing room, holding the hanger delicately, as to not harm the wisps of fabric that make up the garment. And standing right there is my boss—the high school principal. He's there with his wife. Maybe he won't see me. He looks up from his phone and right at me. He's seen me. There is no avoiding this. And even worse, his eyes dart from my face to my intended purchase.

"Hello Sadie."

"Oh, um, hi John." He's standing there, right by the cash register. In order to check out, I'm going to have to walk right by him and put the sex clothes up on the counter. I drop my hand to my side, hoping to camouflage the negligee. I know he's seen it. My face has got to be as red as the cloth. I do the only thing I can think of. I hang the hanger on the nearest rack and hightail it out of there.

I'm in my car before I can breathe again. Of all the people to run into—my principal! I pull into Target, just wishing I was home and in my jammies. But my gray hairs won't go away by themselves, so I head into the store.

CHAPTER FOUR

I cannot believe that just happened to me. I finally get up the cojones to buy something sexy, and then I run into my boss, of all people. That's the problem with small-town living. Oh sure, it's great most of the time. Well, some of the time. But there are definitely times when it sucks. Like right now.

I don't mind shopping at Target as much, because it gets traffic from several surrounding towns so the population is a bit diluted. I can almost guarantee I'll run into at least one person I know, but it won't be like everyone in the store knows who I am.

I grab a cart, since I am physically incapable of walking into the store and buying only one item. One time, I came in for cat food and left after spending $127. I like to blame the cat for costing me so much money, but I think it had something to do with the new shower curtain (and garbage bags, sports bras, tuna fish, cookies, pens, and a book) that came home with me that day. Anyway, I was here for hair color, but I might as well get some groceries. Oh, I need a card for Rob. I have his gift—a nice watch. I should get wrapping paper while I'm here. I need some more ibuprofen as well, and some deodorant. I wind up snaking back through the health and beauty aisles. I see the family planning stuff near the end of the aisle, but there's a greasy looking guy at the other end of the row. I go and get my deodorant and when I pass back, the aisle is empty.

Heading down the aisle, I glance out of the corner of my eye at the products. I'm walking more slowly than I normally would, but am certainly not stopping. I see what I'm looking for. It's one of those his and hers lubricant things that's supposed to spice things up when the two are mixed together. Without even pausing, my hand shoots out, grabs it off the shelf, and tosses it into the cart. I then reach down and re-arrange all the other crap in the cart so that my adult purchase isn't visible from any angle. I don't want people seeing it in my cart, whether I know them or not. My speed doesn't even decrease.

I grab the last few things and head toward the check out. The frozen pizza on top of my pile is calling my name, as it is now almost nine. I scan the checkouts, not for the shortest line, but for the one in which I know neither the cashier nor anyone waiting. I spot the perfect candidate. A disinterested looking woman of about twenty. She doesn't look familiar in any way, shape, or form. She didn't go to my school. I didn't have her in class. She's too young to have kids I would have in class anytime soon. The perfect cashier for me.

I unload the contents of my cart onto the conveyor belt. Such a random selection. Hair dye, wrapping paper, frozen pizza, sexual lubricant. That's smack in the middle of my stuff, so hopefully she won't even notice when she scans it. I try to distract her further by engaging in conversation, talking about how we haven't gotten any snow this winter. She's happy about that. As she picks up the lubricant box, I tell her that I'd be happy for at least a few snow days. She looks down at the item in her hand.

"Oh, I've been wanting to try this."

Seriously, this is not happening to me. "Um, okay."

"Is it any good?"

Oh. My. God. Is she really asking me about this product? "I don't know. I've never used it before."

"Oh, trying it out for Valentine's Day?"

Please, floor, open up and swallow me. "Yeah, I guess."

"You'll have to let me know if it's any good." She winks at me.

Like that's ever going to happen. I mumble something and swipe my card through the card reader. Why can't this day just end?

The cashier pulls the receipt off the register and looks at it. "Have a great night, Ms. Perkins. I know you're gonna be in for some fireworks!"

For the second time in just over an hour, I hightail it to my car and want to die. Apparently the universe it trying to send me a message that I'm not meant to do romantic things like this.

I manage to get home without any further mortification. I want to call Therese and tell her about this. She would probably piss herself laughing at me. Not that she's ever been really shy about this stuff, but after going through fertility treatments and giving birth with her mother and mother-in-law in the room, Therese has no shame about her girl parts. She proudly breast fed in public, whipping those puppies out whenever and wherever we happened to be. Now I know that's all-natural and it's perfectly normal, but I don't know if I would ever be able to do it. I'm just not that comfortable with my body.

Speaking of aspects of my body that I don't like, I have gray hair to cover. I got my first gray hair when I was seventeen. It was junior year, and I remember sitting in health class, playing with my hair, which was long and permed at the time, when I found that gray hair. All of my mom's family went gray prematurely. I wasn't that concerned about it. For me, going gray was something I inherited, like my dad's blue eyes. It had nothing to do with me getting older. I'm trying to ignore the fact that more and more of my hair is going gray, and I have to touch up my roots every five weeks now.

While the hair color is sitting, I put the pizza in the oven and pour a glass of wine. I only sip it, afraid it will go to my head since lunchtime was so long ago. I can't afford to get drunk before I get the hair color off.

I pull out my overnight bag and pack for the weekend. I'm sort of—okay, a lot—bummed that I didn't get lingerie for the weekend. I look in my drawer. There is a little teddy set that my ex-boyfriend gave me. I think about packing it but can't bring myself to do it. It would be too weird, and I could see Rob getting upset about something like that.

I'm hoping this weekend spices things up for us. We're sort of in a rut. I guess that happens. It's even more boring since everything last fall. That thing that we don't talk about. I like to think that we've moved past it. And now we're middle-aged people, and we've fallen into a comfortable pattern. Well, we're not yet middle aged; we just act like it. And I don't want comfortable. I want something exciting. At least I've got the special sauce. I toss that into the bag. I can't wait to tell Rob what happened in the store. And for the record, no, I will not be updating the clerk about the effectiveness of the lubricant.

On second thought, he probably won't appreciate my stories. He might be mad that John saw me with the lingerie. John is one of those people who Rob doesn't want to know about our relationship. We're both tenured, but Rob is afraid that it could make us look bad. It's not like it will change our promotions, since there are none. Whatever. He's not comfortable with it. Someday he will be, and I can wait. Right? It seems like I've spent my whole life waiting for one guy or another. It's what I do. This pattern was established a long time ago.

The first guy I ever waited for was Henry Fitzsimmons. Dark blond hair, light green eyes, and a kind heart. Of course, he was my brother Brady's best friend, so that made him the forbidden fruit. I fell in love with him when I was about nine. When I was eighteen, I made a complete ass out of myself in front of him, and then I never talked to him again. It took me a few more years to get him out of my system. Word in town is that he moved out of state. I'm sort of glad I never had to cross paths with him. I'm sure if I did, I'd be reduced to a bumbling teenager again. Thank goodness for small favors.

I rinse the dye out, and my hair is now its correct shade of medium brown. This is my natural color. I mean, it would be my natural color if I weren't now salt and pepper.

I'm trying to distract myself from thinking about the weekend and what it will mean for our relationship. I'm giving Rob a watch. What will he be giving me? It's time to take the next step. Maybe. I guess. If he's ready. I'm not sure if I'm afraid that he won't propose or that he will. Thinking about it gives me a stomachache, so I turn on the news to distract myself.

Well, that's no better, since the lead, and apparently only, story is about Tristan. I see his mother on the TV, clad in her hoodie and sweats, yelling about how her son was innocent and never did anything to anyone. I'm mad at her. Now, I know I'm not a parent, but I do spend enough time with kids to know that having a good parent makes all the difference. From everything I know about the family, she is not a good parent. She's making my anger at the senseless loss return, so I snap off the TV.

I should call my mom to remind her that I won't be around this weekend. I look at the clock. It's just after ten. Too late to call. And it's too late for me to still be up. Drying my hair quickly, I turn back my covers.

What an awful and hectic day today has been. Tomorrow, getting away with Rob, will certainly be better.

CHAPTER FIVE

"Oh hell, no—this cannot be happening!"

"What? Sadie, are you okay? What's wrong?"

Balancing my phone precariously between my ear and my shoulder, I angle in for a closer look. "I cannot believe this. It's a total disaster."

Therese tries to reassure me. "Whatever it is, we can figure it out. When is Rob picking you up?"

"Um, I have to leave in ten minutes. I'm meeting him at the B&B. I want to get there by five so I can get ready for dinner." Today has been just as hectic as yesterday. I've run home right after school, showered, and am now trying to complete all my necessary grooming. I'll swing by the nursing home to say a quick hello to Dad on my way out of town.

"Wait—he's not picking you up? What kind of romantic getaway weekend is this? But that's getting off the topic. What were we talking about?"

Leaning even closer to the mirror, I acknowledge the fact that my eyes are not deceiving me. There it is. As plain as, well, the eyebrows on my face. "Therese, this is serious. I'm tweezing my eyebrows and there's a gray hair!"

"Oh my God, that's terrible! That's, that's ..."

"I know. We're getting old."

"We? There is no 'we' here. You. You are getting old."

"Therese, you are only seven weeks younger than I am."

"But it is an important seven weeks."

"Okay, but we're getting off topic. Again." Conversations with Therese were often like this. We could be talking about three different topics all at the same time. Sometimes it works. Sometimes, like now, not so much. "What am I going to do?"

"Well, obviously pluck that sucker. Duh."

I wince as I pull the offending hair out of my eyebrow. Staring at it in the tweezers, it's just an unassuming little fiber. But it's what it symbolizes that scares me. I'm getting old. And I'm alone. Well, not alone, because I have Rob, but I also have a vacant ring finger. "It's gone. I gotta get going soon."

"You'll call me if he proposes?"

"Of course. And what do you mean 'if?' Don't you think it'll happen?"

"I should be asking you that. You're the one with the intuition about these things."

I sigh and lean into the mirror again, just to make sure there are no more offending gray suckers infiltrating my eyebrows. "I don't know, Therese. I mean, I haven't gotten a sign or had a dream or a premonition about anything. It just makes sense. We've been together for almost two years. I'm thirty-five. He's forty. We're going away for Valentine's Day weekend to a romantic B&B. This is the perfect time for him to propose."

"Why do you sound like you're trying to rationalize it? Do you want him to propose?"

There's the loaded question. I should want him to propose. As my mother (and sister and brother and sister-in-law and friends) like to remind me, "You're not getting any younger." I should want to settle down. And I do. I think. I mean, I do.

I want to come home to someone every night. I'm sick of an empty apartment. I want to own a house. I want to be part of something larger than just me and my cat. Rob makes sense. We're both teachers. He's all the things that I'm not—organized, pragmatic, structured. That's why I'm pretty sure the proposal is coming. We haven't really discussed it. He's forty, and I'm his first long-term girlfriend. I know, I know, that should be a huge red flag right there. I knew him for a few years before we started dating, so I don't think he's a serial killer or anything. He's just reserved and set in his ways. He's just what I need. Stable and dependable. "Of course I want him to propose. Why wouldn't I?"

"That's the question. Why wouldn't you? You still don't seem sure. What do you want?"

"I want my eyebrows not to be turning gray."

"Sadie, that ship has sailed, so you'd better figure out what it is you do want."

Now, since I've had gray hair on my head for more years than I care to admit, it doesn't, in my mind, symbolize aging. A gray eyebrow hair does. I'm getting old, and I'm still alone. I think about this as I'm packing and driving to the B&B in the quaint village about forty-five minutes away. On paper, Rob looks like the ideal fit. He's about 5'10", which is not too bad, considering my 5'5" frame. We both teach in the social studies department of the local high school. Our rooms ended up being next to each other and we became friends. I tend to be a bit more of a dynamic teacher than Rob is, but it's not about our teaching styles. It's about the fact that he's stable and will make a good husband and provider. When I think about it, I know that's what I want: someone to take care of me. Oh sure, I'm more than capable of taking care of myself, but I want someone who can swoop in and take me in his arms and ravish me.

That's not Rob.

He hates it when I call him Rob, by the way. But I have a serious issue with calling him by his given name. I just can't, in the throes of passion, call out, "Oh Robin." I just can't do it.

He didn't have a choice about his name, any more than I did. If I had a nickel for every time someone told me they had a dog named Sadie, I would be able to buy a coffee at Starbucks at least. It's certainly not his fault that his mother has poor taste. She had to know that a woman would never find her son sexy with the name Robin. It brings to mind too much gender confusion and images of spring birds. I can't make that a deal breaker in determining my future happiness. Rob will be a stable provider. I know that life isn't like a romance novel, so I just need to dial back my hunky man expectations. Obviously those expectations have been letting me down since I was in high school.

I get to the B&B, having daydreamed the entire way. Probably not the safest thing in the world. My driving leaves a lot to be desired, but I've been lucky so far. Rob can't stand it when I drive. He yells at me the entire time. So I am perplexed as to why he wanted to meet me up here. I thought he'd prefer to drive us both to spare other motorists from having me on the road. It has to be because he has behind-the-scenes setting up to do. Nothing else makes sense. I try to get excited about what's going to happen. We've never talked rings or anything, but Rob certainly has paid attention to my personal style. Like the fact that I never wear yellow gold. Or that I don't like the pointed edges of marquise-cut stones.

Looking around, this B&B is truly amazing. Rob told me that it used to be a convent. I've parked in the back, so I'm entering through in a hallway near the kitchen which is to my left. Several small, round tables are spread out, giving the kitchen a cafe atmosphere. A large stone fireplace divides the kitchen and dining room. It is one of those fabulous fireplaces that is open on both sides. Sitting in the formal dining room, you can see right through to the cafe-kitchen. I see a sign indicating that the guestrooms are in a wing to the left off the kitchen, making it necessary to pass through the kitchen on the way to the rooms. Straight ahead of me is a sunken living room that has bookshelves from floor to ceiling. My eyes travel up and up and up, as the ceilings are cathedral height with massive hanging chandeliers. This library room leads into another sunken room, which appears to be a sitting room. The walls and the floor are made of stone. At the far end of that room is the most enormous fireplace I've ever seen. Worn couches surround it, with small end tables scattered about, holding lamps that light the otherwise dark room.

"Dear, can I help you?"

If I didn't know better, I'd say this lady was a left-over nun. Maybe she didn't get the memo that the rest of the group moved out about thirty years ago. "Um, yeah. I'm supposed to be meeting my boyfriend here. We have reservations for the weekend."

"Okay, come this way. You came in the back door. The check-in desk is through the library."

I follow her, apologizing for coming in the wrong door. Walking through the place, it's even more impressive than I first thought. I wish I could curl up with a book for about a week here. It looks so peaceful and relaxing. Maybe I can convince Rob to bring me back here every year for a special treat. I know, I'm putting the cart before the horse, but I've convinced myself that we're getting engaged. I wonder if we'll be married by next Valentine's Day. At my age, I don't want to wait that much longer. Glancing around the library, I wonder if we could have our wedding here. It's not that big, but I don't want a huge shindig anyway. I'd be content with our parents and siblings, and maybe a few close friends. Of course, I'd have to invite my aunt and uncle. And if I do that, then Rob would have to invite his, and his mom is one of seven kids. Just with family, we're up to over sixty people, and that's not including any of our teacher friends. I doubt this place could hold everyone. Maybe if it were in the summer and we were outside—

"Dear? I asked what name the reservation is under."

"Oh, sorry," my attention snaps back to the elderly lady who obviously owns this place. "Henderson. Robin Henderson."

She flips through her ledger and finds the information she's looking for. She opens a small cabinet on the wall and pulls out a key. There is a second key hanging on the same hook. I guess that means Rob's not here yet.

"Here you go, Robin. Room Eleven. Through the kitchen, down the hall, up the stairs and first room on the right."

"Oh, I'm Sadie. Robin is my boyfriend."

"Oh, sorry about that dear."

"No problem. It's not his fault he has an unfortunate name. Has he checked in yet?" I can't believe I said that. I don't know why I'm asking this. I know the answer.

She looks at the ledger and then back up at me. "No, dear. You're the first one here."

Putting on a brave smile, I take my bags and head back up to the kitchen to get to the wing of rooms. There's a heavy fire door that separates the rooms from the public part of the building. I guess that's good. There is still some privacy between the bedrooms and the common areas. I try not to let my spirits get too down as I trudge down the hall. I really had it in my head that Rob would be here, and he would have the room all lit in candlelight with rose petals strewn about and a bucket of champagne waiting.

Not that he's ever done anything that romantic, but that's the sort thing you do on Valentine's Day when you're going to propose, right? Turning the key, I push open the door and find the room empty. Just as I knew it would be. Woven scatter rugs dot the worn wood floors. There's a queen-sized bed in the middle of the room that has a Laura Ashley-type flowered comforter on it. The bed ruffles cascade down in coordinating stripes and plaids that are also featured on the multitudes of pillows on the bed. It is a nice room. For a thirteen year-old girl. There is nothing about this quaint room that even hints at romance or seduction. Certainly nothing that would be conducive to anything spicy in the bedroom.

Not that Rob has ever been spicy in the bedroom. Or anywhere else. I mean, when he was super frisky, that one time, the living room rug was suitably creative for him. We don't need fancy props or lingerie or rose petals to be romantic. We love each other, and that's enough. Right?

CHAPTER SIX

Two hours later, Rob finally arrives. I've had a glass (or three) of wine while waiting for him. Dorothy, the innkeeper, kept me company. I've found out that she and her husband, who is now deceased, God-rest-his-soul, opened the B&B when he was forced to take an early retirement. They bought the old convent and set about restoring it while preserving cool features, like all the stone work. I'm fascinated by the architecture of the place. Even the restoration process sounds like fun. According to Dorothy, at least two to three engagements happen here every year.

I don't know if I'm relieved to see Rob or pissed at him for being so late and not calling. What if he was picking up the ring and there was a snafu there or something? I can't be too upset with him. After all, he is going to a lot of trouble for me.

But I wish he wouldn't.

That thought runs through my mind. And it shocks me. Why would I think that? Is it just the wine talking? Rob, except for his name, is perfect for me. I'm just irritable because I'm hungry. And tired. Once I get some food in me, I'll feel worlds better and be in the mood for some romance.

Dinner is delicious. Pan-seared flank-steak with smashed potatoes and homemade bread that is to die for. Steamed veggies and salad. I go lightly on those for fear of tummy troubles later on. Who wants that? We're the last ones eating tonight. All the other diners have come and gone, but we got off to a late start because Rob got there so late. Dorothy clears our plates and brings us a dessert of chocolate mousse, served in a martini glass with a chocolate wafer garnish. I dive into mine, wishing I could mainline it. As I'm practically licking out my glass, I look up and see Rob's untouched.

"Aren't you going to eat that? It's so good. I could eat this everyday for the rest of my life."

"No you couldn't."

"Sure I could."

"You'd be the size of a house."

"Quite possibly, but you'd love me anyway."

He's silent. I try to pretend I don't notice but I do. He's probably just nervous. Finally he says, "You wanna go sit by the fire?"

Okay, here it comes. This is it. I wish I could go brush my teeth and comb my hair, just so everything is perfect. "Sure," I reply, standing up and following him down the hall to the library. I bring my wine with me. I feel like I need something to do with my hands. Man, I'm getting really nervous too. Unbelievably, we're the only people in the room. I don't know where everyone else is. Perhaps they've all retired upstairs already. I look at my watch. It's after nine. We're probably the youngest couple here, so it makes sense that we're the only ones still up. Fine by me. It will give us more privacy. I wonder if Rob would be up for getting a little frisky on the couch in front of the fireplace. We may not have rose petals or sexy lingerie, but that would be damn romantic.

Sinking back on the couch, Rob and I sit side by side, but not touching. I'm about to jump out of my skin. I can only imagine how he feels. He starts talking about school. Probably the last thing I want to be talking about now, but I can play along. We get on the topic of the union, something that we don't see eye-to-eye on. And never will.

He's a union rep. I'm only a member because I have to be. And frankly, I'm resentful of how much my dues are and how many annoying e-mails they send me. I've shifted so my knees are pointing towards his and I'm leaning forward.

My body language is totally indicating that I'm giving him the go-ahead for action. We're in a heated debate about the ongoing contract negotiations when I'm startled by movement at the other end of the room. I look up, nearly dropping my wine glass, and see a large man coming in a side door and heading towards the kitchen. He's dressed ... as Cupid? He's probably over six feet tall, with a white-blond curly wig. He's wearing leather chaps, biker boots, and a black leather vest. That's it, well, except for the wings, of course. No shirt, just a large heart-shaped tattoo on his arm with the word 'Mother' inscribed on it. He heads into the kitchen and I hear the fire door open to the bedroom wing. I could not really have seen what I just saw. Could I?

"Did you see that?" I ask Rob.

"No, what?"

I start to describe what I've just seen, but I stop myself. Rob will think it's a bunch of hooey, like my premonitions. I can't explain them, but that doesn't mean that they're not real. Speaking of dreams, I've drunk a little more than I had intended, and I'm getting sleepy. Rob had better make his move soon or the heat of the fire is going to put me out. If Cupid is in the house, then it must mean that some romance is due to happen.

Wait, why do I need to wait for Rob to make a move? It's the twenty-first century. If I want to get some action with my boyfriend, I can initiate things. I've been pretty passive in this relationship. I let Rob take the reins and run things right from the get-go. Which has left me stuck in a holding pattern, waiting for him to make the next move. Since the fall, things have been even duller. I'm dying for some spice, as my adventures last night proved. Why should I have to wait? If I want a little nookie, I should be able to get some. And maybe, just maybe, my increased interest will spark him to get off his duff and onto one knee.

I put my wine glass on the end table and snuggle into Rob, resting my head on his shoulder. My hand lightly caresses his thigh. Running my fingers up and down his leg. Up and down. His arm is around me, and I'd like to think that he has pulled me in tighter. I hang in this position for a while, waiting for him to lean in and kiss me. But no, nothing. I sit up a little straighter and lean in. Rob is looking at me, leaning in. He just sits there.

Okay, a relationship between two passive people just won't work. He's got to meet me halfway. But he holds still, so I lift my body up, trying to close the distance between our lips. Just as we're about to connect, something brushes by my hair. Rob's hands are down, one behind me and the other on my lap, so I know it's not him. I lift my right hand up to brush the fly, or whatever it is, away, when I feel something brushing my hair again. Out of the corner of my eye, I can see it. A bat.

Perhaps it's because I've had about two bottles of wine, or perhaps it's because I did a lot of camping as a kid, but this doesn't faze me. I let out a noise that sounds like a "whoop, whoop" as I continue waving my hand about my hair, just to make sure the bat has not landed on my head. I jump to my feet and try to relocate, still waving and whooping. Moving around to the back of the couch, I notice Rob. He's on his stomach, underneath the coffee table. Dropping my hand to the side, I watch him for a minute. He begins to army crawl out from under the table. I see him look around for the bat, never quite processing that I'm still even in the room. He jumps up, yells, "I'm outta here" and sprints up into the cafe. I hear the fire door open and close.

Still standing there in the living room, I look up but can't see the bat anywhere. Afraid it's going to dive-bomb me again, I hurry into the kitchen. Where I see Rob through the small window in the fire door. He's holding it shut.

He not only didn't protect me from the bat, but he ran out and left me there. What if that had been an ax murderer? Would he have just left me to perish while he saved his own hide? I see his eyes grow wide, and he starts waving frantically. The bat dive-bombs me again, causing me to drop to the ground and crawl under one of the tables. This time, I'm yelling. Okay, shrieking is more like it. I can hear Rob through the glass, screaming like a little girl.

That's enough to silence me. Holy crap, if we get married, this is the man who I expect to protect me and my kids, should we ever have any. Screaming like a six-year-old girl, barricading me from safety just to protect himself. Now, I don't need a caveman. I don't need someone to think that I am a helpless female incapable of doing anything for herself. But I do want a partner who won't leave me to die at the hands of a rabid bat.

I grab a cloth napkin off the top of the table and cover my head with it as I run in a crouch to the door. I bang on the door, yelling at Rob to open it for me. Finally, he opens it a crack, and I squeeze myself through. He slams it shut behind me. He's panting, as if he'd just run a sprint. Which I guess he did, the speed with which he ran out of there.

"I don't do bats," he finally says. He's frantically brushing at his hair and shoulders and arms, as if it is on him.

"Yeah. I got that."

He just stares at me. Then, it hits me. "Your name is Robin."

He continues looking at me blankly.

"Your name is Robin and you're afraid of bats. What kind of sidekick would you make?"

"You think I've never heard that one before?" Oooooh, he's pissed. We stand there is silence, staring at each other. It is obvious that there has been a shift in our relationship. All because of a tiny flying rodent.

"You left me out there to fend for myself," I finally retort.

"You did fine. You managed."

"And that's what life would be with you, right? Managing."

"Sadie, I don't know what you're talking about. I don't think I can sleep here. Knowing that all those things are out there. I'm going to drive home."

"What? It's late. And I've had too much to drink to drive."

"I didn't say you had to leave. You can stay." He turns and walks down the hall. I follow him up the stairs to our room.

"You're seriously going to leave me here?"

"You'll be fine. Call me when you get back tomorrow, and I'll come over."

"Really? That's it? That's all you have to say?"

"I can call you when I get in tonight, but you'll probably be asleep. You have had a lot to drink. I don't want to wake you up."

"Um, okay. Thanks I guess." I watch him pack up. Of course, he's hung up all of his clothes, even though we were only supposed to be here for a night. Anal freak. I can't hold back any longer. "Really? Nothing else? You weren't going to ask me anything?"

He stops and looks at me like I have three heads. "Sadie, what are you blabbering about?"

In this moment, I know it's over. And a feeling of peace washes over me. Rob—Robin—is not the man for me. Who cares that I'm thirty-five? Who cares that my eyebrows are turning gray? Who cares that I keep considering adopting another cat and just turning into a crazy cat woman? I want a boyfriend who's not afraid to hold my hand in public. I shouldn't have to settle. I don't have to settle. And Rob would definitely be settling.

"Don't call me tomorrow."

"Okay."

That's all he says. Okay.

"Don't call me, Rob."

"I said I wouldn't."

"No, Rob. Don't call me again. I don't think this is going to work."

"What?"

"I don't think we're a good fit for each other. You left me to die at the hands of a rabid bat."

"I doubt it was rabid, although this is not the time of year bats are normally out."

"The point is that you left me. You saved yourself and didn't even stop to think about me. I want someone who puts me first."

"You really want to be alone at your age?"

Ouch. Low blow.

"If I'm alone, at least I know I'll put me first. And I can do that. I want love, Rob. I do. But I'm not sure you're capable of giving me what I need. Of loving me how I want to be loved. And I've waited this long, I can wait a little longer. I don't need to settle. And I'm afraid it would be settling with you. "

"If that's how you feel, I'm not going to beg you. I'll see you at school on Monday. "

And with that, he was gone. And I was alone in a romantic B&B on Valentine's Day. I guess that wasn't Cupid I saw earlier. Or, if he was here, he certainly wasn't here for me. I start to cry, but then stop. There was no reason to cry. I'm better off being alone than with someone who doesn't meet my needs. I'm not going to settle again. I will wait for the man who will sweep me off my feet. And one who isn't afraid of bats.

CHAPTER SEVEN

I sleep surprisingly well considering the events of the previous night. I'm guessing the wine had something to do with that. I will miss sharing my bed with someone. Not in a sexual way, although I will miss that a bit too. Rob and I only stayed together about two days a week, but those days were nice, waking up next to a warm body.

I need more than just a warm body. I deserve more than that. Don't I?

I take a shower and get dressed. Now in a comfortable sweater, leggings and boots, I wrap a scarf (my accessory of choice) around my neck and head downstairs for breakfast. It's sort of a reverse walk of shame, going down to breakfast alone. I wave at Dorothy who is flitting from table to table in the cafe, filling mugs with steaming hot coffee.

Standing in front of the door of death, I wait to catch Dorothy's eye so she can tell me where to sit. Her gaze is focused behind me, obviously looking for Rob. "Just one. The other party had to leave," I say coolly.

Well, maybe not coolly. My voice is high pitched and squeaky and about fifty decibels louder than I intended. And every person in the cafe turns to look at me. In my solo glory.

Sigh.

Just as the occupants of the cafe go back to ignoring me, my phone rings, drawing their attention my way. I slink backward through the fire door and look. It's not Rob. I don't know if I hoped it would be or not. I know I told him that I didn't want to talk to him again, but if he fought for me, I'd probably take him back.

"Hey Therese."

"Oh my God—you left me hanging all night! What happened? Did he do it? Of course he did. How was it? Oh my God—are you two still in bed celebrating?"

"No, actually, I'm going to breakfast. I have no idea what Rob is doing."

"He didn't do it yet? Maybe tonight? Maybe he's setting everything up so it's perfect?"

"I highly doubt that," I say, dejection seeping into my words and heart.

"Oh come on. You know it's coming. I hope he did a good job with the ring. Then we have to start talking wedding. Have you thought about when? Where? I'm your Matron of Honor, right? You'd better not pick Jenna over me."

"I'm not picking anyone, Therese. Rob left."

"Wait—what? Come again?"

"Rob went home last night. There was a bat here and it freaked him out. He said he couldn't stay, knowing it was in the building. So he left. I'd drank too much to drive home so I stayed."

"Um, wow. Sort of speechless over here. Not at all what I expected you to say."

"But wait, there's more."

"More than a bat? How can there be more?"

"Before he left, we broke up."

"WAIT—WHAT? WHY?"

"Therese, please stop screaming into my ear. What part of 'too much to drink' did you not hear? I have a bit of a headache. Rob freaked out when the bat dive-bombed me. He crawled under a table and then ran for his life, screaming like a little girl. He got behind a fire door and then *held it shut* with me on the other side, the bat still attacking me."

There's silence for a moment. "I have no words for that."

"It sort of occurred to me as he was shrieking and preventing me from getting to safety that he is probably not the man I want to spend my life with. Frankly, I'm sort of surprised that no one came out of their rooms with all that yelling. And then he told me that he was leaving, regardless of whether or not I could drive. He didn't offer to take me with him and drive back up tomorrow. He just said, 'Oh, you'll be fine' and started to go."

"So it's fine for you to stay in the bat house but not him?"

"Apparently. He's totally petrified of bats."

"His name is Robin."

"I know, right? That's exactly what I said. He didn't find it humorous. Not in the least."

"He's such a stick in the mud."

"He is, isn't he?"

"Truth."

"I can do better, right? I don't need to settle for someone who will leave me like that."

"No, you shouldn't settle. But on the other hand, are you okay being alone? There's got to be someone out there better than Rob, right?"

"I hope so. Dear Lord, I hope so. And no, I don't want to be alone, but I sort of was with Rob anyway. We only saw each other a few times a week. He wouldn't even hold my hand in public! I want someone who will do that. Who is not afraid to be seen with me or to let the world know that we're together and he loves me."

"Okay then, we'll set about finding your Mr. Right."

"Not this weekend though. I'm just going to hide out up here and lick my wounds."

"Do you think Rob will call?"

I think about that for a moment. "No, I don't think he will. I don't think I'm ever going to talk to him again." A weird feeling washes over me as I say this.

"Won't you see him at work?"

"Yeah I guess, but I don't think he'll ever get over this. I don't see us ever speaking again. You should have seen him when he left. I can't explain why I feel this way, but I'm never going to talk to him again. It's like he's dead to me."

"His loss then."

"Damn straight. Now I need to get some eggs and coffee and try not to look too pathetic while everyone else is all snuggled up for the most romantic weekend of the year, and I'm all by my lonesome."

Disconnecting from Therese, I head back into the cafe. Dorothy comes over and offers me coffee. "Yes, please."

"Are you all right, dear?"

"I think I will be. No, I know I will be. This will be a good thing."

She gives me a sympathetic looks and brings me a plate of breakfast food. Scrambled eggs, hash browns, bacon, and toast. I scarf it down, not caring what I look like shoveling the food into my mouth.

"I like a lady with a healthy appetite." A voice from above my head startles me. I sit up quickly and inhale. Unfortunately for me, I still have some scrambled egg in my mouth and I somehow manage to get it lodged in my throat. Not in an I-need-the-Heimlich kind of way, but in an embarrassing fit of coughing kind of way.

My eyes are watering and I'm still spluttering and choking. Finally, I can breathe. I look up to see Cupid standing over me. He's not dressed as Cupid today though. His hair is dark brown with a little wave to it, now that it's not covered by that hideous wig. He's wearing comfortable jeans and a plaid flannel shirt over a Henley. His eyes are blue, and he's got the perfect amount of five o'clock shadow. He's got that solid, steady appearance that is only slightly reminiscent of the guy on the paper towel package.

"Sorry, didn't mean to make you choke."

"No problem. Kind of just how things are going these days."

"Aunt Dorothy said you're flying solo. Mind if I join you?"

I wave towards the seat, giving him the go-ahead. "Make yourself at home."

"Well, since it sort of is my home ..."

"Oh, right. So you live here?"

"I'm more of a caretaker. I help my aunt out with maintenance and when it's a full house. Speaking of which, you weren't alone last night when I saw you."

"So that was you dressed as Cupid!"

His face turns the same shade of red as his shirt. "You saw that."

"A burly man in a wig, leather vest, chaps and with wings is hard to miss. What was that about?"

"Just trying to help my friend out. She was having a Galentine's party and I showed up and—"

"Oh my—did you strip?"

"Good God, no. I just passed out romantic messages that Tracy gave me to hand out."

"What is Galentine's?"

"I don't even know. It was a bunch of chicks in a room. Most of them are single, so I think it's about celebrating their friendships or something. I don't know. Tracy asked. I have trouble saying no."

"Is the tattoo real?"

He laughs, his face breaking into a wide grin. He's like movie star handsome when he smiles like that. I try not to swoon. "No. My mom would kill me if I ever did that."

"Didn't it say mother?"

He smiles again. Oh. My. God. So cute. "When I was little, my great uncle had a tattoo on his bicep from his time in the service. I was fascinated by it. I always wanted to touch it. He told me that I should never get a tattoo, because if you change your mind, they have to cut your arm off."

"Jeez! How old were you?"

He shrugs. "About five, I think? He died not that long after. I promised him that I would never get a tattoo because I didn't want my arm cut off. Kind of always stuck with me, I guess."

"I'm not even sure how to respond to that story." I pause for a moment. "You know, I'm normally not into tattoos, but the right one on the right guy can be a real panty dropper."

His mouth falls open. "Okay, I'll head to the tattoo parlor later today. Does the 'mother' thing work for you?

"Well, maybe not that one. I hope it doesn't traumatize you after the story you told me about your uncle. I'm still trying to process that one."

"Oh stick around. I have lots more stories. But what about you? What's going on with you? You never did answer my question about what happened to the guy from last night."

CHAPTER EIGHT

"I was here with my boyfriend. We sort of broke up."

"Oh ... I'm sorry?"

"Thanks, I guess. I'm still trying to figure out if I'm sorry or not. I came up here with all these preconceived notions. I thought he was going to propose. Turns out, I realized that not only was he not going to propose, but that I didn't want him to. Being with him was settling. And I don't want to settle."

"Why do you say that?"

I lean in and motion for him to lean in closer to me. I don't want to say this too loud and freak out the other guests. I tell him the bat story. "... All because he was afraid of the bat. I don't want a man who leaves me in a panic."

"The bat's name is Murray."

"You have a name for the bat?"

"Yeah. Bats are supposed to hibernate, but this one bat has been around for the last few winters. I named him Murray."

"Okay. That's odd, but whatever. Speaking of names, I'm Sadie."

"Max."

"Well, Max, thanks for keeping me company. I think I'm going to get packed up and head home. No point in me hanging out here all day by myself."

"Are you going to see the boyfriend?"

"Ex-boyfriend, and no. I don't think he's ever going to speak to me again. Which should get interesting considering that we work together."

"Yikes."

"Yeah, well, it'll be fine. I really feel fine about this." I stand up, picking up my plate to clear it. Walking to the sink, I notice Max walks with me.

"Just be careful driving back. There was a bad accident on Marysville Road this morning."

That feeling passes through me again. Furrowing my brow, I look at him. "Call me crazy, but I think someone I know was in that accident."

"Why do you say that?"

"Just a feeling I have. I don't know how else to explain it."

Now I need to get home. I start to panic. What if it was my mom? Or Brady? Or Jenna? I don't always like my siblings but I wouldn't want them involved in an accident. Mostly because I wouldn't want them hurt but partly because I don't want to have to listen to them whine about it.

Heading up to my room, I look around and then sit on the bed for a moment. Alone, I can let the dejection wash over me for a minute. I don't know if I'm more sad that Rob and I broke up or that I just wasted the last two years of my life on him. Maybe breaking up with him was the impulsive thing to do, but it just felt right. I try to go with my gut instincts as much as possible. Thinking about it, I'm really all right about not being with Rob. He was dull. If all the spice is gone before we even get married, then that probably doesn't bode well for a lifetime of contentment.

This is just another setback. Nothing I can't bounce back from, right? If only it were that simple.

I'm almost home when my cell rings. "Hey Therese. I'm almost home. I'll call you when I get in and get settled."

"How far out are you?"

"About ten minutes. Why? What's up?" I try to ignore the sinking feeling in my stomach.

"I'll talk to you then. I don't want to distract you while you're driving."

"Oh, just tell me. You've never worried about it before."

"Nah, it can wait. Talk to you soon."

The feeling of uneasiness is making my skin crawl. I have never felt so creeped out before. Except for the times when I realize that I've predicted someone's death. But I've already done that once this week. What are the odds that I did it again?

Turns out, pretty damn good.

I pull into my parking spot and trudge up the stairs to my apartment. I swear, one of these days, I'm going to bite the bullet and buy my own place. I look at the real estate listings all the time, but I've never been brave enough to pull the trigger. I guess I've been waiting to settle down with someone, but after breaking it off with Rob, it's more apparent than ever that I need to stop waiting and start acting.

"Holy shit—you scared me!" I shriek as I open my door to see Therese sitting in my living room. "What the hell?" I know I gave her a key but that was for emergencies.

Oh shit. This is an emergency.

"Therese, what's wrong? What happened? Is it my dad? Why didn't my mom call me?"

Therese is standing and closes the gap between us. Taking my hand, she leads me to into the living room. I don't know what's coming, but I know it's bad.

"Please just spit it out." My voice is a whisper, hoarsely pleading with her.

"I don't even know how—Sadie, early this morning, there was a car accident."

"Yeah, I heard about it up at the B&B. Oh my God, who is it?"

Tears well up in her eyes. "Rob."

"Wait—what?"

"It was Rob, honey. He's gone."

"I ... I don't understand."

"There was an accident on Marysville Road this morning."

"I heard that. I got a bad feeling. I thought it was Brady or Jenna."

"This is where it gets even worse. I don't know how to tell you this. Crap, this is hard."

"Jesus, Therese, just spit it out!" I've actually grabbed her shoulders and am shaking her, like in a movie.

"Rob wasn't alone. Jenna was in the accident with him."

That makes no sense. "Like she was in the other car that was involved in the accident?"

"No, they hit a tree. They were in the car together.

"I ... I ..." I can't even process what she is telling me. My arms drop down and my legs become jelly. Good thing the couch is behind me to catch me. "Why was Jenna with him?"

"I don't know. You're going to have to ask her."

"Why was she with my boyfriend?"

There's a long pause before Therese can come up with the words. "From my understanding, he was her boyfriend too."

"I don't understand." I feel like a broken record. Like I'm swimming though Jello and I can't see anything or reach the surface.

"I don't either. I don't know how either one of them could do that to you."

"Rob's dead?"

"Yes."

"I'm never going to talk to him again." My words echo in my head.

"No, honey, you're not."

"No, that's what I said to you. That I wasn't going to talk to him again."

"That's not what you meant, though."

"No, but it's what I said. I did this. I killed him."

"Sadie, how can you say that? You didn't kill him!"

"Therese, how else do you explain it? I had the thought that I was never going to talk to him again, and now I'm not. It's like I sentenced him to death."

"I'm going to go with the whole 'you're grieving and in shock' for justification for that statement, otherwise you're coo coo for Coco Puffs."

"What else can it be, if it isn't my fault?"

"I don't know. You didn't make it happen. You didn't even wish for it to happen. All you did was predict it. Sort of."

"But these predictions have to mean something, right? Like I'm given this opportunity to stop bad things from happening and I'm not doing it?"

"Sadie, this isn't a TV show, and you're not a superhero. You can't feel responsible."

I know that Therese may be right, but I can't help but feel the way I do, no matter how irrational it may be. Because of this freakish ability, knowing things that I can't possibly know, there's part of me that wonders if there's something mystical or other worldly that the normal human brain doesn't understand. Therese looks at me, her eyes full of sympathy. But behind the caring and empathy, all I see is that spark of doubt. She's thinking I really did, in some cosmic way, kill my boyfriend.

CHAPTER NINE

Therese has left, after I repeatedly told her I was fine. I totally lied. I am not fine. I doubt I'm ever going to be fine again. Certainly not with my mother calling over and over. I just can't talk to her right now. I can't talk to anyone.

I keep playing over and over in my mind the 'what if' game. What if there hadn't been a bat? What if I hadn't told him we were done? What if we fought for more or less time? Would any of that have changed the outcome of the night? Then the "whys" start. Why was he with my sister? I can't bear the thoughts bombarding me.

I get in my car and drive to the nursing home. I want my daddy. I want him to hold me and tell me that today isn't real. That I didn't kill my boyfriend. That my boyfriend was not really dating my sister as well. Speaking of which, how the hell could she do this to me? It certainly explains why Rob didn't like hanging out with my family. I thought it was because they all are a bunch of nut jobs. How was I supposed to know that it was because he was hooking up with my sister? And Jenna? How could she do this to me?

We haven't had a great relationship in a long time. I'm two years older than she is. I was thrilled to have a little sister. I was sick of being the youngest after Brady. I took care of Jenna from the get-go. If I had only known that I would be doing that for the rest of my life. My mom made excuses for the messes Jenna got herself into. I used to as well. I stopped buying the bull about three years ago. I just got tired of her constant crap. Jenna is thirty-three now. Old enough to be responsible. And believe you me, she is going to take responsibility for this one. Not that accident, of course. That's all on me. Not that anyone needs to know that.

I get into my dad's room, and he's in bed. It's the weekend, so there aren't any therapies. Activities are at a minimum as well, since they figure that lots of family members will come to visit. I don't know the weekend staff that well, since I'm usually here during the week. I sit in the chair next to the bed, unable to speak. I don't know where to start. In my head, I'm making a list of all the people I've killed with my premonitions: the comedian that started it all, Great Aunt June, Bob Tomkins (the mayor), Misty Eve (the female pro-wrestler), cousin Keith, Tristan Austin, and now Rob. Oh, and I also feel some blame for the plane crash in India that killed 350 people, because I complained that it was a slow news day and there was nothing on NPR, and we needed a catastrophe to happen. Wow, the list is really getting big. I just sit there, holding my dad's hand, and wishing he would hold my hand back.

I must doze off like that because the next thing I know, there is darkness outside the window, I have a terrible crick in my neck and there's an aide in the room, bustling about. She's making a tremendous racket. If I didn't know better, I would think she was trying to wake me up.

"Oh, I must have fallen asleep. Sorry."

"Are you Simon's ... daughter?"

"Yeah. I'm Sadie."

"I didn't realize he has two daughters. I've met your sister before."

Even thinking about her makes me bristle. "Oh, what? On Christmas or Easter when my mom forces her to visit?"

"Yeah, it was a holiday I think. But I don't recall ever seeing you here." Her tone is snooty and judgmental.

I do not need to justify myself to this woman. Not at all. But you bet your ass I'm going to. "That's because I leave the holidays and the weekends to the family who doesn't give a shit and only comes around when my mom forces them. I'm here every day during the week, so you can check your attitude."

"Well, you don't have to get nasty with me. We do have the right to ask you to leave."

"Who is the nurse supervisor today? Tonight? Whenever it is? Who's on now?"

She stiffens. "Margot."

I smile. Margot is one of my favorites. She makes the best Christmas cookies. The last two years, I've been in a cookie swap with her.

I stand up and head toward the door. "Dad, I'll be right back."

The aide starts running after me. "Now, I don't think we need to involve Margot in this, do we?"

I turn and look at her. "Your words have consequences. Don't use them if you can't pay the piper."

I turn back into my dad's room and resume my place by the bed. I didn't need to snap at her like that, but she didn't need to threaten me either. Just the mention of my sister and the implication that Jenna is here more than I am really got to me. Today of all days. I put the TV on and resume a matching catatonic state with my dad.

A little before nine, my mother comes racing in, hair frazzled and coat misbuttoned. "I should have known you would be here."

I just look at her. I can't even summon up the energy to speak to her.

"I've been calling your phone over and over."

I shrug. It occurs to me that I haven't heard my phone ring. "I must have left it in the car."

"But this was important. Your sister has been in a serious accident."

"I'm aware," I say dully.

My mother stares at me, waiting for more. "Don't you want to know more?"

I snap. "Yes, Mother. Tell me more. Tell me about how I go away on a romantic weekend with my boyfriend. I think it's odd that he wants to take separate cars but whatever. I think he might be getting things set up to propose, so who am I to question his actions. But then, he freaks out over a bat and leaves me there alone. He doesn't offer to bring me back with him. Nope, he splits, deserting me on Valentine's Day. I find out today that he was killed in an accident. And that in the accident with him was my sister. Now unless she teleported into the car at the last second, I don't want to hear it. I don't want to hear any of it. I'm here with Dad, and this is where I want to be."

"I know this must be uncomfortable for you, but you know how much trouble Jenna has handling difficult situations like this. Do you know how hard she is taking this? Rob *died*. In her arms. Think about how traumatic that's got to be for her."

That's it. I snap. Jumping up, I grab my mom's arm and drag her out of the room. "I'm not doing this in front of Dad." I drag her down the hall and through the front doors. We're in the parking lot, and I don't even notice the cold as I start lighting into her.

"Do not even try to defend her." I wave my finger, and my mother's open mouth snaps shut. "You have given Jenna every single get-out-of-jail-free card that exists. You have made excuses for her her entire life. You wanna know what the issue is? She's a spoiled brat. You wanna know why? You." I point my finger directly at my mom's chest. "You have never held her accountable or responsible for anything. You have never made her step up and deal. You enable her childish behavior. Guess what? She's turned out to be a horrible person. Congratulations on that."

"Now, Sadie, you will not talk to me like that. I am your mother."

"Yes, you are. But you are Jenna's mother first and foremost. You can't be mother to both of us and I won't ask you to choose since I know what the choice will be. I don't need to feel any more horrible than I do right now."

I turn and head back into the nursing home. The February air is cold and suddenly I feel it. As I'm walking away, my mother calls out to me, "Sadie, will you at least call Jenna and check in? She's absolutely devastated right now. Apparently Rob had just proposed."

You always knew the best way to kick me when I was down, Mom. Good to see you haven't lost your touch. I don't even acknowledge her words, and I head back in. Too bad the only family member who has my back is catatonic.

CHAPTER TEN

"I think I've eaten my body weight in chocolate," I groan into the phone. I haven't left my apartment in three days. Showering and putting clothing on is going to be a challenge. But I have to. The wake is tonight. Rob was at least courteous enough to drive his car into a tree over a vacation week. Since even John didn't know we were dating, and we *technically* had just broken up, I wouldn't have been able to use my bereavement days; it would have pissed me off to no end to have to use my personal days.

"You have to get up and move," Therese scolds me.

"I know. I'm going." I flop back into my pillows. My bed stinks. I stink. I don't care. What's there to care about? My life is a disaster. I all but killed my boyfriend. I guess, in hindsight, he most likely deserved it but still. Okay, not deserved it per se, but he at least should have had to pass a kidney stone for cheating on me with my own sister.

"Is Jenna going to be there?"

"Who knows? I'm guessing she will. It's a chance to have everyone fawn over her and make it about her."

"She does suffer from L.A.M. syndrome."

"What's L.A.M. syndrome?"

"Look At Me."

"Yeah, that's my sister. Her L.A.M. is further complicated by her F.M.O."

"Now you've got me. What's F.M.O.?"

"Fear of Missing Out. It can be serious, but when combined with L.A.M., it is downright crippling."

"Or you'll end up being crippled because you become so annoying that someone will want to take a bat to your knee caps."

"That's Jenna."

"Have you talked to Rob's parents?"

"No, I chickened out. Plus, this is an awkward situation. The woman lost her son. Turns out, he was a lying, cheating louse, but I don't need to make her feel worse about that."

"Are you going with anyone?"

"I'm meeting the rest of the department there. We're all going in together."

"Surely some of them know you were together, right?"

"I don't know." I slowly get out of bed and look around my room. It looks like a bomb went off. Empty food containers, a few spent bottles of wine and beer. Clothes and miscellaneous crap fill the entire space. "Oh my God, Therese. You should see my place. It's disgusting. I can't believe I let it get like this!"

"You're changing the subject."

"You're observant. I don't know if anyone knows we were together. I mean, sometimes we showed up at school functions together, but Rob was very adamant about not having any public displays, especially at school."

"Sort of ironic, don't you think?"

I avoid looking in my mirror as I start scooping up some of the debris while on my way to the bathroom. "How so?"

"Because people usually act like that when they want to hide their relationship from someone. The person that he should have been hiding you from is the one person who most certainly knew about the relationship."

"Yeah, don't even get me going on that one. I still can't believe my own sister—"

"I can. After all the shit Jenna has pulled over the years, this doesn't surprise me one bit. She can't stand to see you happy. Not that Rob made you all giddy or anything, but I bet she was afraid you were going to get married."

"And to think, I was contemplating having her for my maid of honor."

"YOU WERE NOT!" Therese's voice rises about three octaves. "You take that back right now. You cannot be serious!"

I'm laughing, so Therese has come through for me, yet again. "No, not really, but it is certainly fun to get your panties in a twist."

With that, she disconnects and I get in the shower.

Walking into the funeral home with the other members of the social studies department, I take a deep breath and try not to pass out. The scent of flowers and candles and funeral home overwhelms me. Even though we're on the early side, the place is already packed. Great. I don't want to see people. I don't want to talk to anyone. I especially don't want to talk to Martha, the woman standing next to me. She teaches freshman social studies. She's already a blubbering mess. I try not to look at her. I can't watch someone cry without crying. I know I'm totally delusional to think I will get through tonight without crying. "I can't believe he's gone. I can't believe this happened!" Martha's voice is a whisper. An Irish one. The elderly woman in front of us seems to crumple a bit as she begins crying. This only makes Martha cry more. She's sniffing and snorting, so I try to focus on that. "You know," *sniff*, "I always," *sniff*, "thought that you and," *sniff sniff sniff*, "Robin were together. I guess you were just close because he was engaged to your sister." And then she blows her nose, making a sound like a goose being strangled.

I'm going to throw up. I can't do this. I can't be here. I need air. I need to get out. I need ...

Black. Everything is black.

I hear the voices and then smell this terrible, terrible, awful smell that causes my eyes to fly open and water at the same time. I try to sit up but there are too many people around me. This is not helping.

"Sadie, are you okay?" It's my principal, John. I haven't seen him since the lingerie incident. I feel my face flushing even more, just thinking of that. I hear somebody say, "Look at how red she is! Should we call an ambulance?"

I succeed in sitting up this time. "I'm fine. I just need some air." I need not to have caused the death of a student and my boyfriend. I need my sister not to have been having an affair with said boyfriend. I need this not to be my life.

Someone hands me a paper cup of water and I down it. It helps. I could drink about forty more of those. "Okay, everyone. Why don't you go back into the viewing room. I'll stay with Sadie and make sure she's okay."

I would have said that John was the last person I would want to be with right now, but I appreciate his quiet command of the situation. In ways like that, he reminds me of my dad. He's about the same age. He's due to retire next year. He's way past the typical retirement age, but he was in the service before becoming a teacher, so he's just now getting his thirty years in.

We sit in amiable silence for a few minutes. Finally he says, "Are you really okay?"

I just shrug. I'm not okay. I'm not sure I'll be okay after this. At least not for a while.

"Um, I know that you and Robin were ... an item."

I turned and looked at him, completely stunned. "How?"

"I'm observant. And my daughter works at the Classless Cafe."

"That was our favorite place to eat. We thought because it was a few towns away, no one would know us."

"One day, one of you must have been wearing a school shirt. My daughter asked me and I figured it out. But that's neither here nor there. I want to know if you are okay."

Finally, I'm able to speak. "This would be a hard situation just based on that. Add in the fact that Rob was having an affair with my sister and it gets a whole lot messier."

"Yeah, I would think that it would. I never pegged Robin for a two-woman kind of guy."

"You and me both."

"So, you didn't know?"

"Total shock."

"I guess it would be. Well, whatever you need, just let me know. Are you going to leave now or do you want to go in?"

"I want to leave, but I guess I need to go in."

"Then let me escort you, if you don't mind."

We stand up and start to head into the other room. Right before we get to the entrance I say, "Thanks, John. I appreciate it."

CHAPTER ELEVEN

I wish I could say that the most remarkable thing that happened at Rob's wake was me passing out. Well, I could say that, but it would be lying. I wish I could say that the other excitement didn't involve me. Again, I'd be lying.

John walks me back into the room and right over to Mr. and Mrs. Henderson and Rob's brothers Barry and Maurice. I don't know why it never occurred to me before, but in that moment it hits me. I know why Rob's name was Robin. Mrs. Henderson named her children after the BeeGee's. A bit of laughter threatens to bubble out of my mouth. I choke it back and make a strange gargling sound. It sort of doesn't matter. Everyone is staring at me anyway. There are hushed whispers going around the room.

Mrs. Henderson can't even look me in the eye as I stand before her. I don't blame her. Maybe I should, but I don't subscribe to the philosophy that one's actions are always a direct result of his or her mother's child-rearing abilities. "Mrs. Henderson, I'm very sorry for your loss." And sorry that I brought about your son's death. Obviously I leave that part out.

Now understand, these are people I've had Sunday dinner with. I've spent holidays eating her crappy ambrosia and deviled eggs. Other than accidentally killing Rob, I am not the person at fault here. I am the wronged party. She doesn't say anything, and so I move onto Mr. Henderson.

Just as I'm about to give him a hug, I hear it. That shrill voice that has made me blow my stack countless times over the years.

Jenna.

She's in a wheelchair, my mother pushing her. "Bernice! George! I'm so sorry I'm late. I had to leave the hospital against medical advice to be here, but I just couldn't miss this. I am devastated. Absolutely torn up. I feel so guilty! I wish there was something I could do to bring our Robin back."

Jenna is like a bad soap opera actress, complete with the back of the hand to the forehead and everything. For being in the hospital and not being allowed to leave, she looks pretty made up. Her hair, which is unnaturally red, hangs in ringlets down past her shoulders. She's wearing a black dress that I'm guessing is brand spanking new and most likely carries a brand-name label. Her makeup is caked on, making her look older than thirty-three, and is topped off by fire-engine-red lips. On her left hand is a marquise-cut solitaire set in yellow gold. It takes every ounce of self-restraint I have not to punch her as my mother wheels her over to me.

I hear Barry mutter under his breath, "Well, if she hadn't been jerking him off while he was driving, he'd probably still be here."

I turn and look at him. I never really cared for Barry. Three years older than Robin, Barry made Rob seem laid back and spontaneous. "What did you say?"

"If you're asking me, then you heard correctly."

"How ..."

"Because the first responders all had a great laugh at my brother's expense. His fly was down, his junk was out, and there was obvious ... stuff all over her. One of the new guys took the call. He came back to the station and was telling everyone about it before he realized it was my brother. I was on duty that night. I could have been on that call."

At that point, I throw up. Right in front of Rob's casket. From some things, there is no rebounding. This is one of those things.

Rob's mother has to be escorted from the room. His brothers give me death looks. My sister starts wailing about how I ruin everything for her. My mother starts yelling at me for getting my sister all agitated in her precarious condition. My colleagues just stare at the freak show.

Sitting in my car, trying to muster up the strength to drive home, I don't know if I can move. If I can carry on. This is my punishment for killing all those people. I think a negative thought about someone and—poof—they're dead. I have to erase all the negativity from my life. And there's only one way to do that.

I have to move.

I know it seems rash, especially in light of the recent turmoil I'm living, but I need to start over. I'm thirty-five years old and destined to be alone. I'm actually sort of okay with that. I'm really and truly nervous that I am responsible for people's lives. If I'm living somewhere new, then maybe I won't have as many ties, and I won't kill as many people. I know I'm grasping at straws, but I need something to hold onto in this moment.

Even if I didn't kill Rob—which seems unlikely, since we had just broken up—I had decided I was no longer settling. Living in my crappy apartment is settling. Putting up with my sister's antics and my brother's douchiness is settling. I don't have the money to quit my job right now. Even anticipating the awkwardness that will result from the goings on at the wake, I'm actually pretty content with my job. I truly love American history. I'm sort of a nerd like that. I do enjoy teaching. I like to think I make a difference, even if it's a small one.

I get back to my apartment and am once again startled to see Therese inside. "What are you doing here? Please don't tell me someone else has died. I just cannot handle any more tonight."

Therese hands me a glass. I make a face as the liquor burns going down. "Good Lord, what is this?"

"It's a Rob Roy. In honor of the dearly departed. You won't need many."

I put the glass down on the coffee table. Which is uncharacteristically clean. I look around. The whole place looks spotless. "Did you clean?"

"Yeah, I figured you could use the help. How was the wake?"

I kick off my heels and head into the kitchen to find something to eat. Drinking on an empty stomach isn't a good idea, and I definitely need to be drinking tonight. I dig a bag of pretzels out of the cabinet and find the jar of peanut butter. Dipping the pretzels right in the peanut butter, I start munching away.

"That's disgusting. Haven't you ever heard of utensils?"

"I live alone. No one eats this peanut butter but me."

"Good point. You didn't answer my question."

"The wake was a disaster of epic proportions."

Over that Rob Roy, and then another, I give Therese all the gory details.

"So ... vomit?"

"All over the funeral home rug."

"So ... she was spanking the monkey?"

"Yup. He died with it all hangin' out."

She's quiet for a minute, and I can tell she wants to ask me something big. 'Cause otherwise, Therese is never this quiet for this long.

"Was he ... like that with you?"

"You mean getting it on while he was driving? Never. I mean, this man wouldn't hold my hand in public. He would only kiss me behind closed doors. God forbid there was any public sex. I mean, once we did it on his living room rug, but otherwise, it was in bed, with the lights off."

"How boring."

"It got really bad after the fall. That's when things fell off between us."

"Do you think that's when he started seeing Jenna?"

"I don't know. I kept waiting and waiting for things to pick up again between us. For him to make a move and to take control, but he never did."

"Maybe he wanted you to take control."

I shrug. "Maybe that's why he ended up with Jenna. I just can't believe he proposed to her."

"Yeah, that makes no sense whatsoever."

"And the ring is the antithesis of anything I would want."

"Marquise cut?"

"You got it."

"Doesn't he know that you're likely to stab yourself with that cut of stone?

"Apparently not." Feeling the alcohol melt through my limbs, I sink even deeper into the couch. "I didn't want to marry him. I broke up with him. But I didn't want him to love someone else."

"I just find it hard to believe that he could be in love with Jenna. It's like he had the Madonna-whore complex or something."

"Yeah, but I would have been a whore in the bedroom. Or living room. Or wherever. He just never gave me the chance to."

"Too bad we can't ask him."

"Oh, I bet he's glad he got out of this one." I stop and think for a minute. I'm getting pretty sleepy. "You know, when I said I didn't think we'd ever talk again, I didn't mean it like this."

"Of course you didn't, Sadie. There's no way you could have caused this."

I'm drifting off and I feel the weight of a blanket on me. Mumbling, I speak, probably just to myself, "But somehow I did and I don't know what to do about it."

CHAPTER TWELVE

The closing is at nine a.m. I can't believe I'm doing this. Rob's death and the chaotic aftermath over the past three months certainly gave me some perspective. No matter my age, no matter my dating status, no matter my ability to kill innocent (or not-so-innocent) people, I need to get on with my life. I need to live for the now. And that, for me, includes buying my own house. And the day's finally here.

After hibernating for a few more days after the wake debacle, I pulled myself up by my bootstraps and got on with my life. Years of watching HGTV has left me with a hankering to own my own place, where I can knock down walls and re-tile something. I started looking for a house—three towns over from where I currently live. I could stand the longer commute in exchange for a change of scenery. I'd still be close enough to go to the nursing home every day after school but I wouldn't have to see the same people all day every day. I probably wouldn't run into students after school.

And I'd be able to focus on my house. My HOUSE! I'm going to own a house. It's an adorable little Craftsman bungalow. Best part—it's blue. Worst part—it needs a whole lot of work. My dream is to restore it to its former glory, with all the modern conveniences, of course. It's gonna take a lot of cash and even more elbow grease. I'm going to do as much work as I can by myself. Yes, I know I'm a girl, but it's no longer the dark ages. And I'm a girl who spent almost every Sunday in my dad's shed, assisting him on one project after another. He was always working on the funeral home, trying to restore and keep up the old house.

Sure, I will need help with the big things, and I'll hire out for those. While waiting for the house to be mine, I've been watching YouTube video after YouTube video on how to do a lot of the projects I have on my to-do list. Here's the secret—I've been in love with this house since I first laid eyes on it. It's just down the street from a bookstore and coffee shop. Far enough off the beaten path but close enough to keep me in the swing of things. It's in a neighborhood that has restaurants and shops as well. I love everything about it. And with the long Memorial Day weekend coming up, I'm ready to start ripping out carpeting and renovating.

Once the closing is done, I head to the nursing home to share my news with Dad. Just like everything in my life, I want to share it with him. "Dad! I'm finally a homeowner! Everything's signed, sealed and delivered. I own 6258 Grove Street. You would totally love it. It needs tons of T.L.C., but you taught me well, and I think I'll be okay. I hope I'll be okay."

I flop down in the chair and wait for a minute. I know there will be no response, but I like to pretend. "It was a steal too. Not a steal, but undervalued to say the least. It was a bank foreclosure. Good thing too, because I need that extra cash for renovations. I guess all these years of tutoring during the week and waitressing all summer have paid off. I have a home because of it."

Stroking Dad's hand, I try not to notice how old it seems. He's only been here a few years. Four now. Some days, it feels like he just got here. Others, it feels like he's been here for decades.

"Hi, Sadie. How are things today?"

Helga's grown on me in the last few months. "Great. I closed on the house today. As soon as I leave here, I'm going over there to get started. There's a bit of work that needs to be done before I can move in. Carpets to tear up, hardwoods to refinish. Stripping, sanding, and painting. Lots of painting. I think I may need to look at some wiring as well. The bathroom needs an overhaul."

"What about the kitchen?"

"The kitchen is fantastic. It's what made me fall in love with the place."

True story. The previous owner re-did the kitchen before he ran out of money. The cabinets are a mint green and may be original to the house, restored and refaced. There's a tile backsplash that pops against the tangerine walls. Sounds hideous I know, but in reality, it's spectacular. And, it's so me.

"Who's working on the place?"

"Yours truly." I try to ignore her raised eyebrow. "Dad here taught me well. I'm a pro with power tools."

"Are you going to hire out at all?"

"I'm sure I will, if it gets to that point."

"Let me give you my son's number. He's a contractor, so he's very good with his hands."

Ick. Not the endorsement I want to be hearing from someone's mother.

"You know I'm not looking to date anyone right now, Helga. Not after this year."

"I know, Sadie. This is purely business. Trust me, you need to call him. You won't be sorry."

Famous last words.

****

Let me set the scene for my life's latest disaster. I put a call in to Helga's son. He agrees to show up after he finishes on his other job site to do a walk through and come up with estimates for both time and price. Great. I've got time to do a few things before he shows up. But, as with any home improvement project, it's all the 'but firsts' that get you. For example, I need to clean the leaves and garbage out of the front yard. The house has been vacant for a while. So I sweep and pile it all up. To finish the job, I need to get to the garbage cans that are at the end of the alley next to the house. But first, to get to them, I have to pick up the cardboard and debris that are blocking access to the cans.

So this is what I'm doing. I've got a large pile of stuff right in front of my front door to be collected. I look, and the garbage cans are totally blocked by this massive stack of cardboard, like a year's worth of recycling left to disintegrate. So, I start pulling up the cardboard. Which then reveals a bees' nest. And boy, are those bees pissed that I disrupted their hiding spot! Oh, have I mentioned that I am allergic—severely allergic—to bees?

With about fifteen minutes to go until Helga's son arrives, I find myself in a swarm of bees. Naturally, I'm wearing shorts, as this warm May day would dictate. So, it's not surprising when a bee, very displeased to be disturbed, flies up my shorts' leg. And stings me. In my groin.

Within moments, my leg—well, my crotch—begins to swell. I hobble into the house, dig some Benadryl out of the box labeled for my bathroom. How I manage to find that box so quickly, I will never know. I take about four pills, hoping to ward off anaphylaxis. The welt in my privates has grown to the size of a softball or large grapefruit. I hobble to the kitchen and procure some ice to put on my groin. For future reference, the words 'ice' and 'groin' should never be used in the same sentence.

The massive dose of Benadryl has started to make me a little—lot—loopy, which is why I accidentally answer my phone when it rings. It's my mother, and if I had been in full possession of my mental faculties, I never would have answered the phone.

"'Lo." I slur.

"Sadie? Is that you?"

"You called me. Who do you think it is?"

"Are you alright? You sound drunk?"

"Nah, I just had to take a bunch of Benadryl. I got attacked by bees."

"You should call 911. You could die!"

"Naaaah. That's why I took so many pills. I have a guy coming to give me an estimate on the work, and I can't miss it."

"I'm not far away. I'll be right over."

"I'm okay, Mom ..."

The next thing I know, my mother is shaking me awake. "Dear God, Sadie? Are you okay? Sadie, do you know where you are?"

I look at her and focus. Shit, she came to my house. This is supposed to be my sanctum away from my crazy family. "Why are you here?"

"I was on my way over anyway."

"Wait, what? Why?"

I'm sitting in a chair at my kitchen table. It's really the only furniture I have in here at the moment. My cat jumps up on the table and I reach out to pet him.

"Sadie, you know, allowing the cat on the table is really in poor form. And look at his fur! It's all matted! Don't you ever brush that thing?"

I try really hard to focus on my mother. She looks at me and shrieks. "Oh dear Lord, look at your face! You got stung right in the middle of your forehead!"

I hadn't even noticed this one. Apparently, when your crotch is on fire, you tend not to notice a little forehead pain. So, here I am, my groin the size of a football, a welt the size of Kansas in the middle of my forehead, in a Benadryl coma, with my mother criticizing my feline grooming skills, when Helga's son walks in.

CHAPTER THIRTEEN

I'm sorry I called Helga's son. I'm sorry he showed up. I'm sorry I swore off dating for fear of killing another boyfriend. I'm sorry I didn't let Helga fix me up with her son years ago. I'm sorry I had a welt the size of a football on my hoo-ha when he showed up.

Helga's son is Max. You know, Cupid from that fateful Valentine's Eve before my life went in the shitter.

Not that it's not in the shitter right now. I am so confused. It's got to be the medicine, right? 'Cause I'm waiting for Mike to show up. Mike, the name on his business card. So when Max shows up, I get all confused.

"Hey! What are you doing here?" I slur like a drunken skunk.

"Coming to meet you, I think. Are you the homeowner here?" He looks like he wants to bolt.

"Yeah, I'm Sadie Perkins. I called you. I know your mom."

"And I'm Sadie's mom, Carol." Of course my mother has to butt in.

Trying to keep my eyes open, I point to my mother. "That's my mother and she's leaving now."

She turns in a huff but makes sure to call out before she leaves, "Remember what I said about the cat." 'Cause obviously grooming my cat is high on the list of priorities right now.

"I know you." His brow is furrowed as he's searching to place me. Considering I look like the Elephant Man, it's no wonder he doesn't remember me. Oh, have I mentioned that because of the groin issue, I'm sitting with my legs spread apart, the right one on a chair, the groin on full display, covered only by the bag of ice? Which, as it turns out, is really a bag of peas. Guess I won't be having those for dinner after all.

"The B&B Valentine's weekend. I saw you as Cupid. You saw me the morning after my boyfriend and I broke up."

"Oh, right. Sadie."

"Yeah, but you're Max not Mike. You have to explain. But go slow, because things are a little fuzzy right now. I may or may not have taken an entire package of Benadryl."

He sits down on a chair across the table from me. I try not to notice how nice the worn jeans look on him or how his biceps are displayed in his fitted black t-shirt. He runs a hand through his dark hair. He's again sporting a five o'clock shadow, which is fitting since it's after five. I wonder if he ever shaves.

"Oh, I'm being rude. Do you want something to drink? Water, soda, beer?"

"I'd love a beer, but you don't look like you're in any shape to get up. Tell me where and I'll get them."

Now, I probably shouldn't be drinking after taking the Benadryl, but I don't want to be rude. I wave in the general direction of the fridge and he retrieves two. He hands me my beer, and I say, "What? You're not even going to open it for me? What happens if I break a nail?" Oh crap, I shouldn't have said that. Now he probably thinks I'm some prima donna diva.

Then, opening my beer, I actually do break a nail. Dammit. Probably because my hands are not the most dexterous at the moment. Honestly I couldn't care less about the nail. What I do care about is that it seems like the universe just fired a cosmic warning shot across my bow. I mentioned something, and it happened. Cute guy in my kitchen; I cannot get involved.

"So, here's the deal. I have some renovations to do before I totally move in. I need to tear up the carpets in the living room, hallway, and bedrooms. That's no biggie. The wood floors will need to be refinished. I want to gut the bathroom, replacing everything but the clawfoot tub. That has to stay. All the woodwork will need to be sanded down, some of it repaired and refinished. There are a few windows that need to be repaired as well, and I think I'm going to need to rehash—rehab—them for energy efficiency, and replace the storms. I'm sure other things will spring up, as they're known to do."

"What's the budget?"

"In my head and on paper, sufficient. In reality, I'll be woefully short, I'm sure, because I know complications will arise."

We discuss the finer points of fees and schedules. Mike—Max—whatever his name is, works at the B&B as a caretaker and does contracting work in his free time. Depending on the business and projects at the B&B, he has varying availability.

"Okay, but what do I call you? Your business card says one thing, but you introduced yourself to me as something else. I'm confused. It doesn't take a lot. Especially not right now."

"Call me Max."

"What's with the Mike thing then?" I'm too damn nosy for my own good. Plus, if I didn't get these details, Therese would have my hide.

"My given name is Michael Andrew Xavier Schultz. Sort of a mouthful for a little kid. My uncle gave me the nickname 'Max' when I was a baby, and it's stuck since. I have to put Michael on the business stuff, since it's my legal name and all."

"Fair enough. Max it is then."

He looks over his shoulder at the living room. "Nice place. Lots of potential."

"I know. I love the style, the architecture. I mean, it's blue, which is great. But most of all, I fell for the kitchen. The previous owner re-did it in the original style and color palate of the house. I think he ran out of money or something, since this was a foreclosure."

"This is fabulous."

"I know, right?"

"Are you okay? Like really okay?"

"I'm allergic to bees and got stung while trying to clean up the side alley. I may have taken too much Benadryl."

"I got that already. Tell you what. Why don't you go sleep it off, and I'll look around the outside. I've got some spray in the truck, and I'll take care of those bees for you. I'll call you tomorrow with my thoughts."

"That sounds like the best idea I've heard all day."

CHAPTER FOURTEEN

     June brings with it an unseasonably warm streak. Which, when I lived in my apartment, was no big deal. I'd just crank the air conditioning and not worry about it. I'm in my house now. Sort of. Most of my furniture is still in storage in the detached garage. A few things, the essentials, are in the house. My bed, a couch, a small kitchen table and two chairs. I brought my TV in and put it on a box but I find that I rarely watch it. I don't have time with all the work I'm putting in on the house.

Finals are just about done, so tutoring has slacked off, except for those few students who need to go right until the last minute. That will be done next week. I'll be at the restaurant again over the summer. I wanted to take the time off but I need the money now more than ever. I did work with my boss to get a schedule that will allow me as much time to work with Max on the house as possible. I'll work a few lunch shifts, Friday night and a Saturday double. That leaves Max and me all day Sunday, as well as the weeknights he's available. I don't miss the coincidence that we'll be working on Sundays, just like I used to with my dad.

     Our first project had been to pull up the god-awful carpets and refinish the hardwood floors. We started that Memorial Day weekend, after the swelling in my crotch subsided. My bedroom was the first room we tackled, just to make it livable for me. There are no decorations or fancy things in it yet. My clothes are in the closet (or in boxes in front of the closet). I have my bed and a box that doubles as a nightstand. I did paint it, so I could probably move the rest of my furniture in here, but it just seems low on the priority list right now. Along with grooming my cat.

Max and I fell quickly into an amicable working partnership right from the get-go. It's sort of hard to reconcile this easy-going guy with his mother, Helga. In many ways, Max reminds me more of his Aunt Dorothy, who runs the B&B. Max has never mentioned a father or siblings, just his mom and aunt. It's pretty endearing to see how close he is with them.

He's also not that subtle about flirting with me. Truth be told, I enjoy it. I enjoy the attention, and I enjoy that someone as attractive as he is notices me. He's funny and I find myself laughing a lot with him. I think I'd forgotten what it was like to laugh. I'm relaxed around Max. It's refreshing. If I were looking for something more, which I'm totally not, I wouldn't have to look far. I wouldn't want to.

This week we're starting the bathroom. I can still shower at school, and I've rented a portable john for the back yard. Yuck, I know, but the house only has one bathroom. I've researched how to refinish and paint the clawfoot tub to restore it to its former glory. For some reason, someone along the way gutted the original tile and sink. The 1970s brown linoleum is getting ripped out, and I'm replacing it with a period-inspired white hexagonal tile. A pedestal sink will complete the look after white subway tile is added back to the walls. I wish I could do vintage tile, but I am on a budget so the tub will be the only authentic part. Max enlisted the help of a few of his friends to move the tub outside for me. I've got it up on sawhorses while I sand it down. It's hard work, and stripping and sanding the interior is even harder. The heat is not helping.

The sweat is dripping off me. My tank top is soaked, as is my sports bra. I'm wearing a baseball hat to keep the sun off my face but it's just making my head hot. I jump when something cold touches my back, right between my shoulder blades.

"Thought you could use this." Max hands me a large plastic cup filled with lemonade and ice.

I take the cup and smile. "How did you know?"

"It's freakin' hot today." He's always doing nice things like this for me. He's a genuinely nice guy.

"Ain't that the truth? Plus, being out in the sun working on this tub. Who knew stripping was this hard?" The words are out of my mouth before I even realize it. I see Max's eyes dart up and down my body. If I weren't flushed from the heat and humidity, I'd probably be turning beet red. With my free hand, I rip off my cap and shake my hair out.

"Aww, come on. You cannot do that to me."

I take a sip of my lemonade and sit down on an upside down milk crate. "What?"

"That whole hair shake thing, like you're in a music video, especially right after you've mentioned stripping." Max plops down on another crate. He's facing me and I'm trying hard not to meet his gaze. His light blue eyes are intense and I could easily get sucked into them.

"It's called I'm-trying-to-avoid-heat-stroke. Whose brilliant idea was this to refinish this tub?"

"That would be you. You're the boss."

"And don't you forget it," I say with a wink. Crap. I have got to stop flirting with him. It seems like the longer we work together, the more and more innuendos and double entendres slip out. It's flirting via witty banter, and I can't have it.

"How are things going inside?" Max is tiling while I'm working on the tub.

"Pretty good. The walls are ready to be grouted, and then we'll get the floor down."

"How do you think it looks?"

"This is your vision, Sadie, not mine."

"Does that mean you don't like it?" I can't help but pout a little. Yes, it is my house. It is going to be done the way I want it. But that doesn't mean that I don't want Max's approval. We've become close over the past three weeks. We work side by side almost every week-night. I don't see him on Fridays and Saturdays because I'm waitressing to finance this project. I don't ask what he does then. I don't want to know. In other words, I'm afraid he's got a girlfriend. Not that he's ever mentioned one.

I like Max. A lot. I know I can't, but I do. He's almost too good to be true. And what's not to like? He's gorgeous. He's funny. He's handy and good with his hands. I'd like to find out how good. Dammit, I cannot be thinking about that! Even though Therese has tried to tell me time after time I'm being irrational (well, she calls it crazy), I can't help but feel that somehow, being involved with me, will mean that something bad will happen. I like Max too much to predict his death. I know, crazy.

"I think it's coming out great. Very authentic to the house and the period."

"That doesn't sound convincing. What's your design style?"

"1980s flea market."

"Oooh, that's an under-valued niche."

"I don't spend much time at home. It's a place I sleep when I don't stay at the B&B. It's not really *home*, you know?"

"I know. That's why I'm working so hard to make this home. Plus, what else am I going to do with my time?"

He's quiet for a minute. I'm looking around my small back yard, already thinking of the things I will need to do out here. "So ... that boyfriend you were with at the B&B ... I take it you didn't reconcile?"

Now I'm looking at the ground by my feet, unable to meet Max's gaze. "No," I say, barely audible.

"Are you still in love with him?"

Why, why, why is Max bringing this up? There can only be one reason Max is bringing this up, and I don't want to think about it. He's fishing to see if I'm available. I'm not. Not because I'm taken, but because I like him too much to kill him off.

"That situation got really complicated." I look up at him and I see his mouth open, I'm guessing to ask for details. I'll never know because we're interrupted by the most annoying sound in the world—my sister's voice.

"Oh Jesus! What the hell are you doing back here? I've been at the door, banging and banging. Jesus, this place is a disaster."

I look up. I haven't seen Jenna since the wake. My mother has begged and pleaded with me to call her, to reconcile. I just can't. Check that—won't—do it. I have no use for her in my life. Yet here she is, intruding on my little oasis of happiness.

"Hasn't anyone told you it's hot out? Can we please go inside where it's cool?"

I just look at her, still too stunned to speak. Apparently, I don't need to, 'cause it looks like she's going to do all the talking today. "What the hell happened to you? You look disgusting. You have shit all over your face?"

"Nice to see you too, Jenna. You can leave the way you came in."

"Is that any way to greet your sister?"

"As far as I'm concerned, I don't have a sister."

I look over at Max, who is trying to keep a neutral look. I know him well enough to know that he wants all the juicy details. He's into gossip. He gets a lot of it at the B&B. He's worse than Therese.

"Well, maybe your friend is less rude. Aren't you going to introduce us?"

"Nope."

"Sadie, don't you think this has gone on for long enough?"

"'Til the day I die will not be long enough!"

Max stands up. "I'm gonna get back to work. If you'll excuse me."

We both watch him walk away. What a fine sight. I only wish that Jenna couldn't see it. She sits down on the crate that Max has vacated. She's wearing a tunic tank top that is light and flowy. In all reality, I think it's really cute and if our universe were different, I'd ask her to borrow it.

"How can you stand to work out here? It's so hot."

"The tub isn't going to refinish itself."

"Why don't you just buy a new one?"

"Because this is still in good shape. Do you know what a new one would cost? Why am I even asking that? Of course you don't. You've never worked a day for anything in your life. You just take, take, take. You wouldn't know what it's like to earn something, to make something. You just think the world should hand everything to you on a silver platter just because you're you."

She's quiet, playing with a strand of her red hair. "I used to be like that. I'm different now."

"No, you're not. You haven't changed in the past three months. You're you and you'll never change."

"That's not true. I have changed ... because of what happened."

"Because everyone knows what an evil, conniving snot you are? That you stole my boyfriend? That you were jerking him off while he was driving and he died because of it?"

She stands up, affronted that I'd even brought that stuff up. "No, because of *this*!" She pulls her shirt tight to reveal a very small bulge.

It's worse than a knife to the gut. All of the pain and sorrow comes rushing back. Pushing that down, I just focus on how much I hate my sister.

"Get out. Now. I don't ever want to see you again."

She starts to walk away. Max slowly exits the back door, I presume to check on me. Jenna looks over her shoulder and then stops. Turning around, she says, "I can't believe my own sister would be so hateful and spiteful. You know what, you're just jealous. I finally have something that you don't have."

I spy a hammer out of the corner of my eye. Before I even know what I'm doing, I've picked up the hammer and am hurling it in her general direction. She jumps out of the way, and the hammer lands with a soft thud in the boxwoods that border my property.

"What are you? Some kind of deranged freak? Are you trying to kill me?"

"Get off my property or I will have you arrested for trespassing!" I shout. My sister has little shame, but prison is probably the one thing that scares her, so she finally hightails it around to the front of the house. Wearily, I sink back onto my milk crate and put my head between my legs while I try to catch my breath.

"I bet your family gatherings are pretty entertaining."

"I wish I could say that this is unusual, but it's a typical performance for Jenna."

We're both quiet for a minute. Before I know it, I'm talking. Not really to Max but more to try for myself to work out what just happened. "I can't believe she's pregnant. She's going to be someone's mother. I ... just ... can't ..."

"She doesn't seem the calmest person, although you were the one who threw the hammer."
"She deserves it. She deserves so much *more.*"

"Wow. Remind me not to get on your bad side."

I didn't want to go here with Max. I wanted to let the past stay in the past and move forward. But the past has an uncanny way of popping up when I wish it wouldn't.

CHAPTER FIFTEEN

"So, you remember Valentine's Day Eve? You were asking earlier about the guy I was with. Well, after the bat incident, he told me he was leaving. We'd come up in separate cars, but I drank too much to drive home. When he still said he was leaving anyway, I ended it. I realized I deserved better than him."

"Yeah, you do."

"You're not kidding. Rob—Robin—to be accurate, left me, and came home to my sister. With whom, it turns out, he was also sleeping."

"Ouch."

"Yeah, but wait, there's more!"

"More? I'm afraid to ask."

"You should be. Do you remember that there was a bad car accident on Marysville Road that morning? You warned me about it. He was in the accident. With my sister. Rob was killed."

"I vaguely remember. He was with your sister? He left a weekend with you and went right to her?"

"Apparently, he had just proposed to her, and she was giving him a happy ending. It was too much; he lost control of the vehicle and drove into a tree."

"Wow."

"Yeah. So, yeah."

"And now ...?"

"Apparently she's pregnant. I'm guessing it's Rob's, although with Jenna you never can be too certain." And with that, the tears start to flow. Through my sobs, I say, "You know, I've cried more than I want to admit about this whole situation. I thought Rob was going to propose to me that weekend. Then, to find out he proposed to Jenna instead. And now, on top of it, a baby." And when those words are out of my mouth, the floodgates open, and I'm doing that ugly cry thing.

I'm not even aware of Max moving toward me until I'm in his arms. Sobbing, snotting all over the place. My tears are hot as they stream down my cheeks. I try to stop but the more I try to stop, the more I cry. It feels good to be able to lean on someone, even if for a brief moment. Max doesn't say anything, but I feel a quiet support in his presence. Finally, he says, "Do you feel better now?"

"No, I'm not sure I'll ever feel better about this. Certainly not when there's a baby to remind me."

"You're not the one stuck raising the kid. She is. As far as I can tell, it's totally not your problem."

"Aaahh, you don't know my dysfunctional family. What's Jenna's problem is the whole family's problem. As you can see, she sought me out."

We've separated now, and I'm in desperate need of a beer. I open up the door and Max reaches forward, holding the door for me as I enter in. I head right down the hall and to the kitchen. Taking out two bottles, I pop the caps and set them on the small kitchen table. Plopping down, I take a long pull before I start speaking again.

"It's not supposed to be like this. I'm not supposed to hate my sister. But for this, I do, and I always will."

Max looks at me thoughtfully. "It's not like you had any idea they were sleeping together. And he's already been punished enough, don't you think?"

"No, it's not the sex thing. Well, it is but not. Oh, I don't know." I don't want to talk about the real issue. But then, suddenly I do. I've kept it pent up for too long, and

Jenna just poured a whole lot of lemon juice on my paper cuts.

"I had a miscarriage about seven months ago. I was eleven weeks along, so I would have been due any day now."

"Oh."

"Yeah, no one knows. I mean, I told my best friend, Therese, but that's it. The only other person who knew was Rob. He was not pleased, to say the least. I don't think he wanted kids. I've wondered since he died if that's what drove him to start hooking up with my sister."

"So this is going to be hard then."

"Any way you slice it."

After a long pause, Max says, "So this is nice and uncomfortable."

It's enough to get me laughing. Yeah, that's the story of my life. Nice and uncomfortable. "It's just not fair, you know? I'm the one with the stable job. I would never have done something so reckless as what she did that caused Rob's death. Why does she get to be the one to have a baby and not me?"

"A baby or Rob's baby?"

I think about that for a minute. "A baby."

"Then there's time. You can find someone else. You will find someone else. You're a great catch, you know. Plus, this house is going to be such a draw."

"I appreciate the vote of confidence, but I'm off men."

He raises an eyebrow. "You're a switch hitter? I never would have guessed that."

Laughing again, I swat at him playfully. "No, I'm off dating."

He grabs my hand and holds it. "Just because Rob didn't treat you right, it doesn't mean every guy out there will treat you badly too." He's looking into my eyes, and I know what he's trying to do. I want to say yes, and I want to let him. But something in my stomach tells me no. I have to listen to that inner voice.

Slowly, I pull my hand back. "No, it's not that. I, I have my reasons. I don't want to get into it, but it's how I've decided to live my life." How do I tell him that I'm a freak with a crazy psychic ability that kills people?

We get back to work, but the easy feeling has slipped away, and it's more an uncomfortable silence. I feel Max watching me expectantly. Eventually he goes back into the house. The thought of the baby pops up again. Not that I'd gotten over my boyfriend sleeping with my sister, because I hadn't, but I was trying to move on. Now, there would be no moving on. Forever, there would be a piece of Rob in our family, inserting himself in the middle of us. Oh, geez, that sounds dirty. You know what I mean.

My heart's no longer in refinishing my tub. However, if I don't finish stripping and sanding it today, I'll be behind schedule all week. I don't want that to happen, so I crank on some 80s music and throw myself back into stripping.

"Sadie ... Sadie ... SADIE!"

I am so lost in my work that I don't even hear Max calling me. I look around. It's dusk. Where did the day go? "Oh sorry. I was sort of focused."

"I get that. It's looking great."

I step back and admire the tub, now free of any rust or cracked paint. I'll seal it tomorrow and then paint it after that. "I'm going to paint the outside black and the inside and lip white so it will really pop. I'm undecided about the feet, whether to paint them chrome or black."

"What about white?"

I squint while I look at the tub, trying to envision it. "Yeah, that might work too. And it would save me from having to buy the chrome paint. Any little bit of savings will help." I wipe the sweat from my brow on my arm. In doing so, I'm exposed to my own rank smell, which is the result of honest day's work spent slaving away in the sun. "Ugh. I need a shower. And since my tub is out here, that's going to be an issue. I hope it's not too late to drop in on Therese."

"Hadn't you thought about this?"

"Honestly, not that much. I figured I could shower in the morning in the gym at school, but I didn't count on the fact that I'd be so disgusting I'd need to shower before I went to bed."

"Where does Therese live?"

"Over in Terrenceville."

Max looks at me for a minute. "I only live about five minutes from here. Why don't you just come over and get cleaned up? We'll order some food and eat too. You've got to be hungry."

One part of me is shouting "YES! YES! YES!" which makes me want to say "NO! NO! NO!" But I am tired, and it will take me at least thirty minutes to get to Therese's. This is so much closer and involves food. And Max. Easy decision.

I gather up my stuff, which is basically just a new pair of shorts and tank top, fresh underclothes, and a toiletries bag. I make sure I have a comb and my favorite pair of flip flops. Have I mentioned how much I love summer?

"That's it?" Max is looking at my rucksack.

"Yeah. Why?"

He shakes his head. "Just used to a different kind of girl, that's all."

I ignore that softball he lobs me, although I'm dying to know what he means by that. I follow him to his house, which is actually seven minutes away. Crap. I don't like that he lives close. It's too-easy access.

Walking through his front door, I can see that Max was not lying about his decorating style. The floors are a brown and gold linoleum in the foyer. In the living room, there are gorgeous wood floors. They're easy to miss because there's an oversized, salmon-colored sectional that takes up more than half the room. Shiny brass and glass end tables bookend the sectional. It's like 1985 threw up in here. He points to the bathroom, and the decor only gets worse. The oval spa tub, extra low toilet and the sinks are all teal green. The teal is offset by geometric patterned wallpaper and again, shiny brass fixtures. Blech.

That being said, he has a functioning bathroom, so as my dad always said, "In the valley of the blind, the one-eyed man is king."

The shower feels great and I emerge as a new and better-smelling, woman. Now I can bust on Max about the decorating style. He's on his couch, feet propped up in the recliner end of the sectional, and a beer in hand. There's another beer and a Chinese menu on the coffee table.

"I'm starving and you must be too. They deliver, so tell me what you want, and I'll call an order in."

YOU! A voice screams in my head. Damn it! Why does everything this man says or does provoke a potential sexual comment from me? I try to regroup and pick the food I think I'll be able to eat the easiest. The last thing I need is for Max to see my ineptitude with chopsticks and think I'm even more of a train wreck than I appear to be.

Max calls the order in, and then we have to fill that awkward silence while waiting for the food to arrive. Looking around the living room, I'm too distracted by the hideous decor to think about anything else. "You weren't kidding when you said your style was 1980s garage sale." I take a seat on the other part of the sectional. Far enough away to behave myself but not so far as to appear rude.

"Actually, I didn't buy all this stuff myself." He smiles proudly.

"Dear Lord, I would hope not."

"It's sort of ..."

"Interesting? Intriguing? Electric?"

"Abhorrent is the word I think I'm looking for. Hideous would work too. And what kind of description is electric?" Although, even though I won't admit it out loud, this couch is very comfortable. I could see taking a nice Saturday afternoon nap on it someday."You know, the opposite of sedate and humdrum." He's freshly showered and in a clean pair of jeans. He must have used the other bathroom while I was showering.

"Well, it is anything but that."

"This was my aunt's place. I inherited it from her."

"Dorothy?" This couch is really comfortable. I'm sort of having a hard time keeping my eyes open.

"Oh, that's right. I forgot that you knew her. No, my father's sister. She passed away about five years ago."

"I'm sorry about that. Were you close?"

"No, not at all. I was pleasantly surprised when I got the call from her lawyer. I didn't really even know her. My dad passed away when I was two, and we drifted apart from his side of the family. I don't think they ever liked my mom in the first place, and she wasn't the easiest to get along with while she was grieving." Max looks around the room, a wistful look on his face. I wonder if he's thinking about his dad or the aunt who left him this house.

"Helga? Hard to get along with? I can't imagine that in the least."

"So, you've never really told me, how do you know my mom?" Max stretches his arms up and folds them behind his head. He looks relaxed and comfortable.

"She hasn't told you?"

He shakes his head. "Nope."

"My dad is one of her patients in the nursing home. He's been there for almost four years. He had a stroke, and all the greatest treatments were not enough to make up for a surgeon's incompetence. So there he is, motionless and helpless. He's on your mom's unit."

"Oh, well, now makes sense that she wouldn't tell me how she knew you. Privacy laws and all that nonsense." He pauses, looking at me for a minute. I can tell by the inquisitive look on his face that he's going to start asking me a lot of questions. That man's face reads like an open book. And then he starts. "Tell me about your family."

CHAPTER SIXTEEN

I don't want to talk about my family. I mean, I love my mom and dad but the rest is sort of ... yeah. That. I think I always thought we were the stereotypical suburban family, except with dead bodies next door (and in my dad's car). As I've grown older, I'm saddened by the dysfunction between my siblings and me.

"Well, I told you about my dad. We were—are—very close. I still go to visit him every weekday. I don't go by on the weekends as much because he gets other visitors then. I miss him terribly. My mom, well, she's a unique character. She's a good mom, she is. Except she can't help but fall under Jenna's spell, which then causes problems between us. My dad used to tell my mom when Jenna was yanking her around, but he's not around to do that anymore."

"Is it just you and Jenna?"

"No, we have an older brother, Brady. He's married to Tina. I'm pretty sure she took his balls when they got engaged. He's the most apathetic, useless person. On top of that, he's pretty much a douchebag."

"Wow, tell me how you really feel."

"After Dad's stroke, we sued the doctor. It was malpractice, no question. My dad had been a small business owner—he was partners with his brother in a funeral home. I know he saved for retirement, but I don't think it would have been enough. This way we could ensure his care and Mom's well being. To me, that's why we sued. So Dad could be where he is and Mom would never have to worry and could keep her house. So, right before the settlement came in, Brady tried to convince Mom and the lawyer that we should split the settlement four ways. That would have left Mom with only one-quarter of the settlement to provide for her and Dad. When I brought that up, Tina's response—with which Brady agreed—was that if I didn't like it, I could give my parents my portion."

"Essentially leaving you with nothing, your mom with barely enough and—"

"And Brady and Jenna would get a tidy little package for doing nothing. Jenna at least goes to see Dad on holidays or when my mom guilts her into it. Brady and Tina haven't been in probably two years. But then, Brady posts on Facebook about how much he misses my dad and writes all these letters to him. When I've confronted him about it, he says he can't bear to see him like that, so it's easier for him to think of Dad as already dead."

"Wow, that is pretty douchey."

"I can't argue with that one."

"It doesn't matter now, anyway, since the settlement will remain in trust as long as Dad's alive. The primary reason for it is to take care of him and Mom. Brady, Jenna, and me—our needs are secondary."

"So you won on that one, I take it?"

Smiling, I nod. It was a sweet victory.

The doorbell rings, signaling the arrival of our food. I get up to go get my wallet, but Max throws his hand in my direction. "I got this. Relax."

I sink back into the couch and wait for him to return. In a minute, he's back with the brown paper bags, spreading the white containers over the table. We're silent for a few minutes as the need for food overtakes the need for conversation. Inhaling the food voraciously, I hadn't even realized I was this hungry until I started eating. I try not to be too clumsy with the chopsticks, but fail miserably, repeatedly dropping clumps of white rice all over the place—the table, the floor, down the front of my shirt.

Okay. So do I fish it out? What is the proper etiquette for food in the boobs?

I'm sitting there, just trying to figure out what to do when Max looks up. He's a pro with the chopsticks. I can get the rice out later.

"You're good with your chopsticks. I'm a mess." Again the thought of Max being good with his hands runs through my head. STOP IT!

"Sonya Lin." He waggles the chopsticks at me.

"What?"

"Sonya Lin. I went to grade school with her. Her family was Taiwanese. She taught the entire class how to use chopsticks. It's never failed me yet." Waggling again. Then, he picks up and pops a piece of chicken in his mouth with ease.

"I need a Sonya Lin," I say, trying desperately to grab a piece of broccoli with my chopsticks. My mouth waters just looking at it. Why can't I pick the damn thing up? Get in my mouth already!

"No, you don't. You've got me."

My girl parts threaten to ignite when he says that. Damn, I've been alone too long.

He apparently doesn't notice me having a small coronary over here. "You have to hold the bottom one like you would hold a pencil."

I pick up the chopsticks and try to follow his instructions, hooking my index finger around the top stick. Holy cow, it works!

"Look at me! I'm doing it!"

"Does that mean you're going to stop dropping rice everywhere?" And he puts emphasis on the word *everywhere*, which means I know he knows about the rice in my bra. I try to pretend that he doesn't. That he's not thinking about my bra right now. And that I'm not thinking about the things he could do with my bra right now. With his mouth.

Oh crap, I need a cold shower.

Have I mentioned that Max is not only hot, but funny and incredibly sexy? Plus, I know he owns leather chaps. I need to STOP. NOW.

Standing up quickly, I thank Max for dinner as I start to pack up my containers. Okay, what is the proper thing to do here? Do I take my leftovers or leave them, since he paid for them? If we were in a restaurant, I would take my own leftovers home, but we're at his home. But if he eats out of my containers, isn't that gross? No, it's kind of sexy. I can see him, standing over his sink, eating out of the box, fancy chopstick action. And no shirt. His muscles would be bulging each time he lifted a bite to his incredibly kissable lips.

"Sadie? Earth to Sadie?"

Snapping out of my entirely inappropriate reverie, "Oh yeah? What?"

"You stood up and now you're standing there all weird. Are you okay?"

"Yeah, I'm fine." I reply. I have got to get out of there. "Thanks again. See you whenever."

He stands up and follows me to his front door. "Tomorrow, right? Tomorrow's Monday and we usually work then, right? I have a light day with my other stuff. What's a good time to come by?"

There's not much distance between us anymore. He's looking at me eagerly. I have to split before I attack him and ruin our friendship.

I kind of get the feeling he wouldn't mind that much. I wouldn't mind that much. But I would. I'm off men. I mumble, "Whenever. Let yourself in. Do whatever you want." To my body. GAH.

I give a shaky wave and head out to my car. I whip out my phone and dial Therese, putting her on speaker so I can drive legally while still talking.

"I'm trying to watch my show."

"A show where a bunch of rich bitches throw tables at each other is not entertainment. They're just a bunch of arrogant, alcoholic, pushy women who have a misguided sense of entitlement. No wonder one of them is going to jail."

"Tell me how you really feel."

"I just did."

"Okay, then tell me why you're really calling. You never call this late at night."

"What time is it?" I look at my dashboard clock. Ten-thirty. "Oh geez, I'm sorry. I didn't mean to call so late. It's been one of those days."

"Dare I even ask?"

"Too much to get into tonight, but I need you to talk me down. I'm going to end up jumping Max."

"What's the problem with that?"

"You know. I can't do that to another person."

"I don't think the world would be so cruel as to take someone else away from you, do you?"

"Yeah, I do. Especially considering the other issue of the day. Apparently, my sister is a Fertile Myrtle."

"Come again?"

"Yeah, that's the other thing, which is why I want to focus on my obsession with my hired laborer."

"Who knows? He could be the next Magic Mike. You should give it a shot."

"You know his name is really Mike, right?"

"Oh yeah, you told me that. Before I get lost in a Channing daydream, don't think you're getting off the hook that easily. What's this about Jenna?"

"Pregnant. Rob's baby."

"No shit!"

"Yes shit, so that's why I'm not tempting the universe right now."

"She's going to have a baby? She hates being around children."

"I know, and she'll be going at it alone, so I'm betting that my mom will end up doing the heavy lifting on this. There is no way Jenna will be able to handle it by herself."

"Maybe she can finally rise to the challenge and will surprise us all."

"Maybe Rob's parents will sue for custody, and she'll get off the hook, totally scot free."

CHAPTER SEVENTEEN

Rob's mother, Bernice, has little patience for Jenna, or anyone else in my family, for that matter. I'm watching all this unfold at Sunday dinner. It's the end of June, and Jenna has finally decided she needs to come clean with Rob's parents. Naturally, my mom offers to put on a big meal so we can all come together. I still want nothing to do with Jenna or her spawn, but there is no way in hell I'm missing this showdown.

My mom's running herself ragged between the meat on the grill and all the rest of the prep in the kitchen. I want a front row seat when Rob's parents show up but for right now, I'm being useful and setting the table for Mom. I've brought a large tossed salad, and I'm fixing fresh dressing for it. Jenna is pouting because she wanted to have the dinner outside, but the insects are terrible this year, so Mom insisted on staying in.

"God, what's in that dressing? It's so smelly," she says, wrinkling her nose as she walks by, stealing a crouton and popping it in her mouth. "You know, it's a pregnancy thing. I am just sooooo sensitive to smells right now. Not that you would know what it's like."

That's the thing with Jenna. She has moments when she can be fine but then just has to push, push, push it over the edge. I just ignore her, like I always do. And when I ignore her, she keeps upping the ante until I lose control and snap at her. I am determined not to let it happen this time.

"I'm soooo tired all the time too. This is hard work, growing a person. Most days, I'm surprised I'm even functional. I'm starting to nest as well. You should see all the cute things I've bought for baby Robin. This baby is going to have so many toys to play with, it's going to be ridiculous."

"The only one here that's ridiculous is you." I can't help but snap at her.

"Well, you don't have to bite my head off."

That's it—I can't handle it anymore. "Jenna, what were you thinking? I mean, hooking up with my boyfriend was one thing, but how could you let this happen?"

She's on her way out of the room but stops and turns to me. "I guess Mother Nature had a plan."

"A plan? You wouldn't know a plan if it bit you in the ass! What are you going to do for money? For child care? Do you actually think you can take care of this baby?" My voice is rising octave after octave. Pretty soon only dogs will be able to hear me.

"Sadie, all your ranting is giving me a headache. I can't handle this kind of stress in my delicate condition. Are you trying to stress me out? It's bad for the baby. Mom, you need to make her stop interrogating me!"

"Girls!" Mom admonishes us. "The Hendersons are going to be here any minute. Stop your bickering. I don't want a repeat of the wake when they get here. You need to be on your best behavior."

It's like we're eight and ten again.

"Well, I'm the only one here who has an excuse for passing out and throwing up now. Sadie just likes to be dramatic."

To keep from punching her, I grab the tray of rolls and cheese and bring it to the table. The doorbell rings, and Jenna calls, "Sadie, be a doll and answer the door for me. I don't want to greet Bernice and George like this."

Like I'm the freakin' hired help. I open the door and plaster a smile on my face. "Hello Mr. and Mrs.—Bernice and George. Please come in." I always had trouble being on a first-name basis with them. Rob called me old fashioned and dated. I like to think I'm respectful. I think it's really more from hearing my dad and uncle address clients at the funeral home. They always used titles.

"Oh, it's you."

What a rousing endorsement. In a hollow voice, I manage, "How have you been?"

When Rob and I were together, I never saw this side of his mother. She was always very cordial to me. Certainly not warm and fuzzy, but I never would have pictured her as a bitch. Guess what? She is. Sort of makes me glad I'm not saddled with her as my mother-in-law. "My son is dead. How do you think I've been?"

So I see her attitude has not improved since the wake.

My mother rushes out. "Bernice, George, I'm so glad you accepted this invitation. I think we have a lot to talk about."

Bernice looks at her husband. "I didn't want to come here. He made me."

George gives my mom a weak smile. "Carol, thank you for inviting us. This has been a very difficult time for us, as I'm sure you can imagine."

"Oh, yes, I'm sure. I'm just getting the meat off the grill. Sadie, please get our guests something to drink."

She turns and is gone, leaving me standing there like a nincompoop. "Um, uh, what can I get you to drink? Wine? Beer? Soda? Water?" A fork to stick in my eye just to make this all stop?

I get their orders and usher them into the dining room. Where the hell is Jenna? And then I get it—she's waiting to make her entrance. Like at the wake, Jenna is always about her entrance. It started the day she was born, when my mom went into labor and delivered Jenna at the movie theater. Seriously, why couldn't my mom ever deliver at a hospital like a normal person? We always said she was born to be an actress. Except for the complete lack of talent, she has everything she needs. Too bad she wasn't born a Kardashian.

Sitting uncomfortably, trying not to make eye contact with Rob's parents, I'm completely at a loss for what to say. Luckily, Rob's dad breaks the ice.

"How's the rest of the school year gone for you?"

"It's been a struggle, but we've made it through. It was tough. First losing a student and then Rob. I think we'll all be glad when this year comes to a close. Will you be at Awards Night for the scholarship announcement?"

"Yes, we plan to be there. It's the least we can do to carry on Robin's name." George is at least pleasant to me.

"I think he would really like it, a scholarship going to a student who plans to study economics. It isn't always the most popular course, but Rob was certainly one of the most popular teachers." Because he let everyone get away with everything. But they don't need to know that he was a pushover.

So, now it's time for Jenna to drop the bomb on Rob's parents. She's changed her clothes into an obvious maternity top. But she's not that big yet so it sort of looks more like an unfortunate wardrobe choice. Bernice gets it right away. I would guess that Jenna is not their favorite person to begin with. I don't think this makes the situation any better.

"Oh, no. Not you. I'd take her—" she's pointing at me, "over you." Geez, thanks for the vote of confidence.

"Well, I'm the one you have to deal with. I'm the one giving you a grandchild."

"The only thing you'll be giving us is a paternity test."

"How can you question this? Like I would cheat on Robin?"

I can't hold back on that one. "Well, I never thought Rob would cheat on me, let alone with my sister. Or that my sister would sleep with my boyfriend, so it just goes to show you, you can't trust anyone anymore."

Jenna shoots me her patented death-ray stare. I swear she could win awards for it. As if my comment has somehow betrayed our sisterly bond. Oh, wait, her sleeping with my boyfriend took care of that one.

"Well, since you all have doubt, I would be happy to submit to a paternity test, and then you can apologize to me and little Robin."

Bernice gasps and then lets out a tiny squeak. Her mouth is hanging open. At this moment, my mom walks back in, carrying a tray loaded with steaming meat. I get up, take the tray from her and place it on the table. Using the tongs, I snag a chicken breast and plop it down on my plate. Everyone else is just sitting there, staring at each other. Jenna and Bernice are engaged in a death-stare showdown. Man, the kid is going to have one heck of a staring ability. Like it could win championships.

My mother sits down, looks around, and then notices I'm eating. "Sadie, for heaven's sake, don't be rude. Didn't I raise you better?"

George looks at my plate and then at my mother. "Carol, I don't presume to tell you your business in your own house, but I don't think Sadie's manners are the ones you should be concerned about right now."

I want to high five this man.

The rest of the dinner is about as uncomfortable as you can get, short of having itching powder in your underpants. I think Bernice may have bested Jenna in the stare down. Jenna is a bit on the subdued side. Now George and Bernice are exchanging glances, having a whole conversation without ever saying a word. My mother prattles on as if nothing is amiss. She's good at doing that. She's bad at acknowledging there is a problem. Hence, Jenna.

Finally, what seems like hours later (but actually is only ninety minutes), Bernice and George are ready to leave. Bernice addresses Jenna for the first time. "After we confirm the paternity, we will be sitting down with a lawyer and drawing up a visitation agreement. If you don't cooperate, we will consider going for custody."

Boom. There it is.

CHAPTER EIGHTEEN

After the Hendersons leave, Jenna is all in a tizzy. Which means, obviously, that she can't help Mom clean up. Instead, she's moving from one chair to another, fanning herself. There's a fair amount of moaning and wailing going on as well.

"What if they try and take my baby?"

I swear she's channeling Meryl Streep in "A Cry in the Night."

Mom, always the voice of reason. Well, usually the voice of reason, chimes in, "You'll just have to hire a lawyer. Until then, try to stay on their good side. If they want to see the baby, let them. Include them in the child's life. This is all they have left of their son. Try to respect that."

See? Good advice that any normal person in her early thirties would heed. Too bad Jenna is not normal. I can tell by her response that she stopped listening at the word lawyer. She fixated on that and didn't hear the rest of it.

"How am I supposed to afford a lawyer? Retail does not pay that much you know. Those people are loaded, I bet. I should sue them for child support."

"If you can't afford a child, then maybe you shouldn't be having one." I can't help myself. Jenna's job is fairly decent. She's the manager at a very upscale boutique. She's good at selling. However, she's also good at spending. Her savings could use a little work. Where I could buy a house on just my salary, sometimes Jenna has trouble making her rent. I don't know how she makes her car payments.

"Well, it's not like I planned to be doing this alone, you know. I thought I'd have Robin with me for support."

I know I should leave well enough alone, but I just can't. Like that thread that's hanging, it begs me to pull. "Do you know that Rob would have supported you?"

Tossing her hair in that defiant manner, she looks at me. "Why on earth wouldn't he?"

"Because Rob wasn't on board with the whole kid thing."

"And how would you know that?"

"Jenna, are you a moron? He was my boyfriend. We'd talked about it. A lot." No way in hell was I telling her about my pregnancy and miscarriage. That would just be one more thing for her to hold over my head about how she's better than I am. There was a time in our lives when Jenna and I weren't competitive. We didn't hate each other. We liked each other. We were the best of friends. We played together every day. We picked out the same outfits so that we were dressed alike. Even though we had our own rooms, we slept in the same room each night. Then, one day, it abruptly changed. It probably coincided with puberty and hormonal changes. I was in eighth grade and Jenna was in sixth. She came home from school, threw her bag at me, and told me she hated me and that I'd ruined her life. Despite trying to talk to her about it, she shut down, and our relationship has been forever changed.

It was trivial stuff too. If I told Mom I wanted something for Christmas, suddenly she had to have it for her birthday (right before Christmas). If I was joining a club, even if she had been interested in it, it suddenly became the "lamest." But as much as she criticized me, there was a one-upmanship that became tiring. I'm not saying I was blameless. I fed into her drama. I whined and complained almost as much as she did. However, somewhere along the line, I grew up and she didn't.

Mom was caught in the middle. We've gone through periods where we're very close. We've been through periods where she and Jenna are very close. That never happens at the same time. I feel like we're always pulling Mom in one direction or another. About the time when Dad had his stroke, I decided I was tired of the game and took myself out.

It's hurt Mom, I'm sure. I miss the relationship we used to have. Jenna wasted no time swooping in and playing the helpless role. Stupid things, like needing my mom to come over and get her Christmas decorations out of storage and putting them up for her. I'm resentful of the attention Jenna gets, like she's a helpless child. Not that I want to be helpless, but it would be nice to be taken care of every now and again, instead of taking care of everyone else. No one sees that Jenna's manipulative. No one expects more of her.

And no one, besides me, sees any problem with her getting knocked up by my boyfriend.

Part of me wants to jump up and down and scream and shout. I want to tell everyone that I was pregnant and lost my baby. I want the sympathy, the coddling. I want people to think that I'm the special one, not her. I'm jealous that she gets the attention. And I'm too damn old to feel that way.

I can't keep putting my mom in the middle. I can't keep swallowing my pride and kowtowing to my sister. And this baby thing is only going to make that much harder. Especially if things get nasty. Well, nastier.

The kitchen is in pretty good shape, so I give Mom a quick hug and leave without saying goodbye to my sister. Walking out into the driveway, I see Aunt Elaine outside pruning her rose bushes. Our family living next door to the funeral home was convenient for Dad, to say the least. I always wondered if Mom minded living so close to her brother-in-law. Uncle Peter was sort of the polar opposite of Dad. Uncle Peter and Aunt Elaine never had children. I always wondered why, but sometimes I think it was because the three of us were a handful.

I usually avoided talking to my aunt, but tonight I decide to go over there.

"How's it going? Nice crop of roses this year."

"They're coming along. How are you doing? I hear that you bought yourself a little house."

"I did. Lots of work, but I think it will be worth it in the end. Of course, it may take me several years to get through all the renovations I want to do. Maybe next summer I can hit you up for some landscaping ideas. I'd love to have roses that look like this." I touch the delicate pink blossom. So beautiful, so dainty, yet tough all at the same time.

"They've been my pride and joy for years, these roses." Aunt Elaine has a wistful expression on her face.

"They're a lot of work, aren't they?" In my head, I'm thinking maybe I want something lower maintenance. Still, now I have to invite her over and get her opinion. It won't be so bad. After all, I'm shaping up to be the old aunt who never has kids, just like her. Won't hurt me to spend some more time with her. I'll be looking for the company when I'm older too.

"I've had a lot of free time over the years, with Peter working odd hours at the funeral home. Roses are my thing."

"I get that. It had to be hard being on your own so much." Mom was always busy with the three of us. She never seemed bored when Dad had a Saturday funeral or was called out of the house at odd hours to transport a body.

"Isn't that why you're taking on this home renovation project?" From anyone else, that comment would have seemed mean. From Aunt Elaine, it was direct but soft.

"Probably. I've been looking at houses for a long time now. I've always wanted to own my own home. I love the old ones too. I don't mind the restoration aspect. It's fun."

"You know, when you were young, you were always the one helping Simon with all the projects. I always thought it was odd that you were the one with the tools, not Brady."

"Brady is a tool."

She laughs. "Yes, he's quite the piece of work. Breaks my heart, really, to see how Brady and Jenna turned out. The three of you were like our own children in many ways. You're the only one who has a decent head and heart."

My eyes fill up. Partially from the compliment, but mostly because someone has *finally* acknowledged me for being a good person.

Aunt Elaine continues. "I know this year has been rough on you."

"And it's only going to get rougher."

"Why do you say that?"

We've migrated to the large front porch and are sitting on the wicker furniture usually reserved for the bereaved who can't go the full three hours of the wake without sneaking outside for a smoke. "Haven't you heard the joyous news? Jenna is in the family way."

"You're kidding!"

"Wish I was. She's pregnant with Rob's baby."

Aunt Elaine has no words for this. I understand it. It's like a bad soap opera being played out in my life. Finally, she seems able to speak. "I, um, take it this was unplanned?"

"You could say that." I think for a minute, "Actually, to tell you the truth, I don't know. With Jenna, it's hard to say. I mean she was, after all, having an affair with my boyfriend."

"Well, there's that."

We sit in silence for a minute, the night sky creeping in and easing out the last moments of daylight. I wonder why I haven't made more time for Aunt Elaine since I grew up and left my parents' house. Although I don't like to think it, in some ways I'm just as selfish as Brady and Jenna.

"I'm sorry I haven't been around more."

"You've been busy. Peter says you still visit the nursing home almost every day."

I look at my toes, nails in desperate need of some polish. I've been too busy with the house to even think about it lately. "I do. Well, weekdays at least. I'm still waitressing and then working on the house."

"What are you working on?"

"The bathroom is just about finished. I restored the original clawfoot tub and redid the rest. I just have to finish putting in the light fixtures and shelving, and then that room will be done."

"Then what?"

"Taking down some woodwork in the living room, stripping it, staining it, and putting it back up. The rest just needs a good cleaning and polishing. There are some gorgeous built-ins. Painting. I've been trying not to move too much in so that I won't have to move too much back out. I have a dumpster for all the debris. The place is sort of a mess, but I love it. It's my mess. When I get it livable, you'll have to come over and see it."

"I will. It sounds like you've got a lot on your plate. Are you doing it by yourself?"

"I've hired a contractor to help me. But otherwise, yes."

"That's impressive. Simon would be proud."

"I'd like to think so. I tell him about it all but it's hard to know what he hears. So, thanks for listening, Aunt Elaine. It was nice chatting with you." I stand up to leave.

"Any time, Sadie. Don't be a stranger. If you need an open ear, I'm here."

I give my aunt a quick hug and then run down the stairs. Once at the bottom of the stairs, I look back up at her. "You know, Jenna's done a lot of crazy things before, but this really takes the cake."

"Yes, it does."

"I mean, who does this?" I'm talking more to myself than to Elaine.

"You don't deserve this."

"No, I don't. But what about Jenna? What does she deserve?"

"Waterboarding?"

I laugh, a bitter, shrill laugh. "That would be too good for her. I swear, I could kill her for this. I really could."

"You don't mean that Sadie honey."

"Unfortunately, Aunt Elaine, this time I do."

CHAPTER NINETEEN

"It's gorgeous."

"I know."

"I'm completely in love with it."

"How can you not be?"

I turn to look at Max. We're standing in the doorway to my bathroom, admiring the gleam of the chrome fixtures, the shine of the white tile, the majesty of the tub. It is perfect. It fits the period of the house with all the modern conveniences, right down to the fluffy Egyptian cotton towels that were a complete and total splurge for me. I cannot wait to wrap myself in them. To keep the black of the tub and the white of the floor and tiled wall from being too stark, I painted the walls above the tile a bright aqua blue.

I'd been nervous about that combination, but Max assured me that it would be great. If I weren't happy, he said he'd repaint it, free of charge. Actually, we'd had some heated discussions about the paint, even as it was going on the walls. I was sort of worked up and accidentally splattered Max with it. From there, it escalated into a paint fight. We finally ended up in the backyard, hosing each other off. Thankfully the water had been cold, because things had been about to get more physical than I was ready for.

"You were right about the blue."

"I know."

"Humble much?"

"Not about this."

I try not to notice how his grin shows off his straight white teeth or how his eyes seem to match the aqua on the walls. Likewise, I'm totally not looking at how his feet, usually trapped in work boots, are long and lean in his flip flops, making me wonder what else on his body is long. I shake my head a bit to clear the impure thoughts that are encouraging me to throw myself into his arms and rip off all his clothes. I don't know how much longer I can hold off his advances, which are getting more obvious and more frequent.

Giving in would not be good.

Or more likely, it would be very good.

But bad, I tell myself, since we still have several rooms to renovate before the end of the summer. My goal is to get all the rooms painted and the trim done by the time I go back to school, as well as finish the mudroom overhaul that has brought the laundry out of the basement. The washer and dryer have already been moved, but nothing else is done in that room. I have to fix up the living room fireplace and built-in bookcases as well. The original lead glass windows above the bookcases are on the schedule for this week. The mudroom project will be the next big thing. Replacing all the light fixtures and outlets will be something I can do on my own in the fall, if I don't get to it before then. Thinking about being in the house without Max here working makes me sort of sad. Lots of sad, actually. I think I've spent more time with Max since Memorial Day than I did in a year with Rob, which, when you consider that we worked together, says a lot.

I'm going to have to come up with more projects just to keep Max around. Or I could just ask him out. That might be easier. Until I accidentally kill him, like I did Rob. And all those other people.

Then I notice he's looking at me. Uh oh, please tell me I was not speaking out loud.

"What?" I try to compose myself.

"I should ask you that. Where did you go? You were all happy for a second, then you looked down, and it was like you got lost in a fog or something. You do that a lot. Are you okay? Are you offended by my toes?"

"No, I'm fine, but why would I be offended by your toes? I can't smell them from here or anything."

Max looks at his feet and wiggles his toes a little. We're still standing side by side just outside the bathroom door. It's a rather awkward position, and we should move, but I'm not going to lie—I appreciate the proximity.

"They're freakishly long. My college roommates always made fun of them."

"They are more like fingers than toes."

"That's why I never wear shoes that show my toes."

"I thought you just wore the boots because it's part of your sexy-construction-worker image."

He turns and looks at me. Somehow, we're even closer than before. My chest is rising and falling, trying unsuccessfully to keep air in my lungs. I could get lost—scratch that—I am already lost in his eyes. They're twinkling with some sort of mischievous thought. It's the sort of look he gets before he does something he's not supposed to, like that time he dropped ice cubes down my shirt.

He steps towards me, and I instinctively back up. My back is now against the doorframe, and I've nowhere left to go. It's hard to catch my breath with him this close. And with his body pressing into mine. And with his lips so very close.

"So, you think I'm sexy?"

I try to hold my ground. "What? Where'd you get that idea?"

"You just said I had a sexy-construction-worker image, didn't you?"

I try to think but all I can focus on is how close those lips are to mine and how easy it would be to close that distance. "I, um, I ... I meant that all construction workers think they have a sexy thing going on. That's all."

"So," he says, licking his lips, "you don't find me attractive?"

God, he's killing me. All the flirting, all the teasing, all those comments have led up to this very moment. I want him so badly right now. But I can't. I cannot do this to him.

"No, not really." I'm so lying.

"Then why are you breathing heavy? And why are your pupils dilated? And why do you keep pressing your hips into mine?" With that, he grinds into me, matching my unconscious movements. Dammit. My own body is betraying me.

Before I can lie some more, he takes my breath away, once and for all claiming my mouth. Oh. My. God. His mouth is warm and delicious and skilled. His stubble scrapes my face, but just makes me want him even more. I'm weak in the knees and hot and bothered all at the same time. My lady bits have awakened from their slumber and are screaming in joy and agony.

I wrap my leg around his waist as his hand begins to caress my thigh. It reaches into my shorts and grabs a handful of my ass, squeezing with a firm pressure. Thank goodness it's summer, so we don't have much clothing to remove to get to business. His mouth moves to my neck and chest, and I'm frantically trying to remove his t-shirt.

We're going to have sex, most likely up against this wall. In the middle of the day. Hallelujah. It's like all my fantasies are coming true.

"Sadie! SADIE! SADIE MELVINA, WHERE THE HELL ARE YOU? YOUR CAR IS HERE SO I KNOW YOU'RE IN THERE!"

Max pulls back and looks at me. He remembers that voice—hell, how can you forget it?

I roll my eyes as Max steps back, my leg falling to the floor. He's pulling down my shirt, which I hadn't even noticed was pulled up, exposing all of my bra. Man, he works quick.

"SADIE MELVINA!" Jenna's voice scrapes through me like nails on a chalkboard.

"Melvina?" Max asks, unable to control his smile. He's taken a step back and is adjusting himself. Part of me is cheering that I've had such an effect on him. The other part is going to kill my sister.

"Shut it. Long story. I hate it and never tell it to anyone. Hence, Jenna insists on using it. I hate her. I hate her so much."

I'm not even aware that I'm muttering how much I hate my sister as I walk toward the back of the house, following the most distasteful sound ever.

"SADI—"

"What do you want?" Jenna is standing in my kitchen, bellowing, just like she used to when she was little and wanted my dad to come tuck her in at night. "Why are you in my house? Actually, I don't care. Get out."

Her mouth hangs open for a split second. Then it snaps closed, and she re-loads. "I cannot believe you have the nerve to talk to me like that." She's nervous, pacing around my kitchen, touching everything on the counter. I don't register that this is her behavior when she's deep in thought or troubled. I only register that I want her out of my house. NOW.

"Seriously Jenna, get out. I don't want to talk to you. I don't want you in my house. I don't want anything to do with you."

"Sadie, I know what this must seem like, but I really need your help."

Now it's my turn for my mouth to fall open. Red rage seethes through me, making it impossible for me to even form words. Jenna's always been ballsy, but this simply takes the cake. Without waiting for me to respond, she continues.

"I don't know what I'm gonna do. I—"

"You're going to leave before I drag you out by your dyed-red hair extensions."

"Um, actually, I'm going to leave." Max interrupts us. He's got a look on his face like he's trying to say something to me without actually speaking.

"I'll walk you out." Anything to get away from my sister.

We step into the living room. I hear Jenna walk down the hall toward the bathroom.

"Are you going to be okay here?" Max reaches out and runs his finger lightly down my cheek and jawbone. That light touch ignites a fire elsewhere.

"Yeah, nothing I can't handle. I'll make her leave, one way or another."

"Do you want me to stay?"

OH GOD YES. "Nah, that's okay. She'll be gone soon. I'm gonna start working on the windows. They've all got to be taken apart to improve the weather efficiency. And the two stained glass windows are getting fixed. I've got a tight schedule to stay on. The window guy is coming tomorrow afternoon."

He looks ... disappointed? "Okay. Call me if something comes up."

"You mean, like if I feel the need to kill her?"

Laughing, Max leans in and gives me a quick kiss. "Something like that. It does seem like she's always interrupting at inopportune times." He turns and is out the door. I close the door behind him and lean back on it. Holy hell, he is one of the sexiest things I've ever laid eyes on. I touch my lips, relishing the memory of him ravaging them. I almost had wall sex. Or at least wall foreplay. Until my damn sister walked in.

Speaking of which, where the hell did she go? Is she still in the bathroom? It's been a few minutes since she went in there. No sign of her in the kitchen or living room. Must be the bathroom. What is she doing in my brand new bathroom? She'd better not be fouling it up in there. Or puking all over the place. If she is, she's gonna clean it up. I literally just put out the towels. I don't think I've even used it yet. Speaking of which, I need to pee, so she needs to wrap it up.

BANG BANG BANG. "Jenna, hurry up in there. You'd better not be destroying my bathroom." I wait. No response. Standing still just reinforces my bladder's suddenly urgent need to empty. BANG BANG BANG. "C'mon Jenna!"

She's got the water running, which is only making the situation worse for me. Dammit, I don't care what she's doing in there. I'm going in.

Are you freakin' kidding me? That bitch locked the door. Cursing myself for buying a house with only one bathroom, I hightail it to the kitchen and dig through the junk drawer for the key. I loved all the crystal doorknobs and skeleton key locks that my doors had. Of course, I never thought I'd have to actually use them. The key takes a bit of jiggling in the lock to do its thing, but finally I have the door opened.

I am so not prepared for what is in my bathroom.

I am going to kill her.

CHAPTER TWENTY

Four hours later, I'm finally done. Every minute of those four hours, I am fueled by hatred and vitriol for my sister. Four freakin' hours. I wash the towels but decide I can't stand knowing her blood was on them, so I end up tossing them in the dumpster with the rest of the debris. My eyes and throat are burning from the bleach that I've used to scrub the tub and the floor. Wiping the walls down with one of those eraser things takes off some of the paint. Crap, that means I'm going to have to paint again. Luckily, I have some left out in my garage.

The cleaning process results in three bags of garbage, including the contents of my new wastebasket, which Jenna had somehow filled up in those moments in my bathroom. The knife is still on the floor. If I can't use a towel that she's bled on, there is no way I'll be able to use the knife on my food. In the bag it goes. I haul the garbage to the dumpster by the garage and find the paint.

It's almost midnight when I finish. I'm hot and sweaty and still have some blood on me. I guess now would be as good a time as any to christen my shower. As I strip off my clothes and pull my phone out of my back pocket, I notice the text alert. Max, wanting to know if I'm okay. I text him back.

Things got bad but I took care of it. Ok now. Thanks for checking.

Once in the shower, the water sluicing down on me, I let my mind drift to Max. It's easier this way. To stuff all the upsetting Jenna thoughts down and put them away in a deep dark corner of my mind. Now I'll think of something pleasant. Max's kiss, his mouth, his hands. Damn, I knew those hands would have skill. Would it be wrong if I texted him to see if he wants to come over and pick up where we left off? Pulling my hands through my hair to lather up the shampoo, I decide that yes, it would be bad. Very bad. Even if I didn't think I was cursed, maybe this would not be the most opportune time. I mean, there's everything with my sister. No matter how hard I try, I can't keep thoughts Jenna from sneaking back into my brain. I wish I could say that I thought it would be better from this point on, but I don't think that's going to be the case. Where Jenna is concerned, just expect the worst. I mean, Rob and the baby are just the tip of the iceberg.

God, Jenna ... and a baby. Two things that should never be said in the same sentence. She doesn't deserve a baby. I deserve a baby. It's not fair that ... well, none of this is fair. At least I have my own house. It's not like anyone gave it to me, either. Years of working my ass off. Nights, weekends. Year round. I never wanted money from my parents like Jenna and Brady did, either.

I need to stop thinking about my sister. She's gone and hopefully I won't have to waste any more energy on her. I close my eyes and will my brain to be rid of Jenna. Now I just need to figure out what to do about Max. I like him. Really like him. He's so ... delicious. And he likes me too. I'm sure once I'm ready to pull the trigger he'll be on board.

Am I ready to pull the trigger? Hell, I almost did this afternoon. Sighing, I turn off the water and grab my crappy old towel off the hook. Damn Jenna. She even took my brand-new, expensive, fluffy towels away. Why does she have to pollute all that is good in my life? Why does she taint everything? What did I do to deserve her as my sister?

I throw on a t-shirt and shorts. Combing out my wet hair, I can't keep my mind from wandering back to Jenna. Back to when we were kids. Inseparable. We could have had our own rooms but we had no desire to be apart. She wanted to be with me and, surprisingly, it didn't bother me. After school, we'd play, picking up our elaborate games where we'd left off the day before. We lived in our own world. Occasionally we'd let other people visit, but we were the reigning queens. And it was great. Then, one day, it was as if someone flipped a switch in Jenna.

Not only was she was no longer my friend, but she was my nemesis. She was angry all the time. Most of that anger was directed at me. To this day, I have no idea why. If I said black, she said white. We fought. Constantly. It drove my parents crazy. Although they tried as best they could not to get involved, lines were drawn. Dad and me, Mom and Jenna. Brady was too aloof and self-centered to care about what was going on in the house.

These thoughts are going to keep me up all night, and I can't afford that. I'm about a half-day behind on work, thanks to my sister. I will need to sleep fast, get up early, and get working on taking apart my windows before the repair guy gets here.

Lucky for me, pure exhaustion wins out over my racing mind and the next thing I know, it's morning. I pick my way around the boxes and piles that litter my bedroom. I'm getting a little tired of living in a construction zone. I long for the day when there are no more tarps, no more tools, and each room has actual furniture to sit on. I'm not going to know what to do with all that space.

Glad that I showered last night, I throw on another pair of cut-offs and a tank top, lace up my boots, and get to work removing the window frames. One window is dismantled, and I decide that I'm not going to be able to go much longer without a cup of coffee. Only fourteen more double-hung windows to go.

I sit at my kitchen table while I take a few moments to enjoy feeding my caffeine addiction. Someday, my front porch will be cleaned off and spruced up, and my summer mornings will be spent enjoying my coffee out there. I need to keep focused on the positives in my life, instead of all the negative energy that Jenna keeps bringing into it. I wonder, not for the first time, if all this competitiveness is typical between sisters. Therese is an only child, so she's no help there. I could ask Max. After all, Helga and Dorothy seem to be able to coexist without inducing bodily harm. I wonder what their secret is.

I've finished my first cup of coffee, so I pour another one and head back to the living room. I was lucky to find someone locally who can help repair and restore the windows that are broken. I absolutely love, love, love the charm of this place and am hell bent on saving as much of it as I can. I'm also fortunate that only the two small living room windows on either side of the fireplace need to be fixed. They're stained glass and are just super cool. All the other windows need to be dismantled, cleaned up, re-glued back together, and then re-strung. This rehashing will help improve their efficiency and keep me warmer in the winter. Once all the windows are put back in, I'll replace the storm windows as well. I'm looking forward to this winter, sitting in my living room with a nice fire going, all snug and warm.

I can't help but think that Rob would have hated this house. It's old and there are no right angles. I think it was built probably about 1920 or so, right before the Great Depression changed everything. The house isn't that big, about 1400 square feet. The mudroom was added onto the back of the house, probably in the 1950s. Someday, when I have the time, I'd like to do a little research on this house. I don't just teach American history, I love it, and the Roarin' Twenties is my favorite time period.

Rob didn't appreciate it. Much like I don't think he appreciated me. I think the only thing he did appreciate was the amount of space and control I gave him. I try not to play the 'if only' game, since it's not productive, but for once I let myself. If I had not lost the baby, I'd have a newborn. I'm not sure if we'd be married or not, but I'd—we'd—probably be living in Rob's sterile, modern townhouse. The thought of that makes it hard for me to breath.

I call Therese with my revelation.

"Things really do happen for a reason." She sounds exhausted, like always.

"I'm starting to think that you're right."

"Of course I'm right. But why the sudden revelation? Mason, get down from there now!"

"What's he doing?"

"Climbing the refrigerator."

"Aren't you afraid it's going to fall on him?"

"No, I'm afraid he's going to find my secret stash of Girl Scout cookies hidden on top."

"As long as you have your priorities."

"So back to the important things. Why am I right?"

"It's just with everything with the house and Max and Jenna and the baby—none of it would be happening if I hadn't had the miscarriage. And while I'm not happy about Jenna, the rest is pretty damn good, and I wouldn't have any of it. And that would make me sad."

"How would you know what you didn't have? Ainsley, put the pots back in the cupboard!"

"I don't know that I wouldn't know, but wouldn't I know that something was missing?"

"I don't even know what you just said, but sadly I get it." A loud scream/cry/yell erupts in the background. "WHAT!" Therese yells, not to me but to whatever—or more accurately, whomever—is creating that ruckus. "What is going on in here? Ainsley, get up, now. Get out of that—what the heck? Sadie, I gotta go."

She abruptly disconnects. Even though someone hanging up on me is one of my biggest pet peeves, it doesn't bother me when Therese does it. It's sort of the norm, since her twins are the original Satan's spawn (her words not mine). I don't take it personally.

The rest of the day passes with the window repairs. It's pretty tedious and time consuming. I haven't heard from Max, which is sort of unusual. He usually calls or texts me throughout the day. Maybe he's regretting what happened last night. Maybe he's regretting what didn't happen. Maybe the repeated altercations with Jenna in his presence have scared him off.

All I know is, it's been one day without talking to him—not even one full day—and I miss him. This is bad. This is so bad. Maybe it's because I'm reacting to the Jenna situation. Maybe it's because I'm sick of being alone. Maybe I'm just in need of some lovin'. Against my better judgment, I decide I'm going for it.

CHAPTER TWENTY-ONE

It's like the universe knows that I've decided to go for Max and is now making a concerted effort to prevent that from happening. I probably should take it as a sign. My phone starts blowing up with texts. The first from the restaurant. Two people called in, and they're getting slammed. They want me to come in and work. The next from Therese. Apparently Ainsley got her butt stuck in a pot and Therese had to call 9-1-1 to come and help get her out of it (since she couldn't very well transport a three year-old who is stuck in a pot). Did I mention that Andy, her husband, is away, yet again? Poor Therese. Then, my mom starts texting. Once my mom discovered texting, it became an addiction to her. She tends to be prolific with her messages, and now she wants to know if I've heard from Jenna. Nothing from Max.

I've got to get into the shower to get ready for work. Mondays are usually slow, but they need me, and I need the money. I don't wash my hair, opting just to pull it up in a messy bun. My work uniform is a green t-shirt with the restaurant's logo on it and a pair of black shorts. As I'm getting older, it's been harder and harder to find shorts that are age-appropriate. I'm in decent shape, but there are some things—cellulite—that can't be helped. Not that I'm saying I have cellulite. Some of the other waitresses wear indecently short shorts, and I don't want to be like that. My work sneakers complete the outfit, and I'm in my car within twenty minutes. Not too shabby.

Bumpers, the restaurant where I work, is a family-owned sports bar type restaurant. We do get a fair number of families early in the evening. Later on, it's more of a bar crowd. Our burgers are to die for and may or may not be partly responsible for some of that cellulite, if I was admitting that I had any.

Mel, the owner, is frazzled, as usual. When I come in through the back door, he says, "Oh, Sadie, thank God you're here. What took you so long?"

I look at my watch. It's only been thirty-five minutes since I called and told Mel I'd be in. Tying my apron around my waist, I can't help but smile. I've worked here since I was in college. Sort of sad to actually put a number to that. I guess I never thought that I'd still be waiting tables at the age of thirty-five, but nonetheless, here I am. Obviously, the money's good. My house is proof of that. To be perfectly honest, I like this job. I get to talk to people. I'm pretty good at it too. It can be stressful, but once the shift is over, there's no more stress. There's no worrying about curriculum or testing or teacher evaluations.

"Go tell Jeannie that you're on," Mel barks, probably more gruffly than he intended to sound.

I head out to the hostess stand and get my table assignment. The only other server is Doug, who is one of my favorite co-workers. He's hysterical. I used to hang out with him and his boyfriend, Scott, before Rob and I started dating. Rob didn't appreciate Doug's humor. I've decided that was because Rob had a gigantic stick up his ass.

"Sweet Sadie, are you a sight for sore eyes. I'm in the weeds right now!" Doug calls to me.

"I'm here to bail your sorry butt out, yet again."

"Sadie, this butt is nothing but fine, and you know it!"

I laugh and greet my first table. It's sort of unbelievable how busy it is for a Monday night. Doug's got a large party, about fifteen people or so, and their order is ready. I put my orders in the computer and head back to the kitchen to help bring out the rest of the food. Three plates balanced on my left arm, one more in my right hand, and I head back out to the floor. Passing by Doug, he reaches up and pats my back. "Thanks for helping!"

I should know better. Doug is famous for this. He's unhooked my bra. I don't know how he does it, and no guy that I've been with has ever been that dexterous with my bras. "Dammit Doug! I'm here to help you." I can do nothing but deliver the plates to the table and hope it's not too apparent that my girls are swinging in the wind.

"Okay, I've got a buffalo chicken sand—" I look up to see Max sitting at the table. With a girl. Okay, it's a large group. It doesn't necessarily mean anything. "—wich." A guy raises his hand. Max's arm is around the back of her chair, and she's sitting awfully close to him. I can't even. Max is just looking at me. No, he's looking at my chest. I am so gonna kill Doug. I hand out the rest of the plates and hightail it to the back.

Why? Why do these things keep happening to me?

Doug comes back, still chuckling as I struggle to recapture my breasts through my t-shirt. "Never gets old."

Needless to say, at my age, the girls really rely on the support of the bra, so once they've been unleashed, I'm working against gravity to re-contain them. "Doug, you have got to stop doing that."

"I can't. It's too funny, watching your face." Doug keeps observing my contortions. "You're hangin' a little low these days, my friend."

"Gravity is not my friend, and after this, neither are you." I smooth my shirt and turn the corner to go out and check on my table. And run smack into Max.

"There you are."

"I've got to get to my tables. I can't talk." I'm trying to side step around Max. Either we're terribly in synch or he's trying really hard to block me because as I step right, he steps left and then back again. I'm no closer to getting by him.

"Sorry I didn't get to text you back today. I was ... um, caught up with something. It was a busy day."

"Yeah, I can see that."

"This isn't what it looks like."

"I don't care."

"Will you let me explain?"

"There's nothing to explain."

"Sadie, I—"

"Max, not now. I have to go." Finally I'm able to push by him as I head out to my tables. Several refills are needed, and then orders are up. I'm doing my best not to look toward Max. Of course, that's about as easy as not pulling a loose thread hanging from a sweater. Every time I look up, Max is watching me. He's not smiling. He's just watching. I don't know what to make of it. It's sort of weirding me out.

So it looks like I was right not to want to get involved. Men are just too much heartbreak. And they cannot be trusted. What a fool I am. Apparently I learned nothing with the Rob fiasco. I've learned nothing my whole life. I can't trust anyone. Maybe this is why I've used my premonitions to keep me from getting involved. A defense mechanism. The realization hits me like a ton of bricks, and that familiar feeling washes over me. That creepy feeling that accompanies my premonitions, if you want to call them that.

I am utterly alone.

It's the strangest thing, to be standing in a room full of people and feel so alone. And the sensation is much stronger than anything I've ever felt before. I shake my head to clear the feeling and set about filling a bucket with ice to restock the soda fountain. My tables have just about finished up, and it's slowed down enough to where I can go home. Max's party is starting to leave, and Doug will certainly be able to handle the rest of the night.

Hoisting the bucket up to dump it out, I'm startled when I hear my name. "Sweet Sadie, there's some dude out here waiting to talk to you. And if you don't want him, I'll certainly take him. Mmm ...mmm ... mmm."

Doug never fails to make me smile. "Thanks Doug, but I think he's spoken for, and unfortunately, not by me."

"That's a pity and a shame. Take your time. I'll get the side work later."

I return the bucket to its place under the counter and head out to find Max standing in the hallway. He's nonchalantly leaning against the paneled wall and looks utterly delicious. Why is he still here?

"Max, what do you want from me?"

"Why are you mad?"

"I'm not mad." I am so mad.

"Sadie, of course you are. I know you—this is mad Sadie. Usually, I only see her when you bend a nail or your sister shows up."

"Well, when my pneumatic nailer jams, and I have to pull out all those bent nails with a pair of pliers, it's frustrating."

"So are you saying you're frustrated then? About what?"

It's time to be honest with him. "You, Max. Me. Everything in my life."

He frowns and then reaches for me. I step back to avoid his touch. "This is because I didn't text you back?"

"No, not because you didn't text me back. Do you really think I'm that high maintenance?"

"No, and that's why I'm confused. Just tell me what's going on."

I look at my feet, clad in my stained sneakers. I'm not used to being direct. This is hard. "I just thought—after last night—you know."

He reaches out again and this time I let him. His fingers graze my cheeks, lingering, before moving to my jaw. His voice is lower, thicker. "Say it, Sadie."

Exhaling a breath I didn't know I was holding, I find the words. "I thought that something was happening—was going to happen—with us. I guess I was off the mark. Wouldn't be the first time this year."

"What are you talking about? I'm pretty sure we were on the same page last night."

The memory of his hands and lips on my body floods my mind, and I feel myself blushing. What I wouldn't give to be able to pick up where we left off. I need to focus on why that won't be happening. Shaking my head to clear my thoughts, I find the words. "So then, why are you here with someone else today?" I see him inhale and prepare to speak, so I rush to continue while I have the courage. "You know the deal with Rob and Jenna. I can't—won't—do that again. I'm not saying that we're anything yet, but I can't—won't—compete. Just take me out of the running."

Max's lips are on mine. What is he doing to me? Didn't I just tell him to take me out of the running? Why is he doing this? I thought he was a good guy but he can't be. How can he be with a girl and now be kissing me? I don't want this to stop, but it has to. Somehow, I find the strength to use my hands, which are already on Max's firm pecs, to push him back.

"Stop. Please." I'm out of breath.

He too is breathless. And ... angry? "Sadie, what do you want from me?"

"Max, you can't just kiss me to avoid the topic. I don't even understand how you can kiss me right now. Isn't your girlfriend waiting for you?"

"Girlfriend? Wait—is that what you're upset about?"

"Um yeah." What is he, some kind of moron? Why would I be upset about something so trivial as a girlfriend? Dumbass—is that what I'm upset about? I thought he was smarter than that.

"That's Tracy."

"Okay." Where is he going with this? It's not like knowing her name is going to make me feel any better.

Quite the contrary. He's looking at me expectantly. "Am I supposed to know who that is?"

"You know, my friend Tracy. The one who I dressed up as Cupid for."

A mental image of a bare-chested Max in his leather chaps and vest springs to mind. I need to focus. "Okay."

"We're friends."

"Like you and I are friends? Friends who take each other's clothes off."

"Not in recent history."

This is about the worst thing he can say. I take another step back, increasing the distance between us. "Max ... I need to get back to work. I can't do this now. I just—can't. If you don't want to keep working with me, I'm sure I can find someone else."

Max turns and walks away without saying a word.

Yup, alone.

Again.

CHAPTER TWENTY-TWO

I feel so crappy after work that I drive right to the nursing home without even changing my clothes. I smell like grease and sweat. With my luck, a pack of rabid dogs will latch onto my scent and hunt me down. I think about this as I'm making a quick pit stop at the liquor store. After a night like this, I need something to take the edge off. Actually, being eaten by a pack of dogs might not be so bad. It would at least put me out of my misery. Even though it's after eleven p.m., the staff at the nursing home is usually okay with me being there. Probably because I bring them cookies fairly often. Note to self: make more cookies. I hope no one gives me a hard time. I'm wound tighter than a drum and ready to snap.

No one stops me as I trudge down the artificially lit hallway to Dad's room, squinting to protect my eyes against the bright fluorescence. My body virtually collapses as I flop in my usual chair, and I let me head sink back. My eyes close and I just try to breathe.

Without opening my eyes, I start. "Dad, I don't know what to do anymore. I'm alone, but I don't want to be. I hurt everyone who tries to get close to me. Everyone close to me hurts me. Who do I trust? How can I trust anyone anymore? Rob, Jenna, and now even Max. Even you. I mean, I know you didn't want to be like this, but I don't even have you. I just want someone to be on my side. To put me first."

My words hang in the dark of the room.

Alone. I feel so alone.

The next thing I know, my mom's standing in front of me. The glow of the lights from the hallway cast eerie shadows throughout the room. Even in the dimness, I can tell something is wrong with her.

"Sadie! Why haven't you called me?"

I vaguely remember seeing about ten texts from her. I didn't read them after the first one asking about Jenna. Mom's really shaken up. I haven't seen her like this ever. Not even when Dad had his stroke.

"Mom, what's wrong?" I look over at Dad. He looks the same, his chest rising and falling. Nothing's wrong with Dad.

"Didn't you get my texts?"

"I, um, saw one. I got called into work and had a bad night. A bad few days really."

"It's Jenna."

Oh crap. "What?"

"She's missing."

"What do you mean, missing?"

"She missed her sonogram today. The Hendersons were meeting her there this morning and she never showed up. I can't get a hold of her. Her apartment is a disaster and her car is gone. I've been talking to the police. I can't file a missing persons report until the morning, but I will as soon as I can. Have you heard from her?"

This is not good. This is so not good.

Mom keeps talking, but I can't listen to what she's saying. I can't process it. I keep flashing back to last night in my bathroom. I swore I'd never think of it again. Her face flashes before my eyes, the panic written across it almost palpable. The blood. Her blood. Crimson staining the bright white.

I have to get out of the room. Now. The bile is rising in my throat, threatening to make an appearance all over my mother's shoes.

Swallowing hard, I mumble, "Um, she stopped by yesterday. Unannounced, of course. We fought." Must. Not. Freak. Out.

"Of course," my mother interjects.

"Of course. It didn't go well, and I made her leave."

"What time was that?"

"Um, I don't know. Seven-ish."

"Did she say anything about going anywhere?"

I don't know why I can't tell my mother what happened. Well, I do know why. I'm ashamed of how I acted. Of what I did. I feel so guilty about it. I am the most terrible sister on the face of the earth. I always used to think that title was reserved for Jenna, but now I know, without a doubt, that I'm the one who's earned it.

I stand up and stretch a little. My back is sore from sleeping in the chair. I need to get away from my mother. Now. Before I totally lose it.

"Okay, Mom. I can't imagine Jenna will come to me. Not after last night. But if she does, I'll tell her you're looking for her."

As I try to move past her, she reaches out and grabs me. "Do you have a feeling about her? I'm so scared that something terrible has happened to her and the baby."

Her touch burns me, as if it's a hot poker. It's probably just my guilt. I pull my arm away and rub it involuntarily. I can't bear to have her touch me right now. I don't deserve it.

"I haven't gotten any feelings." Except shame and dread that my family is going to find out what happened between Jenna and me last night. With my head down, I hurry to my car, leaving my mom and dad alone together. Part of me wonders if she will stay and tell him what's going on.

I'm lucky I don't get pulled over while driving home. I know I was going way over the speed limit and may have missed a stop sign or two. It was sort of hard to see with all the tears flowing. Once in the safety of my home, I do the only sensible thing. I start drinking. A lot. The first tumbler of vodka on the rocks is a little rough going down. The second and third, not so much. I know, drinking myself into a stupor is not the most responsible thing. I don't care. I'm just looking for my mind to stop whirring and the blissfulness of a blackout.

As I'm sprawled on my sunny, yellow couch, I try not relive the events of last night—and fail miserably. The cotton twill is soft under my fingers and I'm momentarily distracted. The couch was an impulse purchase. I try to focus on how the room will look when it's done—dark, stained wood, the walls in a soft bluish-grayish-green. Soft white curtains fluttering to the ground. The pop of color from the couch. My eyes are heavy and it seems like too much work to hold up my glass. The vodka has done its work, and I let myself fall under.

****

The bar is crowded and filled with smoke. The atmosphere kind, not the stinky cigarette kind. I'm scanning the bar, looking for someone, although I don't know who I'm looking for until I see him. Max. He's wearing his leather vest, chaps, and not much else. His privates are covered by something—although I can't tell what from so far away. Max is ... dancing? Yep, that's what he's doing. He hops up on the bar and continues with the gyrating and thrusting. But he's not alone. Tracy is with him. She's jumped up on the bar and they're grinding as hordes of females reach for him, dollar bills waving. Even though I'm totally disgusted and want to leave, I find my feet propelling me toward the bar. Max sees me and his eyes are boring into me. They are pulling me to him. As I get closer, I see him separate from Tracy. I'm within arm's reach of the bar now. Max squats down and extends his hand to me. I can see the sweat glistening on his hard arms and chest, and have to resist the urge to lick it off. He wants me to get up on the bar and dance with him. So much of me wants to. But if I do, I'm not sure where this will stop. If it will stop. Suddenly conscious of the audience, I take a step back from his outstretched hand.

"You come to me," I say, shaking my head. In all reality, there is no way Max can hear me over the din of the bar, but he seems to have no problem.

"I'll come to you in a little while," he says, a mischievous grin spreading across his face. "But when I knock, you'd better answer, and you'd better be ready to dance."

BAM. BAM BAM. BAM BAM BAM.

I don't know how I got back to my couch, but someone's pounding on the door. Quite urgently, I might add. And then I remember—Max. He said he'd be here for me. Sitting up proves a little challenging, so I find myself rolling to the floor instead of getting up. My lack of furniture means nothing to lean on, so I crawl to the doorway and pull myself up. The banging is getting louder. I am very drunk. I don't remember drinking this much at the club. The whole club thing is pretty fuzzy, and I'm not really sure what's actually going on. But I know it's Max on the other side of the door, so I rush to answer it.

Only falling twice, I finally make it to the door. For some reason, Max has changed out of his leather chaps and vest and is now in a policeman uniform. Whatever. I still plan on taking him out of it ... if only I could stand up. For some reason, Max isn't as enthused about me as he seemed to be at the bar. Maybe he's playing hard to get. Usually that's my role, but being the aggressor brings out a new side of me. The untamed Sadie. Then, there are two Maxes. No, the second one isn't Max. It's Henry Fitzsimmons, my high school crush. My first love. Wow, I'm reaching deep into the archives here. I've kind of figured out that this is a dream. Of course it is, since nothing else makes sense. This is one of those weird ones, where I thought I woke up, but I must still be asleep, since this is still obviously a dream. Why else would Fitzy be here? Oh, man, he was the stuff of my earliest fantasies. Well, since this is a dream, I might as well have my way with both of them ...

****

Death. I feel like death. I wish for death, because it has to be better than what I'm feeling right now. I would like to peel my eyes open to see where I am, since I have no idea. However, the banging in my head seems to be superseding all motor control and my eyes just won't open.

The racket in my brain won't stop. I need to do something. I just don't know what. Maybe get something to drink. Maybe take some ibuprofen. Maybe vomit. Maybe just lay here and die. All except the last option require me moving, so I'd better try to get up. With Herculean effort, I pry my eyelids open. I try to sit and my eyes focus in on something across the room. Not something—someone.

"What the hell!" I yell, jumping to my feet. The sudden movement doesn't agree with me, and I'm overcome by the urge to vomit. My hands fly to my mouth, trying to stop the impending purge as I run toward the bathroom.

Mental note: the next time I plan on drinking my face off, I should make sure there is something in my stomach first. Puking yellow bile is not fun. Well, not like puking is ever fun, but this really sucks.

The cool porcelain feels good on my clammy forehead. I never want to leave this position. I should never have gotten up from the couch. The waves of nausea pass for the moment, and suddenly I remember why I jumped up in the first place.

Henry Fitzsimmons.

What the hell is Henry Fitzsimmons doing sitting in my living room?

I haven't seen Fitzy since he and Brady were sophomores in college. The day of my high school graduation party, to be exact. I thought my heart would never get over the likes of Henry Fitzsimmons. It did. And now he's in my house. What the hell?

"Can I get you anything?"

His voice should startle me, but even in my run-down state, I take a moment to relish the deep timbre that fueled my fantasies as a teenager. Speaking of fantasies, this is one heck of a premonition. First I dream about him, and now here he is. I'm starting to freak myself.

"Can you remind me never ever to drink again?"

"Didn't we already go through this at your high school graduation party?"

Oh no, not again.

CHAPTER TWENTY-THREE

Is it possible for a trapdoor in my bathroom floor to open up and swallow me whole? Even though I'm almost positive I didn't install that feature, I'm holding out hope.

"I see some things never change. Last time I saw you, you were in a similar position. Except Therese was holding your hair and lying to you about what an ass you made out of yourself."

"Thanks for reminding me." I groan as I shift my body onto the cool tile floor. At least I know it's clean. Hell, I wouldn't care if it were the bathroom at Grand Central at this moment. Now, Fitzy is upside down to me. I try to take in the sight from the ground up. Scuffed black shoes, flat-front gray twill pants. A button-down shirt that hovers somewhere in the dark-gray-to-purple-palate, if one exists. Gray suit coat to match the pants. His shirt is open at the neck, and a gold chain with a cross hangs at his throat. The years have been good to Henry Fitzsimmons. Too good. I didn't think it was possible. "What are you doing here?"

He's stepped into the bathroom and is looking around. "Your mom asked me to stop by. She was worried about you."

That makes no sense. My mom is only focused on Jenna right now. As right she should be. If I weren't so dehydrated, I'd probably start crying again. I sit up and scoot back so I can lean against the wall. My mouth feels terrible. My tongue tries to lick the awful fuzziness off my teeth but it does no good.

"Be right back." Fitzy darts out of the bathroom. The need to close my eyes overwhelms me. Next thing I know, he's back in the bathroom, putting the toilet seat down and taking a seat. He hands me a Coke. "You look like you need this."

I look at the bottle of soda in my hands. I have no idea where it came from and I seriously doubt I have the strength to open it. I make a feeble attempt and then look up at Fitzy. He sighs but reaches over and opens it for me anyway. It's things like that that made me love him in the first place. Even though I was the annoying younger sister, he was always kind to me. Where Brady was always a jerk, Fitzy was never mean. He seemed to be interested in what I had to say. When someone picked on me, it was Fitzy who stood up for me.

After I take the bottle of soda back, it occurs to me that the bottle is cold, so it must have come from my fridge. But it couldn't have come from mine since I only buy Diet Coke. The cold bottle feels good against my forehead, nonetheless, and the carbonation is surprisingly settling on my stomach. Curiosity wins out.

"Where'd you get the soda?"

He smiles, a slow grin spreading on those full lips that were the subject of endless teenage fantasies. "From your fridge."

"Oh. Max must have left it," I mumble, more to myself than to him.

"Who's Max?" Fitzy's eyes are alert and scanning the bathroom. Even in my maybe-still-drunk-wicked-hungover state, I still take some pride in my bathroom.

"He's my contractor. We did this bathroom together."

"What's his last name?"

"Shultz."

"Are you two involved?"

"With Max? No, not really. I don't know. Why?"

"Just wondering. You mentioned him before." Fitzy is cool, calm, and collected.

"When?"

"When I first got here."

That gets me. Sitting up a little straighter, I look hard at Fitzy. "And when exactly was that? Why are you here?"

"I told you, your mom was worried."

"Not about me."

"What do you mean by that?"

"She's worried about Jenna."

"Why is she worried about Jenna?"

"She thinks she's missing." My voice breaks. I will not cry.

"Do you think she's missing?"

I take a long swig from the soda, trying to think of how to answer that question. I evade by simply shrugging.

"When was the last time you saw your sister?"

"Sunday. She came over. I threw her out. We don't get along."

"Oh? Why don't you get along?"

She's a vindictive bitch who stole my boyfriend, killed him by jacking him off while he was driving, and is now having his baby. I can't say that out loud. I want Fitzy to like me. As that thought hits me, I start to laugh. Here I am, hungover as all hell, still in my clothes from work yesterday, and God only knows what my hair looks like. Not to mention the vomiting and the body odor. The ship of good impressions sailed a long time ago, and I never even had a ticket to board. "Long story."

"Why don't you tell me?"

"I don't have the strength to go into it right now. It's not something I like to think about, let alone talk about."

He stands up and offers me a hand. Pulling me to my feet he says, "Why don't you take a shower?"

And with that, he's out of the bathroom. My brain is still fuzzier than my teeth, although I hope a shower and tooth brushing will help both. While in the shower, I find my motor dexterity is poor, and I have to concentrate so I don't fall. The bottle of shampoo evades my grasp not once but twice. I skip shaving, afraid I will require a blood transfusion. That, of course, makes me think of Jenna again, and I have to sit down in the tub. With the water beating down on my back, the tears start to flow.

How did life get so hard? Why is this happening to me? And why the hell is Henry Fitzsimmons in my house?

With him out there, I know that—no matter how much I'd like to—I can't stay in my bathtub curled in the fetal position. Tentatively, I stand up, turn the water to cold, and let it shock my system. The new peace I've achieved is gone the moment I reach for a towel, and grab one I bought when I went away to college. I want my new fluffy towels. I know, in the grand scheme, towels are something so trivial, but for me, they are the symbol of everything Jenna had done. Every time I get something nice, she finds a way to ruin it. Now, instead of feeling sad or guilty, I'm mad at her again.

Wrapped in my towel, which is old enough to vote, a thought crosses my mind. Fitzy is out there. I'm in here, with no clothes. I quickly brush my teeth and pray to God that he's in the front of the house. For the first time in my whole home renovation process, I wish that my house had a bathroom attached to my bedroom, just so I could avoid one more humiliation.

If only I had known that me being in a towel would be the tip of the humiliation iceberg.

I make it to my room without incident or observation and throw on a pair of shorts and a tank top. It's looking to be another hot day. Or maybe I'm simply sweating out the vodka. Either way, I need ventilation. A cursory comb through my hair, and then it's piled up on my head in a messy bun. It looks like an obscene pineapple. Some deodorant finishes my prep. I don't bother with makeup. It's not going to help.

Fitzy is in my kitchen. There's a sentence I never thought I'd say. As much as I want to look at him, the first thing I see when I walk into the kitchen is the bottle of vodka, sitting innocuously on my table. I have to suppress the urge to vomit again. Swiftly, I grab the bottle and put it in the cabinet. Out of sight, out of mind.

"You know, you're lucky you didn't get alcohol poisoning. Why did you drink so much?"

Fitzy's question bothers me. I don't know why, but it does. "Why does it matter to you? How do you know how much I drank?"

"The receipt for the vodka is right there," he says, pointing to the table. "What's so wrong that you had to drown your sorrows in a bottle?"

"I don't want to talk about it. Let's talk about something else."

"Why do you have a dumpster out back?"

"Oh shoot! They're coming to pick that up today! What time is it?" My wrist gives me no answers no matter how many times I look at it, since I didn't put my watch on. My back pockets are empty. I have no idea where my phone is either. And I can't see the clock on the microwave from where I'm sitting. I'm patting my butt, hoping my phone magically appears. I head out to the living room and don't see it anywhere. A frantic search finds it under the couch with the battery almost drained. It's only nine in the morning. The dumpster guys aren't coming until eleven. I need to finish picking up some debris from the garage and in the house.

Back out in the kitchen, Fitzy is poking around the fridge. I can't help but notice how fine his rear looks as he's bent over. What the hell am I thinking? I'm still reeling from Max and what almost was but wasn't. I cannot even think about another man. Once my phone is charging, I plop down in a chair and finish the last of the Coke.

"Make yourself at home, why don't you."

"I detect a little bit of sarcasm." Fitzy's grin makes me feel like I'm sixteen again. "What did you say before you ran out like your pants were on fire?"

"The guys are coming to pick up the dumpster. I didn't know what time it was. I have a little more to add before they get here."

"Oh? What time are they coming?"

"Eleven. I need to pull myself together and get to work."

For the first time since I woke up, Fitzy looks a little ... uncomfortable. I have to admit, it's a bit unnerving how at home he seems to be, wandering around, taking everything in. Almost ... examining.

"Will you excuse me for a minute?"

Before I can answer, he's out the door. With slow, deep breaths, I try to shake off the last few days and get my head back in my renovation project. I've got to pick up the debris ahead of the dumpster retrieval. Then, back to the windows. That's a multi-day project that hopefully can be wrapped up by Sunday. Then, it's onto rehabbing and fixing the storm windows. That will be critical in making sure they're not drafty come winter.

Fitzy is out in the back, talking on his cell. He's headed back in, heading up the back steps and through the laundry room. I hear him finish up with, "Let me know as soon as you can execute it."

Huh. That's a weird thing to say. I want to ask him about it, but I don't want to pry. Ironic, since he's been poking around every nook and cranny in my house.

"So, who's your contractor again? Will he be by soon?"

I'm a little taken aback by the abrupt interrogation as soon as he's disconnected from his call. "Um, Max Schultz. He's not coming by today." Or any day, I'm guessing.

"I thought you said there was work to be done before the dumpster got picked up? Did I misunderstand?"

"Um, no." I don't know why, but suddenly I'm a little on the defensive. Probably because he brought up Max. "I'm doing most of the work from here on out. I needed help in the bathroom. I'm working on the windows and the storms next. Taking them apart, refinishing them, and redoing all the sash cords. Need to make sure they're all set before I head back to school."

"Why don't you just buy new windows?"

"Are you crazy? These windows are original to the house! A treasure! Not to mention that to refurbish them will cost me about $2,400. New windows would cost over $12,000. So, to me, it's worth the elbow grease on my part."

"Wow, that's a lot of money and a lot of work. You're doing the work?" He sounds skeptical. "Like with power tools and everything? Can you do that?"

This irks me to no end. "Listen, just because I don't have a penis doesn't mean that I can't work a reciprocating saw. You know, I spent more time with my dad working on home projects than Brady ever did. You should know that."

"Sorry, didn't mean to offend. Can I make you some eggs?"

His demeanor has shifted, and it again catches me off guard. Maybe it's because I killed off a lot of brain cells last night. Either way Fitzy, popping up from my past like this has certainly tilted my world for the time being. "Um, sure. Eggs would be great."

CHAPTER TWENTY-FOUR

He waits until I have a mouthful of scrambled eggs before he asks his next question. Fitzy is really good at catching me off guard; I'll give him that.

"So, what's going on with you and Jenna?"

He knows a lot of the history. He saw us close, and then not close. Well, at least he should have. He was just a boy and could have been quite unobservant at the time.

"What do you remember about how Jenna and I got along?"

He pauses for a minute and takes a sip of coffee. He's not eating the eggs. He made them just for me. It makes me feel special and loved, which I know is stupid, but let's face it, my brain is not firing on all pistons at the moment.

"You were always in cahoots, and then you couldn't stand each other. Used to drive Brady crazy the way you two fought. He always wanted to come over to my house, just to be away from the drama. Have things not improved?"

"Um, that's putting it mildly." Chewing again. This man could cook. He's still looking at me, waiting for an answer. "Jenna has spent her life being Jenna. Spoiled, selfish, and mean. For some reason, she has taken it upon herself to make me miserable every chance she gets."

"How so?"

"I think the big one is that she had an affair with my boyfriend, got him to propose to her instead of me, and then ended up causing a car accident that killed him."

"Oh, right. I remember hearing about the accident."

"So you remember the gory details." He nods, encouraging me to go on. "And, the icing on the cake is that she's pregnant with his child."

"Jenna's pregnant?" Even though he's asking a question, there isn't any surprise to his voice. Maybe no one sees how badly this is going to go but me.

"Yeah. It's going to be a disaster. She isn't fit to be someone's mother. She's not even fit to be a human being."

"You know, your mom thinks something happened to her. That she's missing. What do you think?"

Do I tell him what I think? Do I tell him what happened here the other night? I can't. I now know, in hindsight, that I did the wrong thing. I'm going to have to deal with it at some point, but I don't want Fitzy to know what I did. Not yet.

It doesn't matter, either way, because we're interrupted by a banging on the door. Fitzy jumps up. "Let me get it. You stay put." It's a statement, not a suggestion. His voice has an air of authority to it. He's a lot different than the last time I saw him. Yet, still, the same and familiar. He definitely likes being in charge. Fitzy being here, showing up like this, picking up like the last seventeen years haven't happened, is sort of off-putting. At least enough to knock me off my bearings. Not as if that's hard at the moment.

"Oh my God, Sadie! Are you all right?" I can hear Max's voice before he reaches my kitchen.

"Yeah." I say glumly. I really feel like crap. I don't want Max rushing in, thinking that—wait, why is Max here in the first place? Didn't we fight last night? All this— Jenna, Max, Fitzy—it's all too much for me to process in my hungover state. I really hate people showing up unannounced all the time. I need some peace and quiet.

And sleep. I just want everyone to leave so I can go back to sleep.

"I'm sorry, I didn't catch your name." Fitzy is addressing Max. The sight of the eggs on my plate is making my stomach churn. Fitzy certainly is bossy. I should ask Fitzy what he does for a living. He must be in some high-power position or something. Maybe we can catch up someday over coffee in the near future. Not now. I need them both to leave so I can pass out again. My head feels like it's about to explode.

"That's because it's none of your business." I've never heard Max so abrupt. Normally, he's jovial and light. Today his voice is hard. It's disturbing. He must be really pissed at me. He has no right to be mad at me—he's the one dating multiple people or whatever is going on with him and Tracy. He can't blame me for wanting no part of that. I'm mad at him. "Sadie," he squats down next to my chair. "Are you okay? What's going on?"

Oh, I get it. Max can do whatever with whomever but now he's gonna get all pissed that I have another man in my kitchen. Well, two can play at this game.
"This is Fitzy. He's a *friend*. You know, like you and Tracy. And he's making me breakfast. Max, Fitzy. Fitzy, Max."

Fitzy extends his hand as Max stands up, still glaring. "Henry Fitzsimmons."

Max has no choice but to accept. "Michael Schultz."

Fitzy cocks his eyebrow. I used to love it when he did that. "I thought Sadie called you Max."

"I thought she called you Fitzy."

They were practically peeing on each other to mark their territories. I guess I should be flattered, but I just couldn't appreciate it at the moment. I was feeling all sorts of crappy and wanted to crawl into bed for about a week.

Max squats back down and grabs my shoulders. "What's going on? Are you okay?"

I shake out of his hands. I don't want him touching me. "I'm fine. I mean, I feel terrible, but that's because I did a battle with vodka and lost. Why are you so antsy?" It was a big word for my limited brain cells to come up with in their alcohol-infused state.

"Why are the police here?"

"Police?" I look around and see Fitzy standing over us, his hands on his hips, pushing his sports coat back. There it is—his gun. And not in a penile-euphemistic kind of way. An actual gun in a holster, his shiny badge on his belt. I guess that answers the question about what Fitzy does for a living. "Oh, yeah. Fitzy just stopped in—" then it occurred to me. "Why *are* you here?"

Max doesn't let Fitzy answer. "It's not just him. There's a police car in front of your house, too."

Police car. Police ... car. Police ... man.

Oh shit. No way. With a speed I didn't know I could muster at the moment, I run to the front of the house. As I approach the front door, bits and pieces start to flash in my mind. Uh oh, I think I'm going to throw up.

"Sadie, what's wrong? You're three shades paler than a ghost." Max puts his arm around my waist, as if he's afraid I'm going to pass out. I let him because I might.

"Max, did you stop by here during the night? Wearing your leather vest and chaps?"

I hear Fitzy behind me, snickering.

"Um, no. Why do you ask?"

A small surge of relief passes through my veins. "No reason. I just remembered a weird dream I had." As more of the dream starts to come to my consciousness, I can't believe how real it seemed. Max was there, first as Cupid, then as a police officer. Then, there were two Maxes. But it wasn't two Maxes, it was Max and Fitzy. Thank goodness that was just a dream. I'm pretty sure I was rather crass with my suggestions about handcuffs and where he could put his nightstick.

You know, if I wasn't somewhat clairvoyant, this whole dream thing would have freaked me out. But I've become used to premonitions that later become real—or turn out to have a basis in reality.

I open the front door and step onto my porch. I can see that there is a uniformed officer sitting in the front seat. He lifts his hand in some sort of signal. Like some gang sign, as if we had gangs in this small town.

"Are you with him?" I ask Fitzy. "What's going on?"

"Sadie, I'm going to need you to come down to the station with me."

"Wait, what?" I look between Fitzy and Max. Max is just as bewildered as I am. Two more cars pull up. Neither their lights nor their sirens are on. Still, it's enough of a spectacle that the neighbors are going to notice. Great. What a way to make a first impression.

"Sadie, let's go."

"Um, Fitzy, I don't think so. I'm not feeling great. I'm going to go back to bed."

"Sadie, this isn't a request. We have a search warrant for your house. You need to come with me and answer some more questions."

Max jumps in. "*More* questions? Sadie, I don't know what's going on, but please tell me you didn't answer any of his questions without your lawyer present."

"Lawyer? I don't have a lawyer. And no, I didn't answer ..." I trail off. It occurs to me that everything Fitzy said to me before was a question. There was a lot of him asking and me answering. Oh no, what did I even say?

"I'll call Tracy. She's a legal secretary. I'll get someone for you."

I make a face at Max. Tracy again? I look at the police cars surrounding my house. Looks like I don't have much of a choice here. "Okay, Max. Thanks." This was all happening so fast. I didn't even really know what this was.

Now I address Fitzy. "Fitzy, what's going on? Why do you want to talk to me? Do I need a lawyer?"

His jaw was set in a hard way that didn't look right on the face that I know. Or used to know. The Fitzy I pined over as an adolescent would not do this.

"Am I under arrest?"

"No. Not yet."

"Not yet? What did I do? What is this about?"

"Your sister."

Oh shit. Did they know what happened? How could they? Did everyone know what I did? Oh shit.

CHAPTER TWENTY-FIVE

Have I mentioned that I hate my sister? Yeah. I didn't think it possible, but I hate her even more right in this moment. This moment, in which I'm being brought to the police station for questioning. I don't think I did anything wrong. Okay, that's a lie. I know I did. It's why I was so upset last night that I had to make like a Russian and drink an entire bottle of vodka. But I didn't think it was a crime. Maybe in the eyes of God it was. Not in the court of law. Or was it?

I guess I'm about to find out.

Max is back in the house, on the phone. Hopefully he's calling for a miracle. Fitzy is escorting me to his car.

And I'm guessing this pretty much ruins my chances with Max. Of course, now I'm not so sure I want a chance with Max. I don't like how he acted yesterday, and then showing up this morning was weird too. And I don't have to wonder whether my chances are ruined with Fitzy too. Not that I had been so much as thinking about Fitzy before today. Either way, I'd bet there are a lot more date-less nights in my future.

Which is fine with me. That's the way I want it. I don't want anyone else to get hurt because of me. Jenna was just the latest casualty. Except she wasn't the one I had a premonition about. Oh no. I often wished misfortune in her general direction, even more so than usual in the past few months. Like the opposite of praying for someone. A curse, if you will. And my curse came true.

How do I tell Fitzy this? He's going to tell my mother. I can't bear to hurt her. I can't bear to see the disappointment in her eyes. For once, I'm glad my dad is in the state he's in, so he won't be able to look at me like that too. I know I've done something terrible. It's not my fault, really. Okay, it is. It is my fault my sister is dead. I'm the one to blame. The eggs make a u-turn in my stomach. All over the rear tire of his Chevy Tahoe.

At least it wasn't inside the vehicle.

"Sorry about that," I say, wiping my mouth with the back of my hand. Fitzy's jaw is clenched even harder. "Let me just get the hose and wash it off." Since I'm not fully under arrest, he can't stop me from this, can he? I wonder if he thinks this is a ploy to delay the inevitable. It isn't—I'm not that clever, but the extra time to think is certainly welcome. The hose feels like it weighs about nine hundred pounds. It's taking every ounce of strength I have to drag it up to the front of the house.

I wash the tire off, aware that Fitzy and several uniformed officers are watching me. They seem to be amused at my predicament. Great. I'm glad they think it's funny that I booted all over a cop car. I can't believe that none of them is offering to help me. Jerks.

I hear one of them call, "Hey, Richards, why don't you give her a hand? Maybe she'll give you a tip." More laughter. "She looks like she knows how to handle a hose." What the hell is so funny anyway?

Then I see the red-faced young officer who appears to be the butt of the joke. Along with me, that is. And, immediately, I know why.

So, remember that dream about Max showing up as a stripper, dressed as a cop? Maybe that wasn't one of my vivid dreams after all. Maybe that was young Officer Richards that I tried to tip with a bunch of singles. Oh. My. God.

I put the hose back, square my shoulders, and try to pretend I have some dignity left. Marching up to Fitzy, I demand, "Tell me again, why you were in my house this morning?"

"Officer Richards called for backup."

"Because?"

"He couldn't fend off your feminine wiles." Fitzy is trying not to laugh.

"And where exactly did you come in?"

"He radioed for backup. I had already told your mom that I would handle the case, so I received his distress call."

He opens the door, and I climb up and sit down with a huff. "So, why aren't you arresting me for assaulting an officer?"

Fitzy is in the driver's seat and clicks some buttons on his dashboard. "Because, honestly, it was the funniest thing I've seen in a long time. I wish all D and D's were this amusing."

"D and D's?"

"Drunk and disorderlies. Although you were in your own home, so there's not a lot we could do about it. Poor Richards—never had a chance against you. You've learned some new moves since high school."

"Thank you. I think."

"Frankly, the guys are here to see what you look like."

Great. "So, then, after I molested poor Officer Richards, then what? You showed up? Why?"

"I told you, I had talked to your mom. We've so far determined that you were the last known person that we knew of to see Jenna. We're trying to trace her steps to see if we can locate her."

"I thought someone had to be missing for twenty-four hours before a missing persons case could be opened?" My palms are sweating and I sort of want to pass out.

"It was twenty-four hours last night. You were the last person to see her. And what time was that again?"

This time, I noticed the shift into interrogation mode. "Did I invite you into my house then?" Two could play at this game.

"As a matter of fact, you did. Amongst other things." He smiles at me in the rearview mirror. It's still a panty-dropping smile.

Swallowing hard, I manage, "Did it involve your handcuffs and um, nightstick?"

"Sweet little Sadie is all grown up, isn't she?"
"Yeah, feeling so grown up right about now." I bend forward, holding my head in my hands. I try to think about last night, or actually early this morning. "So, if I invited you in, and you started hammering me with questions, then all of that must be grounds for your search warrant." I watch a lot of *Law & Order*, what can I say?

He's quiet for a minute. "Talking to you was not what I thought it would be. You said some things that were a bit on the questionable side."

"Can't I argue that I was not fully in control of my right faculties when I said those things, and so they would be inadmissible?" I wonder what I said? I tend to be loose-lipped on a good day about my feelings toward my sister.
"Been watching *Law & Order*, I take it?"

"Fitzy, we go way back. Apparently, it's my lot in life to constantly make an ass out of myself in front of you. But can you at least be up front with me and tell me what's going on? Why are you bringing me in?"

"Sadie, I ..." he breaks off. We're parking in front of the police station. I know he doesn't have much time before he has to be all official again. "You said some things. They were ... disturbing. If you can answer the questions, then maybe we can figure out what's going on with Jenna."

He gets out and is coming around to let me out. There's a news crew in front of the police station. I'm hoping against hope that they're covering another story. All I can picture is them hammering us with questions: "Detective Fitzsimmons, can you tell us about the disappearance of Jenna Perkins? Is there suspected foul play? Is this a person of interest?" "Aren't you the missing woman's sister? Did you have anything to do with her disappearance?"

Thank goodness they don't seem to know who I am, and really are there to cover another story. Maybe I do watch too much TV.

Fitzy's arm is around my back, and he's ushering me inside. Through the front office, down a corridor, and into an honest-to-God interrogation room. Even though I'd been mostly watching HGTV these days, this was something straight out of Investigation Discovery. I looked around for the cameras, wondering if this would be recorded for posterity. Or prosecution. Whichever came first.

"Can I get you something? Water? Coffee? Soda?"

"A file in a cake?"

Fitzy smiles at me. "I hope it doesn't come to that." His voice is serious under his light words.

"Fitz?"

He stops in the doorway. "Yeah?"

"Why are you being so nice to me?"

"Don't you know—I'm the good cop."

He wasn't kidding. His partner—the bad cop—is a brick wall of a woman named Michele Abbott. She's in an ill-fitting suit and has unfortunate curly hair that probably wouldn't look half bad with the correct product. Detective Abbott didn't mess around with hair product. Or an iron. Or a tailor. Too bad. She's probably trying to project a tough image. I wonder if her outward appearance is a physical manifestation of her inward unhappiness. But I don't have that much time to armchair quarterback her psyche before she starts in on me.

The good news is that while my words seemed to flow endlessly when Fitzy asked me questions, Detective Abbott's piss-poor demeanor makes me clam up tighter than my jeans after Thanksgiving dinner. I'm a little less likely to say something stupid to incriminate myself. I mean, incriminate myself again.

"Tell me about your relationship with your sister," she barks.

"When was the last time you saw your sister?"

"What did you discuss?"

And so it goes. On and on. If I hadn't already had a headache when this started, I certainly would have had one by now.

I'm not saying much. In my head, I know I should wait for whatever legal help Max can find for me. Assuming he can find someone. What if Tracy works for a tax attorney or a patent lawyer? That would certainly be of no help.

The more I think about it, the more I realize that I've actually done nothing wrong. I mean, I was a terrible sister, no doubt about it. But I hadn't committed a crime. This realization helps me to sit a little straighter and take charge.

"Am I being charged with a crime?"

"Not at this moment," Detective Abbott says dryly. Her threat is thinly veiled.

"Then I think I'll be going. I've got work to do on my house."

"The search is still being conducted at your premises. You cannot enter until they are done."

"When will that be?"

"When they find what they're looking for."

"And what are they looking for?"

"The proof that you killed your sister."

CHAPTER TWENTY-SIX

Okay, so how do I get out of this one? Am I responsible for my sister's death? Absolutely. Did I do it? No way. I just didn't prevent it. It's totally not the same thing. Right?

Oh God, I'm going to hell.

This is even worse than getting some odd premonition about a comedian and then him dying. Or making a comment, like the one about never talking to Rob again, which then resulted in his untimely demise. No, I knew—or should have known—what the outcome was going to be with Jenna. And I did nothing to stop it.

I am responsible for her death. But not in the way that Detective Abbott seems to think. What if Fitzy—and Max—and everyone think that I'm a murderer? Murderess? What is the proper term?

My brain cannot even process this train of thought. Will my mother still love me?

What do I do now?

Through my tears, I drive by my house. There are cops everywhere. In the house. Combing the yard. Crawling in the dumpster. The dumpster. Oh crap, this is bad. Sooo bad. Like I need to start working out so I don't become someone's bitch my first week in prison. I don't even watch *Orange is the New Black*. I wonder if I'll have time to binge watch it before I'm locked away. Jesus, what an inappropriate thought. I have always used humor to deflect the unpleasantness around me. Good to know some things are the same.

Therese puts me up, letting me sleep fretfully before even asking me a question. Later, thankfully, her children don't allow me to answer her questions. Never have I been so happy for their attention-demanding presence. The nightly news, however, fills in blanks that I wish it didn't. Did you know that I tell a lot of people I want to kill my sister? Apparently I do. There's Mrs. Henderson, only concerned about her grandchild, begging for the last remnant of her son. At least she doesn't support the Saint Jenna image that the rest of the media seems to favor. Then there's the interview with Tina, Brady's wife. "Sadie was always resentful of the attention Jenna got. She couldn't get over the fact that her boyfriend left her for Jenna. She's been horrid ever since she found out Jenna was pregnant." Brady, my douchewaffle brother, just stands there in the background, wearing a dumbass look on his face. Ugh.

To make matters worse, the national morning news programs pick up the story. *A woman, six months pregnant, is missing. Her sister is the main person of interest in her disappearance. Sources close to both women say that theirs was a tumultuous relationship, with tension worsening when Jenna Perkins was in a car accident with Robin Henderson.*

I can't stand to watch my name be dragged through the mud on national TV. Okay, so they never actually said my name, but we all know who they're talking about. They're playing it up like a mystery, but I know if I were watching it—as a bystander, not the subject—I'd be convinced of my guilt too.

My house is in shambles after the police search. Especially the bathroom. I'm guessing they found trace evidence they were looking for. Or they will, once it's all processed. I just keep waiting for Fitzy and Detective Abbott to come pulling up, sirens blazing, and handcuffs waiting. And not in a good way this time.

The buzz around town is incredible. I can tell every time I walk into a store. I see the looks. Hear the whispers. After some people asked to be switched out of my section at the restaurant, my manager told me to take a few weeks off, "until this blows over." Un huh. Doug gave me a smile and a hug as I left the restaurant, head hanging in shame. I wonder if he'll come to visit me in prison.

It takes me three days to get the house back in order and start working on my windows again. I wonder if I'll need to sell the house to pay my legal fees. I don't have a lawyer yet. Max got the name of someone for me, but I've been too chicken to call. Like retaining counsel is sure proof of guilt. Few friends and family have been in touch. I don't blame them. Actually, I do. Once again, everyone is taking Jenna's side. Just by assuming I'm guilty, they're siding with her.

My mom is the worst. I mean, talking to her is the worst. I don't know what to say to her. Her daughter is dead, and I'm to blame. That much is true. She really can't talk to me about it either. I get it. There's an ongoing investigation. I'm the primary suspect. She's a witness. I need to come clean about what happened. I'm scared because I know how bad I'm going to look. I can barely look myself in the mirror. I don't know how she'll ever speak to me again.

I've been spending some extra time at the nursing home as well. My dad is the one person who won't judge me without hearing my side. I'd like to think that I'd have his backing if he could give it, but I think he'd be disappointed in me, too. Heck, I'm disappointed in me.

Guess it's a good thing that I don't want anything to happen between Max and me. After the truth comes out, I'll be a marked woman. A pariah. I wonder if I can get fired from my job over this. I should probably contact my union rep to be proactive. Ironic. Rob and I always fought about the union, and now here I am, needing it. Or at least I think I'll need it. I put it on my mental list of things to do. Hire a lawyer. Call the union rep. See if I still have a job. Kiss my love life and social standing goodbye.

I know all of these things, so there's really no explaining my next phone call.

"Fitzy? It's Sadie."

"What's up?" His voice is brisk and businesslike.

"Can you talk?"

"I'm in the middle of something at the moment. I can meet up in about thirty minutes. I don't suppose you want to meet me at the station?"

"I'd rather not meet there right now, if it's all the same."

"Gotcha. I'll pick you up, and we'll go for a drive."

What to do in the thirty minutes until Fitzy arrives?

Max.

I need to say goodbye to Max before this gets ugly. Uglier, I should say. I call him next.

"Hey."

"Hey yourself."

"Are you busy right now?"

"I'm just wrapping something up. Lemme go out to my truck."

I wait while I hear him rustling. His truck door shuts and the background noise quiets. "Hey."

"I'm sorry to bother you."

"How are you doing?"

"Not good, but that's to be expected, right?"

"I've been questioned."

"About that night?"

"About what I know about that night as well as your relationship with your sister."

"Oh great. Well, maybe you can come visit me once in a while in prison."

"Sadie, I don't understand."

I sigh. How do I put this into words? "Max, I don't think I'm a horrible person."

~156~

"I know you're not. I don't understand why things are so bad with you and your sister. She brings out a terrible side of you. But mostly I don't understand what happened between us. You seemed all into me, and now you're pulling back. I don't get it."

Max is sort of ... whiny. It's not what I would expect from him. Not at all. I mean, I have a lot going on right now, and he's fixated on the lack of progress in our relationship. "I wish I could explain it Max. I can't even understand it most of the time." How do I put into words that I'm a freak who kills people with a mere thought? That my freaky visions have evolved into being full-fledged curses. Now he's added a possible ex-girlfriend into the mix, not to mention getting a little too intense at an inopportune time. "Maybe it's a good thing that things didn't go too far. I wouldn't want you to be hurt by me."

"Sadie, you could never hurt me."

"That's the thing. I don't mean to. It just happens. I don't want to hurt people but I still do."

"Sadie, you don't have a mean bone in your body. I know you would never hurt me. I know it would be good between us, if you gave us a chance. You're a good person. That's why I don't understand you and your sister."

"There are some things that defy logic. Like how she could—"

"Maybe you shouldn't say anything else to me. You know, in case ..."

"In case you are called to testify against me?"

The silence is deafening. Finally, he mumbles, "Yeah, something like that."

"I never thought I'd break up with someone so they couldn't incriminate me in a court of law."

"It's a first for me, too." Again, silence. Then he speaks, his voice full of hope. "So, does that mean that you were considering dating me?"

CHAPTER TWENTY-SEVEN

"You look down in the dumps."

"Thanks Fitzy. Why don't you tell me I've gained weight too?"

Eyebrow cocked, he looks me up and down. If I wasn't all depressed about breaking things off with Max and the impending murder charges, it would be enough to get certain areas tingling. Okay, maybe it still is enough.

"You look just as good as always."

"Okay, that's enough!" I slam my hand down on the counter. Fitzy raises that damn eyebrow at me again. "You cannot say things like that to me. Don't you understand that you messed me up for years. I'm finally in a good place—"

"You call this a good place?"

"Shut up. You know what I mean."

"No, I'm afraid I don't. How did I mess you up?"

"You knew I had the biggest crush on you."

There's that wicked smile again. "Really? I had no idea."

Now he's just jerking my chain. "Stuff it Fitzy. You knew I was head-over-heels for you. I was always doing stupid stuff, trying to impress you."

"You mean like stuffing a dollar bill down my pants."

Of course, when he says it, I can't help but look at his crotch. He catches me looking. Dear Lord, please make the floor swallow me whole. "I'm never going to live that down, am I?"

"Um, no. It's still the talk of the station. Poor Richards. I think he's going to be in therapy for a long time."

"Can you please tell me exactly what happened? My recall is fuzzy. Honestly, I thought I was dreaming."

"I think Richards thought he was dreaming too. I asked him to stop by and check on you. See if you were home. Your lights were on, and so he knocked on the door. Apparently when you answered, you somehow were under the impression that he was there in an entertainment capacity. I believe you encouraged him by dancing yourself."

I want to die. I sink down in a kitchen chair, hoping the floor will open up, and I can disappear right through it. I try the next best thing, which is folding my head in my hands on the table.

Fitzy sits down in the chair to my right. He's playing with the edge of the woven placemat. "He called me to tell me about your, um, condition, since he knew that I was following this case."

"And then?" My voice is muffled from inside my arms.

"When I got there, it was, frankly, hysterical. You kept calling Richards Max, but you knew who I was. You may have brought up—" he breaks off.

That's enough to make me sit up straight. "Oh God, what? What did I bring up?"

Fitzy's trying to compose himself. He's relaxed back in his chair with a wide grin. "You may have mentioned something about how you always wanted to give me your V-card, and even though it wasn't still valid, it had been a while, so it would be pretty much like the first time again."

It was even worse that I thought.

"I can't even."

"What, Sadie? What can't you even?"

How do you reply to that? "I have no words. I have never been so mortified in my life."

"So I probably shouldn't tell you that you may have brought up a threesome?"

"I DID NOT!" I jump up from my seat, part indignant, yet part worried that I really did say that.

Fitzy's flat-out laughing at me now. "Okay, no you didn't. You're still the good girl you always were."

"Yeah, I'm the good one. That's how I'm the primary suspect in a murder."

"There's been no recovery of a body yet." The word yet hangs in the air.

"How did I get here?"

"If you told me twenty years ago that we'd be sitting here, I wouldn't have believed you either."

"Twenty years ago, Jenna and I were still friends. Sort of. Actually, we weren't by that point. Isn't it sad that it's been over twenty years since we were friends?"

"What happened? You two were thick as thieves when you were little."

"I don't suppose that I can talk to the Fitzy who knew me back then, not the Detective Fitzgerald who is trying to find a body?"

"So you're telling me you know there's a body then?"

"No, that's not what I'm saying. I just wish I had a friend in the world right now. I don't seem to. Everyone's afraid to talk to me because they know they're going to be questioned. It would be nice if I could talk to someone who knew Jenna and me when we used to be close." I sink back down into my chair.

"So what did happen?"

"That's the thing. I don't know. We were close, then we weren't. It was like someone flipped a switch in her and all of a sudden she hated me. It was her mission in life to beat me, to win. Where we used to be a team, suddenly we were competition. I don't know why."

"You know, when I think about you as a kid—"

"I am only two years younger than you."

"Yeah, but when I was fourteen and you were twelve, all gangly and spindly. I used to wonder how your legs could support you. They were so skinny that I thought they would snap."

"I seemed to fill out but you never noticed."

"I noticed. But you were Brady's sister. There was a rule. Like dating someone's ex-girlfriend. Sisters are off limits." He's looking down at my legs now. Why couldn't this be happening in the middle of winter when my legs could be covered up?

"I wish you had told me. Maybe it would have saved me a lot of heartbreak and lonely nights, hoping you'd drop by."

His fiddling with the placemat is irritating me. I put my hand on his to still it. He looks at me and I feel like he can see into my soul. "You know what I remember about you?"

As if it has a mind of its own, my hand pulls back and settles into my lap. I knot my hands together. "What?"

"It was the weirdest thing, but you would say something, totally out of the blue, and then it would happen."

After a moment I say quietly, "You noticed that?"

"Yeah. I remember one time Brady and I were playing baseball in your yard. You were at the picnic table, drawing. You weren't paying attention to us at all. But, clear as day, I heard you tell Jenna to go in and get ice. She didn't want to, and you two started fighting. Finally, you yelled, 'Get the ice for Brady. He got hit in the head with a ball.' Your voice caused Brady to turn, and sure enough, the ball hit him in the head."

"I remember that." That was back when I was just injuring people.

"It's like you had a sixth sense about things."

"Yeah, well, I don't see dead people."

"That wasn't the only time that happened either."

"No, I know."

"What is it? Does it still happen?"

"I don't know what it is. Clairvoyance maybe?"

"Have you ever looked into it?"

"No, not really. I don't like to talk about it. My dad had it too, so we talked about it some. I've talked about it with my friend Therese, but she doesn't understand. She doesn't get that I have no control and that I don't know the future. She constantly asks me what lottery numbers to play."

"Damn, that was my next question." His smile puts me at ease. He's playing with the placemat again.

"You know, I bet you're really good at this interrogation thing. I bet you get a lot further than Detective Abbott."

"Not a big fan of Michele's, I take it?"

"She's scary, needs a better tailor, and needs a lesson in how to use hair product."

"I would tell her that, but frankly, I'm scared of her too. She's beat my ass in the boxing ring on more than one occasion." He pauses. "You wanna hear something funny though?" Without letting me answer he continues. "She has a huge crush on Officer Richards."

That makes me laugh. "Oh, now I feel bad for her. If he can't take me in my inebriated state, he'll never be able to handle her."

"I agree, but I think they could be good together. There's a side to her that not many people get to see."

We sit in a heavy silence. I want to tell him about how I feel responsible for the deaths of the celebrities, relatives, the plane crash, the kid in my high school. Rob. How do you even broach that without sounding like a complete wackadoo?

CHAPTER TWENTY-EIGHT

I'm saved by the bell. Not the bell, but the chirping of Fitzy's phone. He looks at it, and as he's answering, stands up to leave the room. He walks out through the laundry room and then the back door. I can picture him, walking around the driveway, kicking rocks while he listens to his news.

Standing up, I walk over to the window, and see the sight I just pictured in my head. Holy crap. What is this? The visions are coming more frequently. Whereas I used to have one every few months, it seems I've had a lot more recently. Or maybe it's just that I'm more aware of them. The more my emotions are in a state of turmoil, the more I can see things. He doesn't appear to be talking, just listening. His brow is knitted as he listens, feet scuffing through the dirt. He locates a rock and kicks it around, following it over the width of my driveway.

I go back to the kitchen and pour myself a glass of lemonade. It's a hot July day. The summer is more than half over. My windows are only half done. I wonder if I'll be able to get them done at this rate. Will I have to sell my house? I know that beggars can't be choosers, but I hope whoever buys it loves it as much as I do and appreciates all the charm this place has. I had really hoped that it would be not only a house, but a home. Maybe for the next person who lives here.

Fitzy's back inside the house. "Geez, it's hot out there. Got any more of that lemonade?"

I pour him a glass, and as I hand it to him, I find the courage to meet his eyes. "News?"

"Yeah. Just police business."

I wonder if it involves my case. Probably. Something is bothering me. Well, many things are bothering me, but this one I need to talk about. Fitzy is one of the few people I've been upfront with about the visions. "Can I ask you something?"

He's guarded again, watching me while he drinks his lemonade. He doesn't say no, so I take it as a go-ahead. "Do you ever call psychics in on cases?"

He places his glass on the counter and licks his lips. I sort of think he's doing it to mess with me. "We generally don't seek them out. They usually come to us."

"And everyone thinks they're a bunch of quacks, right?"

"Most of them are pretty granola."

"Granola?"

"They're full of fruits and nuts."

Just as I thought. "This is why I don't tell people about my ... whatever you wanna call it."

His phone vibrates on his belt, and he checks it reflexively. "I've got to go. I want you to come with me."

"As in a 'hey, I like hanging out with you' kind of way, or as in a 'you have the right to remain silent' kind of way?"

"The first." Fitzy smiles. "There's something I want to show you."

I drain my lemonade, pull my hair into a ponytail, and grab my purse. As we head down the back steps and toward his city-issue black Tahoe, I ask, "Do I have to ride in the back seat this time?"

"Only if you want to." He opens the passenger door for me.

"Even though I dreamed of it as a teenager, I hope I never see your back seat again."

"I never pictured you as the type of girl who would have gone parking."

"A, it's not 1950. No one goes parking. And B, I would have done anything you asked."

"Filing that away for future reference." Then he gives me a wink. What the hell is he doing to me?

"Don't you think that ship has sailed? This is not exactly the best timing, you know."

"Why? Is it that Max guy? What's the deal with you two anyway?"

"Nothing."

"It doesn't look like nothing to me. He's very protective of you."

"Well, it's not like this is a great time for me to start a relationship. I'll have a lot to offer in terms of conjugal visits." I look out the window. We're headed out of town. I wonder where Fitzy's taking me.

"Why do you think you're going to prison?"

"It's what everyone seems to think."

"Maybe not everyone."

Apparently we've reached our destination, because Fitzy parks the car. We're at the lake a few miles outside town. There are several police cars here. And then I see it— Jenna's car. The old white sedan is half in the water. The driver's door is open, muddy water lapping over the floorboards.

"That's Jenna's car."

"We know."

"Are you dragging the lake for her?"

"Should we?"

I shrug. "Don't know for sure but it seems like a logical plan."

"There's a problem with that statement."

"What?"

"We're talking about your sister—the word 'logical' does not apply."

"Good point."

Fitzy alights from the car. I stay in, waiting for instructions. I can't tear my eyes away from Jenna's car. Not in a premonition-feeling sort of way, but in a remorseful sort of way, I know she's dead in that lake. I mean, she has to be, and it's all my fault. I am a miserable excuse for a human being. I let my sister die. I feel the tears forming, but I don't want to start crying. I know I won't be able to stop. I try to distract myself by watching the goings on. Detective Abbott is there, apparently running the scene. She glances over at the Tahoe, glaring in my general direction. I'm trying to reconcile this woman who is so pissed off that I'm here with the one who has a school-girl crush on Officer Richards. She sends another withering glance at me. I can't say I blame her. I don't know why Fitzy brought me here. Maybe he likes to see me squirm. And not in the good kind of way.

I pull out my phone and text Max.

I'm sorry to drag u into all this. I'm with Fitzy. They found J's car. No sign of her yet.

He responds immediately.

Where?

I wonder if I'll get in trouble for divulging details of a police investigation. Well, no one told me not to.

By Snyder's Lake. The car is ½ in the water.

His next text surprises me.

Why are you with the police?

That was not what I expected.

IDK. He asked me to come with him. Call me crazy but I think he believes in me.

I believe in you.

I know you do.

Then can u believe in me? I know you have trust issues but u can trust me.

I want to.

I know I mean it. I want to believe in Max. Rationally, I know there's nothing going on between him and Tracy. Still something won't let me trust him. As I watch the police officers wander around, I, not for the first time this week, wonder how my life got here. I'm not a bad person. Not really. Okay, maybe a little. Jenna certainly brings out the worst in me. But other than that, I'm a good human being. I teach and tutor children. I'm preserving the beauty of an old home. I visit my father every day. I recycle.

My pity party is interrupted as Detective Abbott yanks the door open. "Get out."

I don't like her tone. She's rude. There's really no reason for it. I'm just sitting here, minding my own business. "Excuse me?"

"You heard me."

Being nice has not gotten me anywhere. Except here, of course. "What crawled up your butt and died?" I know it's not a good idea to piss off someone who has a gun. But still, this woman needs some help.

"Get. Out. Now."

"Fine. Sheesh." I undo my seatbelt, tossing my phone down as I struggle with the buckle. Once I finally free myself and get out of the car, Detective Abbott has been called away by a guy in coveralls down by the water's edge. He's got to be hot, covered up like that. I'm glad I'm not him. Of course, he's probably not going to jail, so maybe his life isn't so bad. Detective Abbott is yelling at him. Okay, maybe his life is that bad.

I wander over to near where Fitzy is standing with a bunch of the other worker bees. The gaggle of men appears to be joking around and talking about baseball, despite this being an active investigation scene. Our tax dollars at work.

I sit on one of the worn picnic benches, looking out at the water. This situation is surreal. I'm with Fitzy. I may or may not be a suspect in a crime. I'm pining after my handyman. And I will never see my sister again. The tears threaten again. Even though I hate her, I guess part of me has always held out hope that we'd get back to being sisters again. I can't believe this is how it ends.

Finally, Fitzy comes over and sits down next to me. "What's up?"

"Nothing. Just trying to figure out why you brought me out here." I'm trying to stay cool and composed.

"Honestly?"

"Um, yeah." I wonder if he's going to arrest me now. He's kicking at the rocks again. It makes me think that it might be a nervous habit. Not that he appears nervous on the outside.

"I was hoping you'd get a vision."

Rolling my eyes, I sigh. "Didn't I tell you that's not how this works?"

"I know, but it was worth a shot. I was hoping you'd see where your sister went."

What he's saying makes me sit up straight. "You mean you don't think she's in the lake?"

"No." His answer is simple and succinct.

"Do you think she's dead?"

It's his turn to shrug. "But you do."

I don't answer. How can I? This time, it's not the freaky psychic vision thing. It's the truth that's going to make me look bad.

"I'm sure the forensics team is having a field day with the evidence from my house."

"Well, you certainly weren't very smart about getting rid of the evidence." Detective Abbott has come up behind us, her sharp voice making me jump. "Maybe you should stop playing prom queen and tell us where your sister is."

I truly dislike this woman. And I know I don't have to stand for this. Standing up and brushing off my bottom, I tell the truth, even though it's not what they want to hear. "I don't know where she is. Fitzy, can you please take me home?"

CHAPTER TWENTY-NINE

My phone shows several missed texts from Max. Oops. I guess I shouldn't have left it in the car. He's awfully protective. Maybe too much so.

"You look upset. Anything wrong?"

Incredulously, I look at Fitzy, mouth agape for a moment. "Um let's see ... my sister is missing and probably dead. Detective Abbott is out to get me. I like Max but don't know what to do about it, and he's sort of getting weird and intense on me."

"Oh, is that all?"

"No, it's not."

"It isn't? What else?"

"I've lost my waitressing job, which may mean I can't finish the renovations on my house like I want. I'm not sure that I'll still have a teaching job when all is said and done. And ..."

"And?"

"And dealing with you is unsettling. When I'm with you, it feels good and comfortable, but then I feel like I'm cheating on Max, which is stupid since nothing will happen with us." Wow, what a mouthful.

He pulls into my driveway. It's dusk, and I can see the last remnants of the purple and pink sky to the west beyond my house. As he turns off the car, he leans his head back. "Seeing you again, I agree, is sort of unsettling."

This makes me turn to look at him. He's staring straight ahead, not meeting my gaze. "Why do *you* think so? It's not like I ever made a blip on your radar before."

"Sadie, I practically grew up in your house. It's not like I didn't see you. I saw you. A lot. Believe it or not, I was a dumb teenage boy who could barely get out of my own way. Plus, Brady threatened me if I ever went near you. But I saw you. You were a cool chick. Still are. I wish I had run into you under different circumstances."

"You mean when I'm not a murder suspect."

"Yeah, something like that," he laughs.

"I take it you're no longer afraid of my brother."

"Um, no. I haven't talked to him—before all this—in about fifteen years."

"You mean, about the time that Tina removed his balls and started wearing them as earrings."

"Tell me how you really feel."

"Well, you tell me. Why did you and Brady stop talking?"

He pauses for a minute. The darkness has surrounded us. The cicadas are chirping and a light breeze passes through the windows making it tolerable to sit in the car. "Because of Tina."

"You know, I would feel badly for Brady, but he's such an ass that it's sort of hard."

"He has changed. I mean, he was always sort of an ass but now ..."

"It's like ass supreme."

Fitzy laughs again. Being with him is like wearing a favorite pair of shoes that look great and fit well. I tell him, "You know, if you had a sister, he would have tapped her without thinking twice."

"I know. He was always sort of like that."

"He and Jenna are sort of alike."

"Then where'd you come from?"

"You mean, how'd I get to be the 'good' one?" I make air quotes with my fingers.

"Something like that."

"I never wanted to be the good one. It's just who I am."

"You do the right thing."

This makes me uncomfortable. "I wish that were the truth."

"Tell me when you've been bad." Oh my, the innuendo is thick.

"You mean other than when I molested you and Officer Richards?"

Fitzy bursts out laughing.

"It's not that funny. I'm never going to live it down. I mean, it's bad enough that I was having a sex dream. It's even more mortifying that I acted it out."

Fitzy's laughter fills the Tahoe. "Oh, but Sadie, it was the most awesome thing. And you had some serious moves. How is it that you're still single?"

I can't handle it. I open the door and get out of the car.

I am single. I'm going to stay single. As I walk in my dark house, all I can think of is how much I don't want to be single. I want to share my life with someone. Fat chance now. When the truth comes out, no man will touch me with a ten-foot pole. Is it too much to ask for a partner in life? I don't even want to be so bold as to ask for kids at this point. I just want someone there when I come home and when I wake up in the morning.

"Sadie? Sadie? I'm sorry. Can I come in?" Fitzy's calling to me from the back door.

"Yeah, I'm in the living room. C'mon in."

He sinks down on the couch with me. "This color is cool," he says, his large hand running over the butter-yellow microsuede. "It's not what I would have expected in here."

"When I get the windows done and paint on the wall, it's going to be amazing."

"I love that you've kept all the woodwork."

"The woodwork is one of the reasons that I love the Craftsman bungalows. Did you know that this house came in a kit from the Sears-Roebuck catalogue?"

"Is that why it's called a Craftsman?"

"No, the Craftsman movement started before that. Sears was just smart enough to produce a kit house that had all the design elements that were popular. It's cool they made them available to the masses. My house was probably built around 1920. Think about all the history here. A family lived here during Prohibition. When the stock market crashed. While FDR was president."

"You always were a history buff. I remember you kicking my ass at Trivial Pursuit."

"I am an American History teacher by day, you know. I never outgrew my inner nerd."

"I think you did. I think you grew up just fine."

"Fitzy, stop."

"Stop what?" His arm is on the back of the couch as he's reclined into the corner, his legs crossed casually in front of him. Today he's in a blue button down and navy pants. Again the shirt is open at the neck and shows a small gold cross. The gun is still on his belt, but it's not intimidating. If anything, it's sort of a turn on. My cat, who usually makes himself scarce, is curled up next to Fitzy, like they're old friends. His green eyes—Fitzy's, not my traitorous cat's—are twinkling. Oh, this could get bad. Or good. Or, crap, what the hell is going on here? And why do I have the sudden urge to climb into his lap?

"You know what you're doing. Why are you doing it?"

That slow, sexy grin spreads along his face. I extend my neck back, resting my head on the top of the couch. I can't look at him. Otherwise, I may—will—do something very bad. But most likely very good. Maybe if I put my hands over my face, I can pretend that this vessel of temptation is not sitting twelve inches from me.

Nope. That doesn't work.

"Sadie?"

Without uncovering my eyes, I grunt an answer. "Hhhrmp."

"You hungry? You wanna get a bite to eat?"

I peek at him from underneath my hand. I am actually pretty hungry.

He continues. "How about Chinese?"

That makes me think about the night Max and I got Chinese at his place. That was the first night I realized that I liked him and, whether or not I wanted to admit it, wanted something more from him. So then why am I sitting here, thinking impure thoughts about Fitzy? I'm so confused.

I stand up. I need to remove myself from this temptation. "I've got to go see my dad."

Slowly uncrossing his legs and rising, Fitzy blocks my way. "I'll come with you. I'd like to see your dad."

"You know he's in a nursing home. He's pretty much catatonic."

Fitzy shrugs. "Okay. I still want to visit."

"Fitzy, I don't want you with me."

He looks uncomfortable for a minute. "I'm afraid you don't have much choice. We're keeping tabs on you right now."

This pisses me off. "And it's your turn to babysit me? Jesus, my life has not changed. Every time I think you're about to throw me a bone, I find out you're being paid to hang out with me."

"What's that supposed to mean?"

"You know damn well. Let me by. I'm leaving."

Fitzy stands his ground. I am so mad. He won't move and I need to get out. Now. Before I do something stupid. Stupid-er that should be. Because the next thing I know, my palms are flat on Fitzy's rock hard pecs as I'm trying to push him out of the way.

"Sadie, don't."

I shove harder. "GET OUT OF MY WAY." I'm growling at him through gritted teeth. He's not budging. And then his hands—massive hands—clasp my wrists. He's not pushing me away. He's holding my hands to his chest. Finally I meet his eyes. He licks his lips. "Sadie, please don't. I'm here because I want to be, not because I have to be. I don't have to be the one to be here. I don't have to be in the house."

"I need to go. Please." It almost comes out as a whimper. If he doesn't stop touching me, I cannot be held responsible for what I do next, but it most certainly will involve the use of his baton.

He releases me, and I storm past, grabbing my purse as I head out the door. I don't care if he follows me or stays here. I don't—shit. He's parked behind me. I can't go anywhere without him.

Why, why can't I get a break? Just once? It's like I'm doing penance for all the bad things I've done. Like all those people who have died because of my visions. And my sister. I don't want to think about her right now. My mind is a mess. Hanging my head, I'm prepared to go in and ask Fitzy to move his car. I turn around and whirl into him. How the heck did he sneak up on me? His hands are on my waist, steadying me. I'm trying to remember how to breathe.

"Sadie, let me drive you. Not because I have to, because I want to."

CHAPTER THIRTY

Complications. More complications. I don't want a complicated life. I want a simple one. I want to teach kids and hope I can inspire them to love American History as much as I do. I want to come home to my cute little house and make it beautiful again. I want to pet my cat without having him bite me. I want a man to share my life with. A partner in crime. Okay, bad choice of words but you know what I mean.

I don't want to have a police escort everywhere because they're looking for evidence. I don't want to be torn between two guys. I know, that doesn't seem like a bad thing, but it's not me. I'm a one-man type of woman. Hell, I pined over Fitzy for most of high school and even into college, which significantly dampened my dating life.

"I need to tell you something," he says finally. The silence in the car has been thick and uncomfortable.

"Yeah?" My voice is flat. This is all too much for me, and I don't have much energy.

"Your graduation party ... do you remember?"

Really? He has to bring this up now? He must get his rocks off at my humiliation. I mean, the first time Max came over was after that bee-sting-in-the-crotch incident, and he never brings that up. Fitzy seems to bring up all my embarrassing moments whenever he gets the chance. Chalk that up as a pro for Max and a con for Fitzy.

Now I'm making pros and cons lists? How did I get here?

"Yes, of course I remember. One typically does not forget a defining humiliation like that."

"I didn't think it was that bad. It certainly wasn't a seminal event."

"Maybe not for you, but it was for me. I'd been in love with you for as long as I could remember. I used to doodle 'Mrs. Henry Fitzsimmons' in the backs of my notebooks. I'd stay home if you and Brady were going to be at the house, just on the off chance that I'd get to spend some time with you. I'd turn down invitations from other boys, simply because they weren't you. It didn't take long before they stopped asking. And then you went away to college and my little-girl heart was crushed into a million pieces. I'd finally convinced myself that going away to college would be my chance to start over and to forget all about you."

"You wanted to forget me?"

"That was the plan. And then, there you were. At my graduation party. You were there for me, or so I thought. You had changed, started to mature. Filled out in all the right places, and I fell hard in that moment. You know, that stupid, irrational teenage-instalove. But you seemed unapproachable. Like you were too cool to be there. So I started drinking to muster some courage. And then you came and found me. And I thought it was to be with me. You were so nice, putting your arm around me, rubbing my back. I thought all the signs were there. I thought I had a big 'ole green light. So I leaned in to kiss you. And you stood up, letting me fall off the picnic table. You were horrified. You kept sputtering about how Brady asked you to check on me and you were just there to make sure I didn't get hurt. Yeah, well, I literally fell for you. And I broke my nose to boot. When you saw me leaning in, you jumped out of the way like your pants were on fire. It's hard not to take that personally."

"You broke your nose?"

"Yes, and had two black eyes for most of the summer. Not that you ever came around again."

There's silence in the Tahoe. I know, I should have the title of the Queen of Humiliation.

What I don't tell Fitzy is that I slept with the first guy who came along after that. His name was Jonathon Dweezledorf. It was terrible and did nothing to make me feel better about myself. I retreated into my studies, avoiding the whole dating scene for a few more years. I still dreamed about Fitzy, although the dreams became more and more sporadic. It certainly explains why I became so passive in my dating and in my choice of men. I made no effort. I was not putting myself out there. It's how I ended up with Rob. We were friends first. He made the first move. I let him. I took no initiative until it was too late.

"Does it help that there's another side to the story?"

"I think it's a little too late, don't you."

"I think you should reserve judgment until you've heard all the facts."

"Fine." My arms are crossed over my chest, and if I could stomp my feet like a child, I would. My lower lip may be sticking out. Just a little.

"Sadie, I already told you, Brady made me stay away. It's not that I didn't notice you. I did. Jenna was the annoying little sister, the one we tried to avoid. You were cool though. Too cool. You were the unattainable. You didn't date anyone. Everyone asked."

"Not everyone."

"If you wouldn't go out with the most popular guy in school, why would you go out with me?"

Unfortunately, I can see some reason in his logic. Damn him.

"At the time of your graduation party, I was dating someone from school. I knew the summer would be hard, but I wasn't going to let a few months and a few hundred miles get in the way. Until I came to your party. I was ready to chuck it all out the window. But I couldn't do that to

Kristen. She deserved more. I couldn't cheat on her like that. Not that I didn't want to. Because all I could see that night was you. I wanted to claim you as mine. I swear I had some real caveman shit going on. But then I realized you were drunk. Not a little tipsy, but slurring your words, having trouble keeping your eyes open drunk. Did I want to kiss you? Hell, yeah. But not like that. Not if it meant cheating on my girlfriend and with you practically incapacitated. I didn't mean for you to fall like that. Physically or emotionally. And I didn't think it was funny. Okay, maybe a little." He stifles a laugh.

I glare at him.

"Oh, c'mon, if you saw it in a movie, you'd think it was funny."

He's right. I know he's right, but I'm stubborn and can't back down.

"So you were there that night for me?"

He shrugs. "I didn't know it at the time. Not until I saw you. And then I tried to talk to you after that."

"I wouldn't take your call."

"No, you wouldn't. I figured you wanted nothing to do with me. That you were embarrassed that you hit on me because it was something you wouldn't have done sober. I went back to college, broke up with Kristen because she wasn't you, and tried to move on. Brady and I drifted apart, and I moved three states away. It's not like I was back in town all the time, but when I was, I always wanted to look you up. I figured you'd be married with a passel of kids by now."

"I had heard that you were working out of state. When did you come back?"

"About a year ago. I was married for a little while and it didn't work out. No kids, nothing tying me down. I wanted to be back around family. This position opened up, I applied and got it. I kept hoping I'd run into you. Not like this, but in some way."

I let out a long sigh. That's a lot of information to process. I don't know if I can believe Fitzy when he says he's had feelings for me all this time. We sit there for a minute. "Can you take me home? I'm not up for seeing Dad tonight. I'll come over in the morning."

"Are you sure?"

"You tell me that I had a chance with you all those years ago and I blew it? That you felt the same way about me? Do you know how you shaped my entire dating life? My party was the last time I approached a guy. I don't flirt, well, not intentionally. I don't hit on people. I sit and wait. And it sucks. Not a lot of guys approach me. I have to settle for whoever drifts my way. Which is how Rob and I ended up together. We were friends, but that spark, a real spark, wasn't there. He wasn't what I wanted. He wasn't going to sweep me off my feet. But he was there, and he didn't reject me. Well, at least not to my face. I was prepared to settle, all because I was afraid of putting myself out there and falling on my face again."

"But you didn't settle."

"No, something gave me the courage to realize that I was probably better off alone than settling. Actually," I smile at the memory, "it was a bat." Thinking about that whole incident brings Max to mind again.

"A bat?"

"Long story. But it helped me see that Rob wasn't what I wanted or needed. Which I guess was a good thing, considering he had already gotten my sister pregnant. But that's not the point."

"I think you've lost me. What is the point?"

"The point is that it's never the right time for us. There's always something getting in the way. Brady, Kristen, alcohol, my sister."

"Max."

"Yeah, Max." I look at his profile, driving in the night. "And it's not like you could do anything now anyway. I'm sure your job frowns upon canoodling with suspects."

"Did you just say canoodling?"

"Yeah. Why? I like that word. Along with caddywhompus."

"Caddywhompus? What's that?"

"It means crooked or cockeyed."

"Don't you start talking dirty to me. Job or not, I don't think I can handle it."

I laugh.

Again, how did things get so complicated?

CHAPTER THIRTY-ONE

I'm holding a bouquet of soft, pink roses in my hand. Baby's breath and pearls adorn the bouquet. I look up into the vintage, gold-framed mirror. My hair is braided in a coil around my head, like a crown. A few tendrils curl out, giving it a soft, romantic look. Everything about it says soft romance. The room is bathed in warm sunlight, streaming through the white sheers as a soft breeze blows.

My dress is nontraditional, but works all the same. It's a long-sleeve fitted mermaid-style dress covered in gold and ivory beads. I know the dress should be heavy, but it feels as light and airy as the curtains. The dress is much more sophisticated than anything I ever thought I would have chosen. There's a large keyhole opening in the back, from just below the high neck to just above my waist. It's sexy without being over the top. On my left hand is a vintage Asscher cut diamond ring with a diamond halo.

The door opens, and my dad walks in. Not my dad who has been withering away in a hospital bed for years, held prisoner in his own body, but Dad. The man who used to carry me on his shoulders. The stoic man, helping bereaved families, at the funeral home.

"Dad! You're here!" I run up and hug him, the tears welling up in my eyes.

"Of course I'm here Sadie-kins. I wouldn't miss this day for the world."

"But you're ... you ... you're back!"

"I'm free Sadie, and I can be with you now. Whenever you need me, and I know you need me today."

"I can't imagine this day without you here."

"You look beautiful. I'm so proud of you. I love you."

I'm not ready to let go of him yet. "Oh Daddy, I can't believe you're here. I love you so much."

"Well, let's get this show on the road, shall we?" He pulls back and wipes the tear running down my cheek. "You have a young man out there who's quite impatient to see you."

A young man? Who is it? I wrack my brain, trying to think of who it is? Is it Max? Is it Fitzy? I have no idea who is out there waiting for me. Anticipation creeps up my spine as we walk through the door, the full part of my skirt swishing and swaying against the worn wood floor.

We're at the bed & breakfast where Rob and I went for Valentine's Day. I'm getting married here. But to whom? It's the oddest thing. I have no memory of how I got here. No memory of planning but here I am on my wedding day. And my Dad's going to walk me down the aisle, just as it should be.

We start to head down stairs, although these were not anything like stairs I saw on my last visit to the B&B. They lead us to the kitchen. Fitzy is standing there. In loose-fitting gray sweat pants. And nothing else. They hang dangerously low on his hips, revealing chiseled abs, defined pecs, and that V that makes women swoon. Tattoos cover his shoulders and biceps, dance across his chest and wrap around his flank. Normally, I'm not one for tattoos, but on Fitzy, it works. It all works. My dad is not there with me, it's just Fitzy and me standing there. And although he looks delectable, I'm confused that he's the one here.

"What are you doing here?"

"I'm here for you."

"You shouldn't be here. It's not right." I don't know why I said that.

"But it can be. You know it can. And you always do the right thing."

I ignore him and keep walking through the kitchen cafe, beyond the door where Rob locked me in with the bat. Down the stone steps into the sunken library, where my groom is waiting for me. My dad is back, supporting me, holding my arm and giving me the strength to continue. I can tell that my groom is dressed in a black velvet tux with a wide black satin lapel and a black satin shirt, but I can't make out his face. I know that he is stunning, and my heart soars just looking at him. I turn to my dad and say, "He's the right one, right?"

Dad leans in and gives me a kiss on my cheek. "You know what to do Sadie. You always have. Do the right thing."

I take one last look in my dad's eyes, so happy to see them full of life and sparkle again.

Then I wake up. The ache in my chest is real. I look at the clock. 3:18 a.m. My dad's birthday is March eighteenth. I know by the feeling running up my spine what this means. And so I wait for the phone call.

It finally comes in around five a.m.

"Sadie?"

"He's gone, isn't he." It's a statement, not a question. My mom is weeping.

"Yes, honey. He is. How did you know?"

"I just did. When did it happen?"

"About two hours ago. They called me about two. He was breathing very shallowly and had spiked a temperature."

She didn't have to say it. I knew what time he passed. "Were you there? Did you get there in time? Please tell me he wasn't alone."

"I was there Sadie. He wasn't alone."

"Why didn't you call me? I would have come. I should have been there."

"I didn't know how long it would take. I didn't expect it to be so quick."

"But he's been gone for two hours now. Why didn't you call sooner?"

"Oh Sadie," I can tell she's crying. "I just wanted some more time with him. We didn't get enough time. I didn't think it would matter when I called you. And I didn't want to wake you in the middle of the night when there's nothing that you can do. The next few days will be long enough. I was trying to let you sleep."

I can't speak, because I'm crying too hard. I wipe my eyes and my nose on my t-shirt, not caring about how gross it is.

"I didn't get to see him yesterday. I was there, in the parking lot, but was upset about something else, so I didn't go in. I was going to see him in the morning."

"You were always there for him Sadie. You were. Don't beat yourself up about this."

"Mom? What are we going to do?"

She sounds old and tired. "We're going to keep going. That's what. Just like always. You're going to pull yourself together and help me make phone calls."

I know I will because it's the right thing to do. My dream comes flooding back, bringing on a fresh cascade of tears. I taste the saltiness as it runs into my mouth.

"Mom, this is going to sound crazy, but he was just here."

"What do you mean?"

"I had a dream. It was my wedding day and he was with me, giving me away." I can barely get the words out before my face contracts into the ugly cry position. It takes me a few minutes to get my breath back. "He was with me and he told me he was proud of me and he loved me."

"Of course he did, sweetie. He was such a good man."

"He's not going to be here to give me away."

She starts crying. "No, he's not. Maybe he needed to go now so he could help Jenna."

He told me to do the right thing. In my dream I thought it was about my choice in men. In the early morning light, I know that's not what he meant.

"Mom, I need to tell you something."

"What?"

"It's about Jenna."

There's silence. I know she's afraid of what I'm going to say. I'm afraid that when I say it, she won't love me anymore.

"Mom?"

"I'm still here. What do you know about Jenna?"

"Mom, I did a terrible thing." Silence again, so I continue. "She was here, Sunday night, like I said." I have to think for a moment to figure out what day it even is. It's Friday. This has been the longest week ever. "Max was here too. When I escorted him out, she went into my bathroom. My brand new bathroom. We had only finished it about an hour before."

"Yes."

"And when I found her in the bathroom, she was in the bathtub." The sight flashes before my eyes. "There was blood everywhere. Like all four walls, and even the ceiling a little. She was in the tub with a knife and had cut her wrists."

"Oh." It's a faint little whimper.

"It wasn't bad. I mean, there was a lot of blood, but her wrists—the cuts were horizontal."

"What does that mean?"

"Jenna used to make the snide comment, 'horizontal for attention, vertical for the hospital.' She wasn't trying to kill herself. Not really. She just wanted attention. More attention. I can't understand why."

"So then what?"

"I kicked her out. I dragged her out of the tub, shoved her down the hall, and out my front door. I told her she was dead to me and I never wanted to see her again."

"You threw her out? Why didn't you take her to the hospital?"

"I'm not proud of myself, Mom. I know I did the wrong thing. I was selfish and angry, and I let it get the better of me. I should have stopped her. I shouldn't have made her leave. I should have made sure she got help. If she's dead, it's all my fault."

"Well, she does bear some of the responsibility, don't you think?"

"Did you just say the word responsibility in regard to Jenna? I didn't think you could use those two words in the same sentence. I thought I had to be the responsible one."

"Sadie, stop. You know what I mean. Why haven't you told this to the police? Do you know what people are saying?"

"Of course I know what they're saying. I've been laid off from the restaurant because no one wants to be served by a murderer. I've been hauled in for questioning. All my friends and acquaintances are being questioned. I'm less popular than a leper at a skin care clinic. Oh, and I'm under surveillance too. They even have Fitzy pretending he cares about me to mess with my head so I'll crack."

"I'm sure that's not what's going on. Fitzy wouldn't do something like that. Nonetheless, why don't you just tell the truth?"

"Because I didn't want to admit what a horrible person I am."

"But it's okay that they think you killed your sister?"

"Well, I sort of did."

"You know what I mean."

"I do, and it's my fault she's dead."

The next thing my mom says surprises me. "We don't know she's dead."

"If she's not dead, then where the hell is she?"

"That, Sadie, is the big question."

"Mom, I'm sorry."

"For what?" That was always a thing in our house growing up. It wasn't enough to apologize, but we had to say why we were sorry. Pretty humbling. Except for Brady, whose standard answer was, "I'm sorry that you're an idiot." He deserves whatever misery Tina causes him.

"I'm sorry that I wasn't the person I should have been and didn't do what Jenna needed me to do. I'm sorry that I was selfish and thought more about what Jenna did to me than what I could have done for her. I just saw that she was trying to ruin another thing of mine that I cared about. She really did a number on my bathroom, which I'd been working on for weeks. It's like any time I have something, something good or beautiful, she has to destroy it. It's her mission, and that's all I could see."

"I'm sorry too."

"For what?" It's my turn to give it back to her.

"That I failed you. That I failed Jenna. That by trying to help her and protect her, I let her grow into a selfish person who acts the way she does. That I excused her behavior to excuse my own failure as a parent."

"I wish we weren't on the phone, because I need to hug you right now."

"I've got the coffee on whenever you get here."

CHAPTER THIRTY-TWO

You'd think that being a funeral home family would prepare us for this sort of thing. You'd be wrong. I mean, there were details that were a given. Perkins Brothers would certainly handle the funeral, but Uncle Peter was contracting out with another set of funeral directors to help handle some of the arrangements. They would run the crowd control at the wake. We expect quite the turnout, and Uncle Peter and Aunt Elaine will be in the receiving line with Mom, Brady, and me.

I hope this wake is less eventful than the last one I attended.

I couldn't care less about the casket. Who knew there were so many options? I mean, I know it's big business. I know there's a cache of caskets in Uncle Peter's basement, but I never paid attention to all the choices. Wood, metal, veneer. Satin, polyester, velvet, cotton. White, black, gray, mahogany. Religious. Secular. If I didn't already have a headache, I'd have one now.

Uncle Peter is in business mode. I know cost is not an object. On the other hand, this is a box to be buried in. I can't see going all over the top for it. I say as much.

"Sadie! That's rude. These boxes straightened your teeth and paid for your college education."

Mom has a point.

"Sorry Uncle Peter. I didn't mean to offend. I guess I never thought that much about the business part of this. I just always thought of you two running out at all hours, riding around in a car with a body in the back. Crying people. Smelly flowers."

"Well, that about sums it up."

Decisions are finally made, and we head back upstairs. There are phone calls to place, flowers to order (hopefully the non-smelly kind), and things to do. Mom needs to get an outfit and her hair done. All Dad's stuff at the nursing home has to be packed up. I suppose that Uncle Peter's got to go get Dad and do all that ... stuff. I wonder if he's going to prepare the body or have a colleague do it.

How do you even ask that? Uncle Peter's eyes are just as watery as mine and Mom's. Dad was not only his brother but his business partner. They were truly best friends. Envy washes over me. Why couldn't Jenna and I have been like that? Sitting at Aunt Elaine's table while Mom and Uncle Peter work on the obituary, I think about what Mom said about failing Jenna. If she had been a better parent. I don't think that's right. Mom was a great mother. She was on her own much of the time, with Dad over at the funeral home. She ran us here and there, helped with projects, cooked supper, baked cookies, tucked us in. If there's one thing I could ask Jenna, it would be why. Why did she turn out how she did? What did I do that was so deserving of her hate?

I volunteer to go pack up Dad's stuff. I'm better if I have something to do. Aunt Elaine is going to take Mom shopping in a few hours. I probably need to get something to wear too. While on my way over to the nursing home, I call Therese and tell her the news. I'm lucky I don't crash my car as the tears pour uncontrollably from my eyes. I make it to the parking lot and sit there for a few minutes. I cannot believe I was here last night. Twelve hours ago. And

I didn't go in. I have so much to feel guilty for, and this is just one more thing.

I've been here so much over the last four years. I've walked through those doors more time than I can count, but walking in this last time will be the hardest of them all.

I wish I had someone to hold my hand.

But who?

And how do I ask for help? I know Therese would come if she could, but the twins are up and raring to go. Her husband is at work. I know he'll take time off for the services, so I can't ask more time of her right now. I'm not calling Brady. I know he's going to be all prostrate with grief, and it will be all I can do not to sucker punch him. He is a hypocrite and will put on a show about how much he's going to miss Dad, despite the fact that he was never here for him while he was alive.

Max. Fitzy. Either one would probably come with me. Maybe. I don't know about Max since we sort of broke things off. Maybe he would. I could call him. Maybe. Fitzy would come, but I'm not sure if it's because he has to. I know, maybe Detective Abbott is on duty and it's her turn to babysit me. She can come, and we'll be besties and braid each other's hair.

That thought makes me laugh, giving me the strength to walk into the nursing home alone, one last time. Cleaning out his room is not nearly as difficult as I'd anticipated. Probably because Dad wasn't really here. Oh sure, this had been my father's room for the last four years, but it wasn't Dad. Dad had been gone for a while. I imagine I'll never know how much he was aware of after the stroke, but I certainly take comfort in knowing that he's no longer trapped in this room.

Helga's on duty. She pulls me tight into a hug, nearly smothering me in her ample bosom. I can't believe that at one point I didn't like her. She created Max. For that reason alone, I am thankful for her. That's secondary to the care she took of my dad. We are—were—fortunate to have such great care for him.

"Oh Sadie, I'm so sorry." She looks around me. "Are you here alone?"

"Yeah, my mom's with my uncle, making arrangements. My brother hasn't shown up yet because it's not time to give out the money, and my sister ... well, you know."

"Where's Max?"

"I haven't called him and told him yet. I've been over at my mom's this morning, and was waiting for a more human hour."

"You know that boy rises early."

So. Many. Impure. Thoughts. I stifle a giggle. If it weren't such an inappropriate time, I would think about how I really need some lovin' right about now. But that would be inappropriate, so of course I wouldn't do that. (I'm so lying right now.) With great effort, I pull my focus back to Helga and the task at hand. I tell her when the services are going to be, and she promises to spread the word to the staff. I can't imagine they go to all the services for all the patients. It would be too much. Too many deaths.

Helga's right. I need to call Max.

And Fitzy.

Who do I call first?

I need to call Fitzy. I need to tell him about Dad. I also need to explain about the Jenna thing. It's time to come clean. Mom knows, and she doesn't hate me. I have to face my fears and admit to the rest of the world how I let my sister down.

That's going to take a while. I'd better call Max quick and let him know.

"Hey—"

"Hey yourself. How's things?"

"Okay. Well, not okay. My dad died." I walk down the hall of the nursing home, perhaps for the last time. I'm glad to have the distraction of the phone.

"Oh my God, Sadie! Are you okay?"

"You know, you ask me that a lot."

"I think I have good reason, don't you?"

"I'm not usually such a mess, really."

"Just since I've met you, that's all." There's a little chuckle in Max's voice. I realize he's right. I am a mess.

"Yeah, that was when things derailed. I mean, I guess they started to skid off the tracks last October, but my life has never been this upside down. Ever."

Max is quiet for a minute. "What do you need?"

This man is too good. Certainly too good for the likes of me, who will probably end up causing his demise anyway. "Nothing right now. Services will be Sunday night and Monday morning. It's going to be weird without Jenna here though. I can't believe we're going to bury Dad without Jenna getting the chance to say goodbye."

He's quiet for a minute. I wish I knew what he was thinking. "You'll keep me posted? If you need anything, and I mean anything at all, you'll call, right?"

"I will ... and Max?"

"Yeah?"

"Thanks."

CHAPTER THIRTY-THREE

"Henry Fitzsimmons. Go."

"You think you're all cool answering the phone like that? You're still the same guy who cried during 'The Land Before Time.'"

"It was allergies. Something got in my eye."

"Un huh. I was there, and I know the truth." Sitting in my car, I can still picture sitting at the movies with Fitzy and Brady and being shocked that Fitzy could be so emotional.

"It's hearsay."

"That's not what I called about though. I need to talk to you. In person."

"I'm not due back on until tonight. Can it wait?"

"Can I talk to you as a person, not a cop?"

There's a pause.

"I don't know." Fitzy's got his cop voice on. I have to get this off my chest.

"You can record me. I need to talk to you now. It's important." I hope he can tell from the tone in my voice that I mean it.

"Fine. I'm driving home from the gym. Meet me at my place in ten?"

He gives me his address, which is not far from my mom's house. Funny. I think of it as my mom's house, even though Dad lived there too. He's barely just gone, but he's been gone for so long already. It's odd, but I think in some ways, this is easier.

I park on the street in front of Fitzy's townhouse. It's in the downtown, near some restaurants and the limited bar scene. It's a funky brick building that I bet is even funkier on the inside. Totally not my style, but I can appreciate it.

I also can appreciate the view when Fitzy answers the door. I cannot form a word or a coherent thought. He's wet, most likely fresh out of the shower. And wearing—wait for it—nothing but gray sweat pants, slung low on his hips.

Holy-Mother-of-Hotness.

And to make it better—no, worse, so much worse—are the tattoos. They adorn each shoulder down his bicep, dance across his chest, and wrap around his flank. Just like in my dream. His body is as sculpted as I'd dreamt as well. He is the man of my fantasies. Would it be poor form to lick him instead of saying hello?

"You're early."

"You said ten minutes." He steps aside so I can enter. There's nowhere to go but up the stairs. I follow him up, resisting the urge to grab his firm buttocks, and try not to stare too hard at his defined back. There are tattoos back there too. One on each shoulder blade, and the writing hugging his side. It looks like it's in German or something. I wonder how much more of him is tattooed. GAH.

There's a landing and then five more stairs that opens into a spacious living room. There's a tile fireplace in the corner with a large flat-screen above it. A cozy, hunter green couch and overstuffed chair provide the seating. Industrial rails line the staircase, which goes up another floor. The whole set of stairs is open from the first floor to the third, giving the feeling that this place is huge. There's a small dining room with a funky light hanging over a bare table. A large kitchen is at the opposite end of the house. I can see stainless steel and black granite. Uber-sleek and modern. And so sexy.

I. NEED. TO. FOCUS.

I'm now thinking appliances are sexy. They are not. They are functional. It's just that Fitzy is so sexy, he's creating this atmosphere that's charged with endorphins or pheromones or baby-making hormones or something.

"Can you please put a shirt on?" I'm agitated, and it comes out sounding annoyed.

"I would have if you had given me three more minutes like I told you to."

He sprints up the stairs, taking them two at a time. I sit down on his couch and try to gather myself. On the glass coffee table, there's a cool candle holder. It's a piece of wood that looks sort of burnt and charred. There are five white candles, burrowed into the wood. I wonder if Fitzy made this. I will not be able to handle it if he's artsy too. Upon examination, I find the artist's name etched into the bottom of the wood. Phew. He's not all sexy artist guy too.

Hearing him come back down the stairs, I say, "This candle holder is really cool. Where'd you get it?"

"Some art show. I thought I needed some sort of decoration. I just got the end tables and coffee table. I'd been using cardboard boxes since I moved in."

"When was that?"

"Two years ago."

He sits down in the chair, which is thankfully on the other side of the coffee table and across the room. Lead me not into temptation.

"Glad you didn't rush into anything."

"I like to take my time and really think things through. Sometimes, I spend years thinking about things before I finally make my move."

I have a feeling we're not talking about furniture choices anymore. I need to gain control of this conversation. Even though he's now in a t-shirt, it's not much better. It's tight in a lot of places, and I can still see the tattoos on his arms. Maybe he needs to put a burlap sack on. I make a fist and put it over my mouth while I close my eyes and take a few deep breaths. Okay, I'm ready to start. I put my hand down and look at him. "Fitzy, I have a lot to say. I don't care if you record it or—"

He's up, out of his chair and coming toward me.

"What are you doing? Go sit down. Way over there."

Still without saying anything, he grabs my elbow and pulls me up.

"Oww, what are you doing?"

He pushes me into the bathroom and turns me to see myself in the mirror.

I have a Hitler mustache.

I look at my hands, which have some kind of black ... soot on them. Damn it, must be from that candle thing on the coffee table. Hastily, I swipe at the black smudge under my nose, but it only smears. Now I resemble Groucho Marx.

"Let me."

Fitzy is standing behind me. He reaches around me, pressing my arms into my sides and turns the water on. With his wet hands, he slowly, gently, agonizingly starts to wipe my upper lip. I turn my body around so we're facing each other. His thumb is cleaning, almost caressing my upper lip, cool water droplets running down my face. He's moving agonizingly slow, it's as if he's tormenting me on purpose. My lips part involuntarily. His thumb is there, and before I know what I'm doing, I'm kissing his thumb. Inviting it into my mouth. Sucking on it. All the while, never breaking my eye contact with him. This has got to be the most erotic thing I've ever done.

Slowly, he withdraws his finger, savoring every caress of my tongue and grasps my waist with his strong hands. He lifts me up and sits me on the sink counter as his lips slam down on mine.

I have waited over twenty years for this kiss. And it does not disappoint. Our lips eager, tongues twisting together. A fire explodes down below. Let me say this about that; from just his kiss, I can tell that there would never be any sort of need for any lubricant. His mouth moves down to my jaw and then my neck as my head tilts back, opening myself to him. His hands have moved down and have a firm hold on my butt. My legs are wrapped around his waist.

I can't believe this is happening. I'm here, with Fitzy. Never in my wildest dreams could I have ever imagined that a man could turn me on this instantly and completely. "Oh my God, Fitzy," I gasp.

"Sadie," he grunts. He stops for a minute and looks at me. His luscious lips are parted and he seems to be breathing as heavily as I am. "You have no idea what you are doing to me."

He steps back and continues to kissing my neck. I feel his teeth gently nip at me. Then, his mouth starts moving down. Down my breast bone, now his hands cupping and kneading my breasts. I arch back, my body alive with his touch. His mouth is now moving down my stomach. I'm leaning back, just letting him kiss, relishing each scorching touch. Each nip. Each lick. Then he gets to my waist. With his teeth, he unzips my shorts.

And if my life were a movie, this would be the point when the audience would hear the sound of a needle sliding over a record, signaling some heinous error.

"Oh my God, Fitzy, you have to stop!" I put my foot on his shoulder and push him back.

He stands and leans in, kissing my mouth again. "I don't know if I can."

"I need you to," I pant. The more he touches me, the more my resolve is crumbling. "I don't want you to."

He's nibbling by my ear. "Then please don't make me stop Sadie. I may have to quote Meatloaf here and say it feels so good. It feels so right. It's the right thing."

The right thing. My dad's words from the dream echo in my ear. It suddenly makes sense. Why Fitzy was in my dream, exactly as I found him today. This is what I was being warned against. Right? With my last bit of resolve, I push him away.

"No, Fitzy, I can't."

He's as breathless as I am. The bathroom is too small to be in here with him. I'm too close and don't have that much will power. I hop down from the counter and re-button and zip my shorts. Damn that was impressive. I always suspected those lips were talented. Now I know just how talented they are. While I don't normally kiss and tell, I'm so going to have to brag to Therese about that one. Exiting the bathroom, I slide by him, my shoulder brushing his chest.

I go back and sit on the couch. Finally he comes out of the bathroom, adjusting himself. He starts to head to the couch. I just look at him and then the chair. He gets the message and sits down.

Now it's time to talk.

CHAPTER THIRTY-FOUR

"My dad died this morning."

"Oh." He looks stunned. "And now I feel like a gigantic asshat. No wonder you ... didn't ..." He can't find the words.

"Fitzy, that's something else entirely. It's not that I don't, because I do, but I'm not sure I should. Anyway, it's beside the point. It's not why I came over here. I needed to tell you about Dad, and it's time for me to tell you what I know about Jenna."

His posture changes immediately and he shifts into business mode. He's sitting up taller, and his facial expressions are shut down.

"I told you, you can record it if you want."

"Are you sure that's a good idea?"

I shrug. "Yeah, it's fine. I didn't do anything wrong. I mean, I did, but not in the way you all seem to think."

"Not all of us, Sadie."

"Well, maybe not you, but that's because you want to get into my pants."

"I can neither confirm nor deny that statement." A tense smile spreads across his face.

He gets up and rummages around upstairs for a few minutes. I wonder if he's looking for a recorder or something. While he's gone, I close my eyes, thinking about what just happened. Nearly happened. It was seriously some of the hottest—I don't even know what you call it—that I've ever done. And with Fitzy, no less.

But he can't be the one I've been waiting for, can he? Don't I want Max? Wait, yes I do. I think. Maybe. I'm so confused. I've been waiting my whole life for Fitzy. My whole life, I've been waiting. I will never feel good enough for him. He's that perfect, that unattainable dream. He's been on such a pedestal in my world that I don't know if we could ever have a fair and equal partnership. I look around at his place. Our styles are so different. Our lives are so different. Thank goodness I stopped it when I did.

He's back, dressed in work clothes. This time, it's a gray shirt with charcoal pants. Everything of his is very color coordinated. "We need to go into the station." I start to object but he continues. "I know you don't want to, but this way it will be official. Plus, there's something I need to show you."

Even thought I know he's right, I'm not happy about it. I follow him to the station. We head back into the interrogation room. Fitzy doesn't ask but brings me a cup of coffee. Then he sits down opposite me and waits.

I tell him the events of the "night in question." I admit that Jenna inflicted harm on herself and that rather than helping her, I threw her out.

After a bit, he stops me. "Why? You're trained in this, being a high school teacher. Why didn't you take her threat seriously?"

"Because I was mad."

"About?"

"About my bathroom. And my brand new towels. Jeez, it sounds ridiculous, I know. But it's just a symbol of yet another thing my sister ruined for me. Anytime I have something good and beautiful in my life, she swoops in and takes it away. It doesn't matter how hard I work for it, or what it means to me, she makes it her mission to take it away from me. I sort of snapped."

"Why do you think that?"

"Years of evidence. The role in the school play. First chair clarinet. My job at the library—and she doesn't even like books! Rob. Then my house. Do you know how many hours of blood, sweat, and tears I put into the bathroom?"

He just sits there, looking at me. His hands are folded in front of his mouth, and he's resting his elbows on the table. I'm glad he's covering those delectable lips so I'm not distracted.

"So, with her being missing, all signs indicate that she went through with the suicide, and it is my fault. I didn't stop her when I had the chance." The tears really start now. My sister is dead, and I did nothing to stop it.

"But that's not the same as killing her."

"I never said I killed her. I said she was dead, and it was my fault."

"That's why you think she's in the lake?"

"Yeah. Where else would she be?"

"That's a good question."

"You know, this ..." I can't go on.

Fitzy is patient for a minute and then nudges gently. "This what?"

Exhaling, I start. "You know about the visions or whatever they are. The premonitions. The dreams." The dream with my dad runs fresh in my head. "Sometimes I say something, and then it happens. I have no control over it. Something pops into my head, and then it's real."

"Yeah, we've talked about this before."

"I don't know if there's like a clairvoyant boot camp or something where I can learn, but I have no control over these things. But as it happens more and more, I'm starting to worry that me saying these things is causing them to happen. I know it's irrational, but maybe there are things out there that we don't understand. Maybe in some sense, it is totally rational."

He just raises his eyebrow. Yep, he thinks I'm certifiable.

"What if, this time, because I was feeling so negatively toward Jenna, what if I *caused* her death?"

"Like ..." he's speechless.

"Like a curse or something."

Finally, he's found what he wants to say. Leaning back in his chair, he puts his elbows behind his head. His body language is relaxed. That's got to be a good sign, right? I mean, you wouldn't be relaxed around someone you thought could kill you with her mind.

"Sadie, there's something we need to show you." He gives some sort of signal to the window. A few moments later, Detective Abbott enters. She's carrying a red, leather-bound journal of some sort. She tosses it on the table in front of me and then perches on the edge of the table, right next to Fitzy.

"Am I supposed to know what this is?" I look at the journal.

"Go ahead, check it out." Fitzy seems pleased. Detective Abbott does not seem amused. Not that she ever does.

It's Rob's journal. The spindly handwriting brings me back. Not because he sent me many cards, but because I often read his class notes and grades on papers. We spent much of our couple time, side-by-side, grading. There are a few pages are marked by tabs, which draw my attention first. The first marked entry is from last October. He describes the pregnancy and subsequent miscarriage. He was relieved. I always thought he was, but here it is, in his hand. I'm not going to lie. It hurts to read it. But I was surprised at the following entries. Regrets. He had regrets. He felt guilty that he hadn't been supportive. He felt that I was pulling away. I skim through a few pages. What I don't see is any mention of my sister. He talks about asking me to marry him. About picking out the ring.

He was going to propose at the bed and breakfast.

Holy crap.

I look up, stunned. "I ... I don't understand."

Detective Abbott chimes in. "Notice anything missing?"

It takes me a minute or two but then it clicks. "Yeah, for someone who wrote down a lot, there's no mention of his mistress."

Fitzy chimes in. "Not only doesn't he mention her, it seems unlikely that he would have proposed to her, when he clearly indicates that he bought the ring for you."

"Unless he bought two rings or something." I cannot wrap my head around this. He was distant after the miscarriage because I was pulling away?

Had I been? He bought the ring for me? Things are so confusing right now.

"But I don't understand. I mean, he was with Jenna when he died, and there was, er, ah, evidence of activity."

"We're still investigating that." Detective Abbott looks smug. Like she's enjoying this. Enjoying seeing me twist in the wind. After a few moments she continues. "We would be very interested to talk with your sister."

"Unless you call Dionne Warwick's Psychic Friends' Network, I think you're going to have trouble with that."

Fitzy starts laughing. "Psychic Friends' Network? What do you think this is, 1989? Try Long Island Medium."

"So sue me that I'm not in the correct decade."

"Or century."

"Or millennium." Holy cow, does Detective Abbott have a sense of humor? Her mouth is twisting involuntarily. It appears to be a smile. I didn't think she was capable.

"What about the knife and towels in my dumpster?"

Detective Abbott cuts Fitzy off. "We'll be the ones asking questions here. We don't disclose the information from ongoing investigations."

Fitzy gives her a look and then gives me a small smile. "While they were an interesting find, we also found blood evidence in Jenna's apartment. We also found that first aid had been applied, and it appeared that Jenna left her apartment after treating her wounds. There's also other firm evidence backing up your story. But, let's keep that in this room." Then he gives me a wink.

"So you don't think I'm a murderer?"

"Ms. Perkins, we're done with questioning. You can leave." Apparently Detective Abbott is done with me.

"Do I have to surrender my passport or anything?" I look from her to Fitzy and back again.

"No, you're not a suspect. While some crimes may have been committed, we don't think you perpetrated any of them. You are free to go."

She doesn't have to tell me twice.

CHAPTER THIRTY-FIVE

Therese has managed to sneak away from her little terrors to help me shop for something to wear to my dad's services. I probably have something in my closet, but a lot of stuff is still packed up, so finding it might be difficult. It seems like too much effort, not that shopping isn't.

"You seem in good shape. I mean, considering how close you and your dad were." Therese's rear end is all I can see, since her head and torso are buried in a rack of clothes. I'm not sure what she's looking for. I don't think she knows either.

"I'm sure I'll lose it at one point or another. In some ways, this is easier because he's been gone for over four years. Really. Part of me, a big part, is glad that he's no longer trapped in that bed. He was alive, but he hasn't lived since the stroke."

"You have a point. What about this?" Therese holds up a sensible pants suit. In theory it's fine. I hate it. There is no excuse ever for a pants suit.

In the end, I find a black boat neck dress that hits just at my knees and has some pleating at the straight waist. It's very Coco Chanel, not that I expect anyone to ask. I find a pair of Clarks that are surprisingly stylish as well as comfortable—black patent leather peep toe pumps. I know it will be a long few days of standing. I wonder if I can get Max to rub my feet.

That is, if he still wants me.

"What if he doesn't?"

"Huh? What are you talking about?" Therese is digging through another rack, looking at blouses. She hands me a white sleeveless blouse with small black polka dots and a black pencil skirt. "This will be good for the wake. What were you talking about?"

"Much better than that pants suit. I was thinking about Max and if he'd be willing to rub my feet, and then I started to worry that he might not still want me."

"Do you want him?"

"Yes. Maybe. I think I do," I say breezily.

"And what about Fitzy?" She doesn't know about the Hitler-mustache, escapade on the bathroom sink. My brain still cannot process what that man was able to do with his teeth.

Once she's filled in, Therese sinks onto a display at the feet of the mannequins, and fans herself.

"Do you need a moment?"

"I might. Knowing Andy, if he ever tried that, he'd get his lip stuck in my zipper, and we'd have to try and explain that at the E.R." She pauses, fanning herself some more. "Tell me why you stopped Fitzy again? Why are you still thinking about Max? Haven't you been waiting for this ever since you hit puberty?"

"I dunno. I guess I've had Max on the brain so much that I don't know how to downshift to Fitzy. Or if I want to. God, Fitzy has me so confused. You know, that's part of why I stopped. I've put him up on such a pedestal that I don't think he can ever live up to it. Max is safer. Much safer. Plus, there was the dream." I fill her in on that. "And, you know, I think it means he's not the right one."

"Fitzy's Team Jacob." Therese has managed to pull herself together, and we're standing in line to check out. I like the clothes at this store, but it always seems like a challenge to find someone to take my money. The cashiers are never at the counters, and when they are, they make themselves busy doing anything but ringing up my stuff. Sometimes I just want to yell, WILL YOU PLEASE TAKE MY MONEY?

"What?" She's lost me.

"He's Jacob. You're Bella and Max is Edward. I mean, minus the vampire-werewolf thing."

I mull over the ways my life parallels *Twilight* while the lady finally rings up my stuff. "You're right. And, ironically, I was always and will always be Team Jacob. I didn't want her to end up with Edward. But I think I now understand. She just couldn't love Jacob. Not like that."

"Wow, deep."

I swat at her with my purse. "But now, what if Max doesn't want me? I've given him the brush off so many times. What if there's no heat between us? What if I can't forget Fitzy?"

"If 'ifs' and 'ands' were pots and pans, a herd of elephants couldn't piss them full."

"If 'ifs' and 'buts' were candy and nuts, it'd be Christmas every day."

"You'll never know until you talk to him."

This is why Therese is my friend.

We head out into the mall and down the escalator to the coffee shop. I need some time to sit and rest before heading back to my mom's. "So, Fitzy and the rest of the police know about the miscarriage."

"Wait, what? How?"

Therese is as shocked as I was to find out about Rob's journal. Neither one of us can make sense of why he never mentioned Jenna.

"But she had the journal—they found it in her car, so that says something too."

Therese is quiet for a minute, which is a lot for her. "Are you going to tell Max about the miscarriage?"

"I already did, a while back. It didn't seem to freak him out or anything. On the other hand, he had just witnessed the Jenna show so, by comparison, I wasn't bad."

"I think Max is good people."

"You know, I think so too. I don't know why he hasn't settled down with anyone. Maybe that's his flaw. He doesn't want to settle down." But even as I say it, it doesn't ring true. He seems too into the relationship not be a commitment phobe. There's got to be a story there. Funny, we've never talked about it.

"So, have you talked to him yet?"

"Yeah, I called him ... I guess it was this morning. Gee, so much has happened today. What time is it?" My eyes are gritty with fatigue.

"It's 7:45. We need to sit here for fifteen more minutes. I can't go home until after I know the kids will be in bed."

"Will Andy put them down?"

"He'll try. I hope. He'd better. So, what did Max say?"

"Just the usual, 'Oh my God, Sadie, are you okay?' It seems like I'm mid-crisis every time I talk to him. He told me to let him know if I need anything. I wonder if he'll come with me to the services?"

"You're asking him out to a funeral? Are you hoping to get condolence sex?"

I stop dead in my tracks. "Condolence sex? What the hell is that?"

"You know, when you have sex with someone who's grieving. Like, to offer condolences."

"I mean, I usually just send a card, but your way sounds ... slutty."

"And fun. You need to start having some fun. You've been a stick in the mud too long. You need to get wild and crazy and freaky, and then tell me everything."

"Um, Therese, my dad just died. My sister is missing and may or may not be dead, and I've only just been cleared of suspicion of foul play. Getting freaky has not been high on my to-do list."

"You need to change it to a do-me list."

"Therese!" I whack her with my shopping bag. She starts giggling, then I do too. "And," I gasp, "What am I supposed to say? Hey Max, even though there was another explorer heading south of the equator, you're the only one I want exploring my South Pole?"

She stops dead. "What the hell is that supposed to mean?"

I blush. "You ... know."

"Wow. You are so bad at this. Please don't ever try to talk dirty to another human being. Please."

I'm laughing again. This is just what I need. Stuff's going to get serious and heavy, and I need a little laugh. Or a lot of laugh. "So I can't call him up and ask if he wants to be my Amundsen?"

"I don't even know what that sentence means."

"Roald Amundsen is the Norwegian who first discovered the South Pole."

"I thought it was that Scott guy?"

"Nope, Amundsen made it there first."

"You are a nerd."

"Thank you."

"That wasn't a compliment."

"I'm a history teacher. My greatest joy in life is restoring an old home. I am a nerd, and I'm proud of it. So, thank you."

"Now if only you could add the right man to that mix."

"If only."

CHAPTER THIRTY-SIX

After a quick call to my mom, I decided to go home rather than to her house. I tell her that the police have cleared me of suspicion. Brady is at Mom's, and I still felt like punching him. I mean, I always feel like punching him, but in my tired state, I didn't know if I'd be able to restrain myself.

Climbing into bed, I hope that sleep will descend immediately, so of course it doesn't. What a day. First the dream, then telling my mom and the police everything, with a little frisky-Fitzy action in the middle. It should be a weight off my shoulders to have everything out in the open. It should be, but it's not. There are still no answers about Jenna. The police seem to think she disappeared on her own volition. I'm still not convinced. But I don't know that I feel responsible for her death anymore. I wish I could have read more of Rob's journal. I wonder if they'd copy it for me. Probably not. And, if Rob had meant for me to read it, he would have given it to me. That makes me wonder why then, Jenna had it.

Despite my racing mind, sleep finally pulls me under. It's dreamless, for once. Thunder rolling through, cracking sharp and loud, wakes me from my sleep. I look at the clock. It's ten a.m. I can't remember the last time I slept this late. Then I hear it. It's not thunder, it's a hammer. What the hell?

I fly out of bed and into the living room. Max is there with his crew of three. They're working on the windows, recording and hanging the ones I had taken apart earlier in the week.

"What ... what are you doing?"

They all whip around and stare at me. I mean really stare, like I don't belong here. They're the ones in my living room. Technically, Armand is on the ladder on the outside of the house, but he's looking into my house as well.

Before I know what's happening, Sinclair loses his grip on the window pane he's holding. Armand leans through the opening and grasps it at the last minute, as Bob lunges at the same time. Armand's sudden weight shift causes the ladder to fall, and then he's hanging over the window frame, feet flailing and kicking. Bob takes control of the ninety-year-old glass, Sinclair grabs onto Armand, and Max comes rushing at me. His hands are on my shoulders, and he drives me back down the hall and into my bedroom. With his foot, he kicks the door shut behind him.

"What are you trying to do?" He sounds ... mad?

"What do you mean, 'what am I trying to do?' I wake up and hear people in my house. Of course I'm going to go check and see what it is. What's your problem?"

"You. You're my problem. Do you understand what could have just happened? Sinclair almost dropped the window."

"No almost, he did."

"Right, but Bob and Armand caught it. Armand could have broken something falling off that ladder."

"Yeah, okay. I'm still not seeing why this is my fault."

He's glares. "Look down."

My eyes glance down and I want to die. Oh. My. God. I'm practically naked. A lacy camisole. No bra, of course. At least my underwear are boy shorts, not a thong. "I ... uh ... I heard .... banging. I didn't know what it was. I wasn't thinking."

Max scoffs. "Obviously not." He looks mad, I think. He's staring at me. Hard. It's making me uncomfortable. Maybe because he's angry. I grab my robe off the end of my bed and throw it on.

"Better?"

"Yes, much."

Wow, it's almost as if the sight of me repulses him. I've never seen Max mad. I've never seen him anything but happy-go-lucky. This is different and not in a good-different sort of way.

"I'm sorry, Max. I didn't know you all were out there. I thought it was thunder. I certainly didn't expect you to be out there with a crew."

"I just figured you were going to get behind schedule with everything." He's standing in front of me, arms folded across his chest. He's in his usual work jeans and a t-shirt. It's a totally different look than Fitzy's.

"Oh, well, yeah. Thanks. Yesterday was a lost day. First my dad and the funeral stuff, then the Fitzy thing and the police station, and then I had to go shopping with Therese to get something to wear to the services. Which, I was going to call you about. Were you planning on coming to the wake? I know you didn't really know my dad, but I'd like it if you were there."

He says nothing.

"What?"

Still nothing.

"Max, say something. Do you not like wakes? I mean, I know it's not like a fun thing but at least it won't be terrible since you didn't know my dad."

"The Fitzy thing?"

Poop. Did I say that?

"It was no big thing. It could have been, but it wasn't."

"As in Detective Fitzsimmons? The one who is investigating you in the disappearance of your sister?"

"Yeah, Fitzy. He was my brother's best friend growing up. It's so hard to think of him as Detective. God, I was in love with him for like half my life. And I'm off the hook with the Jenna thing."

"Go back and explain the Fitzy thing." He is so pissed, and it's making me nervous. And when I get nervous, I ramble. Such an awesome quality.

"Um, you know. I had a dream and he was in it. You were too I think, but he was half-naked. And then I went to his house and he really was half-naked. But when he kissed me, and even though I've been waiting for him to kiss me since I was like nine, it was not what—"

"You can stop right there." Max turns toward the door. "Every time I thought something was going to happen, something got in our way. You kept saying that you weren't interested in a relationship. I thought you meant in general. I should have realized you meant with me. We'll finish up the windows today, but then you're on your own. I'm afraid I won't be able to help you out anymore."

The door opens, slams, and Max is gone.

Wait, what?

I do not need this right now. Figures. I finally get over my phobia of reaching out to someone, and get over the guy who's occupied space in the back of my mind all these years, just to have Max walk out. I mean, Fitzy kissed me. I didn't invite it. I just didn't stop it as soon as I could have. That's a lie. I totally invited it. I guess I should just forget about it. Maybe it's better this way. At least I won't end up accidentally killing him.

CHAPTER THIRTY-SEVEN

Wakes are supposed to be solemn occasions. At least, that's what I always thought. I mean, I did grow up next door to a funeral home. It was always freakishly quiet, and we had to be quiet as well. I can't tell you how many times my mom, in exasperation, loaded us into the station wagon to haul us to the park so we could play outside and not disrupt the bereaved piling in at Uncle Peter's.

Somehow, Dad's wake is sort of festive. Not like hey-let's-get-a-piñata-festive, but the overall tone is more positive than sad. I mean, he was kind of a stud in the undertaker world. Wow, there's a sentence I never thought I would say. Dad and Uncle Peter had a very successful business, had staved off the franchises creeping in, and were well liked by, it seems, everyone in town, as well as the three surrounding towns. It is a real celebration of his life.

And I was smart to buy comfortable shoes.

Nonetheless, my feet are aching, my back is aching, and I have a headache from the thick scent of the flowers. I hadn't wanted to go overboard with the flowers, knowing that they go to waste. The nursing home could only take so many arrangements. Brady wanted the full casket blanket. Mom went along with it. Now, here I am, eyes watering from the lilies. Brady is standing next to Mom, having elbowed me out of the way. Tina is sitting in one of the chairs, stone-faced. She has not shed a tear during this whole process. I'm not sure which is worse—her lack of crying, or Brady's over-the-top crying.

"It's just, it was so hard to see him suffer all these years." *Sniff, sniff.* "It broke my heart that he couldn't move. He was always so strong." *Sniff, sniff.*

Gag me with a spoon.

Therese sidles up behind me and taps my shoulder. "Do you need this?" She hands me a water bottle. I open it and take a swing. My throat burns as I choke and sputter.

"Oh, by the way, that's vodka, not water."

"What are you trying to do, kill me?" I wipe my mouth.

"No, I'm trying to save you from the malarkey that you're standing next to." Therese knows how I feel about my brother.

"I guess since Jenna isn't here, Brady felt he needed to step into the role of drama queen."

"And what about the Ice Princess?"

"You mean my sister-in-law who hasn't shed a tear? That's pretty much normal. I'm pretty sure her face would crack in half if she ever smiled, so tears would be entirely out of the question."

"I just don't get it. What does he see in her?"

"What does she see in him?" I glance over at Brady. I guess at one point he was attractive. Not as attractive as Fitzy (I get a hot flash just thinking of him), but not bad looking. Now, he's, well, he's sort of let himself go. He looks like he's gestating twins, and his breast size rivals mine. He unfortunately inherited my mom's father's hairline, which starts about halfway back on his head. I think he would look better if he just shaved his whole head but for some reason, he doesn't. His hair, which is showing some gray, is long in the back, and he wears it in a ponytail. It looks stupid. Then, there's the mustache. I don't think I even need to explain about that one.

People keep shuffling past. My dad always called it the funeral shuffle. It makes me smile. At a wake, keep shuffling your feet and keep moving forward, and just get out as quickly as possible. The line of people seems never ending. I'm glad to see everyone got the memo about the funeral shuffle. I glance around Brady at my mom. She seems to be holding up all right. Every so often, her eyes fill, but I'm seeing more smiles than anything else. Like me, she is relieved that Dad's suffering has ended.

A small, very old woman with a walker is standing in front of me. I don't recognize her but I don't always have the best gift for face recognition. She looks to be by herself, which gives me no clue as to who she is. I hope I'm not related to her and am clueless about it. I have to bend down to hear her soft voice.

"Are you the one who was born next to my mother?"

The smile spreads involuntarily across my face. My birth story is quite colorful. My mom was nine months pregnant. Her labor with Brady had been very long and drawn out, so she expected the same with me. She'd apparently had some twinges of pain but thought it would be hours before any action would really happen. My dad got a call that an elderly woman had passed at home, so it was a pretty straightforward case. Mom went with him to pick up the body. The woman's name was Melvina Morris. I know this because just after they got Mrs. Morris loaded and into the back of the hearse and pulled away from the house, Mom's labor went into high gear. Dad pulled off into a parking lot, and my mom went into the back of the car to lie down (yes, next to the dead woman). The paramedics— the ones who had also been at Mrs. Morris' house—drove by and saw my dad pulled over with the back doors open. They stopped to help, in just the nick of time to deliver me. I was born in the back of the hearse next to the expired Melvina Morris. Hence my name, Sadie Melvina. Why couldn't Mrs. Morris' first name have been Helen or Alice or Claire?

I signal to my mom who steps around Brady's girth. "Mom, Mrs. Morris' daughter."

"Oh, bless your heart. Thank you for coming." Mom gives her a hug, careful not to squash the frail woman.

"No, thank you. All of these years, whenever I think about my mother's death, I think about Simon. How much caring and compassion he showed to our family, putting his own family on hold."

"That was how he was. He knew that the families of the bereaved needed some TLC. It was one of the many things that I loved about my husband, although I didn't always appreciate it."

"And you dear, you came into this world just as my mother exited it. I've always wondered how you turned out, and I can see that you turned out beautifully."

I blush. "Thank you. You know that my middle name is Melvina, right?"

Tears fill her cloudy eyes. "No, I didn't know that. Firstly, I'm sorry. That's a horrid name. I was always happy that I wasn't named after her. But secondly," she turns to my mom, "thank you. I'm sure Mom knows and has gotten a big kick out of it."

I'm so glad this woman came. This is what wakes are about. Dad always said that wakes are not for the dead, but for the living. He was right. Hearing stories like this, meeting the people that Dad touched, truly does make me feel better. "Thank you for coming. This means so much." She shuffles on, not in the I-don't-want-to-be-here-any-longer-than-necessary kind of way, but in the geriatric shuffle that befalls one with age.

Fitzy comes through the line. He hugs me awkwardly. I wish I could stay in his arms a moment or two longer, but the tension between us is palpable. One day certainly makes a difference. I can't believe I could have slept with him. I can't believe I didn't. I can't believe I'm thinking about this at my dad's wake. Brady's all hugs and grins and gets out of line to introduce Fitzy to Tina. Hours pass, more quickly than I would have thought, but the day feels eternal still. I know I should be hungry. All I feel is drained. I look at Mom and can tell she feels the same way. Uncle Peter is telling the pall bearers and readers in hushed tones what time they need to be at the funeral home in the morning. I take Mom's arm, ready to escort her back over the lawn to her house. This is one time when living close to the funeral home is a good thing.

"Hey—" Brady steps in front of us. "Are we going out to dinner? Tina's hungry."

Mom sighs wearily. "Brady, I'm just too tired. There's plenty of food back at the house. Tomorrow will be a long day as well."

"You know Tina is on a special diet. She can't eat most of the stuff that you have."

Mom looks at me. I can tell she's about to cave and go out, even though it's the last thing she wants to do. Time to be the bad guy. Sadie to the rescue. Again. "We're going back to Mom's. I'm sure there is something there she can eat. If she were so concerned about it, she should have made something in advance."

"Well, we just figured we'd go out."

"Then *you* go out. Mom and I are going home. There's ziti and meatballs calling my name." It was true. The amount of food that people delivered was insane. There was no way we would be able to eat it all. I would need to look tonight and see what I could freeze for Mom so it didn't go to waste. Ziti, casseroles, deli meats, fruit baskets, muffin trays, salads, pastries, you name it.

Brady and Tina don't join us in the end. Probably better for me, but I know it hurts Mom. Uncle Peter and Aunt Elaine come over, as well as some other friends and cousins. The alcohol is flowing relatively freely, and if not for the reason we were all together, I would say it was a good night. I sleep in my old room, the one Jenna and I shared. I can't help but be sad. Not about Dad. I mean, I'm sad about him, but in a way, this is closure for the grieving process that started more than four years ago. I'm sad that things aren't the way they used to be when Jenna and I were little. I'm sad about the way our family has disintegrated.

Brady is too self-absorbed and frankly, too much of an asshole, to be a part of our family anymore. He's in Tina's family and apparently the two are mutually exclusive. Jenna is ... who knows? Is she even still alive? I highly doubt so. I know I said those terrible things to her, and while I sort of meant them, I also know that her baby would have changed everything. I wouldn't have been able to stay away. It's how I ended up with my cat. He was a stray who needed a home, and I couldn't resist. I want to have a heart of stone, but I don't.

That leads me to thinking about Max. He didn't come tonight. Helga came, pulling me into her ample bosom yet again. I get to second base with that woman an awful lot. But no Max. She seemed to know that things were over between us. Not that they had even really started. And why? For what stupid reason did I hold Max at arm's length all this time?

Because I was afraid. Afraid to take a chance and fall. Afraid to love and lose. I made a play for Fitzy all those years ago and fell on my face. Literally. I think I loved Rob. I loved our baby, or the idea of our baby, and lost it. I'm sure Rob was right—I'm sure I was distant after. With the whole clarity of hindsight, I know Rob was not the right man for me. I wanted him to be. On paper he was. But in reality, it wasn't there. I guess I can't blame him for moving on.

And my fear of being alone has left me alone.

CHAPTER THIRTY-EIGHT

Epic.

Dad's funeral will go down in history as one of the most epic events this town has ever experienced. I think it may even make people forget that I passed out and then vomited at Rob's wake. Maybe. I hope so.

The funeral starts like any other. We process from the funeral home, in the steel gray limo, to the church where I was baptized and made my First Communion. I always thought Dad would walk me down the aisle here, but instead, today, I'm walking him down one last time. I can just barely hear the click of my heels on the granite floor over the organ music. The incense hangs in a thick haze and is enough to make my eyes water. The readings are meaningful, the eulogy touching, the songs emotional. "On Eagles' Wings" brings me to tears. Mom is crying, and Brady is on the verge of hysterics. Tina is still stone-faced. She looks bored and pissed. You know, normal for her. It shouldn't be surprising to me that she has yet to shed a tear. Even if she didn't care about my dad, you would think that the emotional pain her husband was going through would mean something to her. Maybe she should have gone into business with Dad and Uncle Peter. She would be good at keeping the stoic look going while people are falling to pieces around her.

I know the last part of the funeral will be the hardest as the priest does his final blessing and we follow the casket down the aisle. I take Mom's arm, ready to escort her down. I don't mind being here for Mom, I really don't. I just wish I had someone to escort me. I wish there were someone for me to lean on. Father Timothy is back at the pulpit. "We will be recessing to a song personally picked by Simon. Internment will be at St. Joseph's cemetery, and friends and family are invited to a luncheon following the burial."

The bearers assemble and start to move the casket. I take a deep breath, trying to find the courage to hold my mom up, and say goodbye to Dad. I'm willing my face, unsuccessfully, not to contort into its ugly cry position. The deep bass of "Another One Bites the Dust" begins to reverberate through the church. We all stop. I'd say we stop dead but that seems in poor taste. I glance at Uncle Peter, who is laughing through his tears. He leans toward Mom and says, "We said for years that we wanted this played at our funerals. We had a pact that whoever was left behind had to play it for the other. We thought it would be great to break into song and dance going down the aisle."

Mom looks at Uncle Peter for a minute and then nods. She lets go of my arm and starts singing as she bops down the aisle. I shrug at Aunt Elaine and follow suit. Like something out of a movie, the entire church begins grooving and singing. It's cathartic and perfect. That is, until we get to the back of the church. The door swings open, surprising the two funeral directors who were on door duty. Max, looking a little worse for the wear, steps in. But, it's not Max who is drawing everyone's attention.

"Will you get your filthy paws off of me? I'm going to have you charged with kidnapping!" Jenna stumbles in, screeching and screaming at Max, swinging at him like a drunk. Her hair has been shorn off in a short bob. It's bleached platinum blond now. But her hair is the least striking change. Jenna is thin and trim. There is no hint of a baby bump. Or any baby weight for that matter. She's only been gone a week. I can't figure out what is happening. She's still screaming. "I'm calling the police! I—" She breaks off and realizes where she is. And who is standing there. And that we're all standing around a casket. "Mom? Mom, what's going on?"

Mom can't tear her eyes away from Jenna's midsection. Her flat midsection. I think that's what everyone is looking at.

Jenna wrenches out of Max's grasp and runs up to my mom. "Mommy, is ... is it Daddy?"

Fitzy steps up from the crowd. "We've been looking for you. You have some questions to answer. I think you should come with me."

Jenna looks at Fitzy and everyone else staring at her, and I can see the panic cross her face. She throws herself on the casket, wailing and sobbing. "Daddy! I came to say goodbye to you. Nothing could keep me away!"

Jenna, despite her lacking pregnancy weight, has enough momentum to knock the casket off the church truck. The pall cloth flies off. My cousin Bobby falls over and is pinned under the casket. There is yelling and chaos, and the cacophony reverberates off the church walls, echoing and amplifying the noise. The funeral directors spring to action to help the rest of the bearers right the casket, freeing Bobby. Jenna is hysterical. Not figuratively, but literally. Taking a page from old movies, as well as all my pent up frustrations, I step forward, haul back and slap that bitch across the face.

Damn it feels good. On a related note, my hand smarts.

Then, I catch Father Timothy's eye, and I feel ashamed. So very ashamed. I am not a good person. Uncle Peter and the other funeral directors manage to right the casket and drape the pall over the top. Uncle Peter smoothes it down lovingly. Jenna has finally quieted down. I look at my mother, expecting to see the seething rage I'm feeling. I don't see it. All I see is sadness and disappointment.

Jenna can see it too. Her voice is quiet, "Mom, I'm so sorry. I would have been here if I could have. I ... I had to go away. This has been a very difficult week." She rubs where her belly should be. "And then he—" she points at Max, "wouldn't let me come back. Until this morning. He threw me in the car against my will and brought me here like this."

"Jenna, we're saying goodbye to your father. It's time to go to the cemetery. If you're available to join us you may. Detective Fitzgerald, is she available?"

Fitzy looks at my mom, searching for an answer in her face. "I think that will be all right. We'll need to talk to both Jenna and Mr. Schultz, but that can wait."

The funeral procession, disjointed and disrupted as it is, exits the church. The solemnity has returned, which I'm pretty sure is not what Dad wanted. I can almost guarantee the circus that just happened was definitely not what Dad had envisioned. The bearers load the casket into the back of the hearse as Mom gets into the limo. Brady and Tina, as well as Uncle Peter and Aunt Elaine, are riding in it too. Sticking close to Mom, Jenna climbs in as well.

I am not getting in that car. There is no way in hell you can make me.

On the other hand, my car is at Mom's, so I have no way to get to the cemetery. Standing there, watching the crowd disperse, I feel alone again. Arms circle me from behind.

"C'mon with us. Andy is moving the car seats."

I turn and hug my best friend. The tears have started again. "Thanks, Therese." We start walking to her minivan. "I don't suppose you have any more of those vodka water bottles in the car, do you?"

"No, but we probably have very old juice boxes that may have fermented. Could be like wine."

"Uhhh, I think I'll pass on that one, if it's all the same to you."

She smiles, her arm still around me. "I can't understand why."

Once we're in the minivan and all buckled in, as the cars begin to creep forward, Andy breaks the silence. "What the hell was that?"

"I have no idea. I mean, Jenna's alive, obviously." I'm talking to Andy and Therese, but more to myself, trying to put the pieces together.

"And she's certainly not pregnant. Do you think she lost the baby? Did she have it early? What happened?" Therese is firing questions faster than a firing squad.

"I ... I don't know. I know I want some answers. And what does Max have to do with it? And what the hell happened to her hair?"

"I know, when you're on the lam, who has time to get your hair done?" Therese is shaking her head.

"I think it's a better look for her. Certainly better than that red crap she had on her head that they've been showing on the news." Leave it to Andy to take that point of view. He's one of the good ones. Therese is lucky to have him. And I'm lucky that they're my friends and on my side.

We're at the cemetery and exit the cars. The burial occurs without incident, which is about all I could ask for at this point. I stand next to Mom, again supporting her during this trying time. Jenna is leaning on Uncle Peter, sobbing. A honking noise is pretty consistently coming from Brady, as he blows his nose. Tina is looking at her nails, obviously bored by the inconvenience of our family tragedy. Sigh.

Can I get a new family?

CHAPTER THIRTY-NINE

So you know that feeling when you're so tired and drained that breathing seems too effortful? Yeah, I'm there. What a day. What a freakin' mess. What the heck?

I try to process the events. Dad's funeral. Brady, hysterical. Tina not. Jenna's alive. Jenna toppling over Dad's casket. I guess we're just lucky that the casket didn't bust open and dump Dad everywhere. Probably a good thing that we went for the pricier casket. Jenna. Jenna's no longer pregnant. What happened there? Did she lose the baby? She had to have, right? She never really said when she was due. I mean, doing some mental math, which takes a Herculean effort at this point, I guess she is—was— probably due in October. Which means that the baby, best case, had to be about twenty-six weeks along. The baby could be alive. Probably in the hospital somewhere, in the NICU. I wonder if it's okay. I'm guessing she lost the baby. If I could feel anything right now, it would be heartbreak for that little child who never had a chance.

Jenna has a lot of explaining to do.

For someone who's been AWOL for a week, and either lost a baby or gave birth to a preemie, I think it's odd that she had time to get a new hair-do. I have so many questions for her. I'm not the only one. Fitzy took her in for questioning. I mean, she's alive, so that means there's no foul play. I should be grateful that she didn't kill herself, and I am. But, yet again, there's Jenna, making a huge spectacle of herself.

I am relieved that she's alive. I really am. My conscience is clear now, not that it means that I want a relationship with my sister. There is so much to process. My brain feels like it's about to implode.

Luckily, it is saved from imminent doom by a knocking at the door. Using most of my energy to get myself vertical, I shuffle to the door and open it.

"Hey." Max, still disheveled, with his scruff more overgrown than usual and his curly hair definitely in the unruly phase.

I respond with a witty greeting. "Hey."

"I tried staying away. I know you told me you didn't want a relationship, but I think we could really have something."

"Max, I can't get into this right now. I'm not saying no. I'm not saying yes. I'm just saying I can't say right now." My brain is screaming a thousand thoughts, mostly centered on what Max was doing with my sister. I'm trying to figure out where to even start.

"I'm not asking you for a lifetime commitment right now. I'm just asking you to say yes to this." And he's kissing me. We're still standing in the doorway. I pull him closer, into the living room, letting the door close behind him. It doesn't feel quite as right as it did the first time we kissed. Something is off. His arms are around me, giving me the support I've been yearning for. Not breaking our embrace, we back up, half walking, half stumbling, until the my legs hit the arm of the couch. I fall backwards pulling Max down on top of me. His weight feels good on top of me, like a safety blanket. His lips and hands are good too. Not in the same way, of course. His touch overrides all the whirring in my brain, and suddenly it's all I can focus on. It's like the primitive part of my brain is driving now.

"Oh, Max. I thought you didn't want anything to do with me," I breathe. He's nibbling on my neck, and his hands are getting busy under my shirt. He pulls back, pushing himself up so that he's looking at me.

"How could you think that?"

"Because that day—I can't even remember what day it was now—when you were here with the guys working on the windows—you left. You said you weren't coming back."

He gets up. I feel a little awkward sprawled on my back, my legs apart where his body had been. Sitting up, I pat the couch for him to sit down next to me.

"I hated the thought that the guys saw you like that. I mean, I've never even gotten to see you like that."

"You know that was a mistake. I didn't know what the heck was going on in my house."

"I know, I overreacted."

"Yes you did, but then you got even worse."

"Well, you admitted you were fooling around with another guy. The one you had been in love with your whole life."

His tone makes me defensive. It's like he's jealous. I don't like it one bit. It's not cute. It bothers me. "I did not say I've been in love with him my whole life. I said he was my first love."

"It's the same difference. I mean, you flipped out that I'm still friends with Tracy even though we used to have sex."

"I flipped out because we—" I gesture between him and I, "almost had sex, you left, and then I didn't hear from you. The next time I see you, you're with another girl. And one that you admit you've had relations with in the past."

"How is that any better than you fooling around with the guy you've been pining for your entire life?"

"To be perfectly honest, until the day he showed up in my living room, I hadn't thought about him in ages. And, when he tried something, I said no. Which," I stand up, "I'm tempted to say to you right now." It's been a long day, and my nerves and patience are shot. Max is pissing me off. I don't find jealousy an attractive quality. Not at all. I sink back into the couch and close my eyes. "You know Max, it's been quite the day. I'm exhausted. Physically and mentally. I just really want to go to bed."

His arm snakes around my waist. "No, Max. That's not what I mean. I mean I just really want to go to sleep right now."

He leans in and kisses me softly on the cheek. "I understand, Sadie. I'll wait. I've been waiting. You're worth waiting for."

Although it's a sweet thing to say, it doesn't make a difference. All I can think about is my bed, as in a passing-out-and-sleeping-for-twelve-hours sort of way. "I need to go to sleep."

"Do you want me to stay?"

"That would be nice." I summon all my energy and stand up. I head to the bathroom, brush my teeth, and collapse on my bed as soon as I get into my room. A few minutes later, I feel the other side of the bed sag under Max's weight. His arms reach around me, pulling my body into his. It's comforting and warm, and I can no longer stay awake.

In the morning, things are awkward. I wouldn't have thought they would be. Lying there, trying to scoot away from Max's outstretched arms, I ponder what the change is. We fought. My distrust of his relationship with Tracy. His jealousy about Fitzy and then the crew seeing me in my skivvies (which, let's face it, is more embarrassing than sexual). Him not showing up at the wake. Him showing up at the funeral with Jenna. Jenna. Why does it all come back to her?

And what the hell was Max doing with Jenna in the first place?

I bolt upright. "Why were you with my sister?" My voice is loud and shrill and reverberates through the room, breaking the calm and silence of the early morning. I'm clutching the sheet to my chest. No matter that I'm wearing a t-shirt and shorts. I feel like I woke up naked next to a total stranger.

Max is groggy and slow to wake up. I nudge him with one hand, still clutching the sheet like a shield with the other.

"Huh?" He rolls over, still not awake.

I kick him. "Max. Max. MAX!"

"What?" It almost sounds like a whine. I guess he's not a morning person. I look at the clock. It is only five-thirty. Okay, I guess it's a little early, but this can't wait.

"Why did you bring Jenna to my dad's funeral?"

He sits up a little, leaning his head against my headboard. "Don't you think she should have been there?"

"Oh no you don't. I'm not falling for that again!" I slide out of bed. I sort of wish I had some other furniture in my room because I'm standing with nowhere to go.

"Falling for what?"

"You, answering every question with a question. Fitzy did it to me to get information when Jenna went missing." Things are clicking around my brain. Something does not make sense. Maybe it is too early to be having this discussion. It's too early to be human right now.

"I'm not Fitzy." It's almost a growl.

Now I'm on the defense. "I'm not saying you are. I'm just saying you need to answer my questions. How did you find Jenna? How did you know she wasn't dead? Where ... how ... I don't understand?"

He sighs, swinging his legs over the edge of the bed. Holding his head in his hands, he starts. "I thought it would help you."

"If you found Jenna?"

There's no answer, so I fill the silence.

"Well, I guess it helped, but I wasn't even under suspicion. I guess they didn't think she was dead at all, so I wasn't a murder suspect anymore. The evidence indicated that she was alive. I think I'm the only one who thought maybe her wrist slashing wasn't just an attention thing but a real suicide attempt."

"Didn't you know Jenna wasn't serious? Isn't that what you said? Isn't that why you kicked her out?"

I shrug. "I guess. I mean, I did think she was just acting out. Again. I didn't think she was truly suicidal. But then she disappeared. I've been so wracked with guilt. I mean, I should have done something."

"I think you should have trusted that your first instinct was right."

"How was I supposed to, when I had the police crawling all over the place? I was under surveillance and all. So, FYI, that's why Fitzy was around. Not because he was interested in me. He never has been and never will be. He was here because he was getting paid to be here."

Max stands up. His hair is unruly and his eyes are puffy. I'm sure I don't look much better. My hair is in that messy bun thing again. "I need some coffee. Do you want some?" I don't care if he wants any or not. I need some, or I won't be able to function much more.

After a quick bathroom pit stop, the coffee maker is calling my name, and I fumble around, trying to get it started. The four minutes until the pot is ready seem interminable. With the magic elixir finally brewed, I sit down at my kitchen table with a mug for myself and one poured for Max. He joins me and takes a sip, still not saying anything. The coffee it too hot to drink, so I just hold my mug and wait.

Then he starts, and I wish he had reserved his right to remain silent.

CHAPTER FORTY

"I, um, didn't exactly *find* Jenna."

"What do you mean, you didn't find her? How did you bring her back if you didn't find her?"

"I, um, ahhh, let me start at the beginning. That night that she was here, that she interrupted us ..."

"Yeah, the night she slashed her wrists in my brand new bathroom. I remember."

"When I left, I was a little nervous that something bad would happen. I mean, she's obviously unstable, and you were very upset, so I sat in my truck out front and waited for a little while."

"So you did think that I had it in me to kill her?"

"No, I was worried about what she would do to you. Then, finally, Jenna came running out. She was holding a towel to her arms, and was covered in blood. I thought she stabbed you. I hopped out of my truck and confronted her. She was on the verge of hysterics. She kept saying that she needed help. I finally got out of her that the blood was hers and not yours. I wanted to take her to the hospital."

"Oh, thank God you were there Max." Relief floods through me. "I've felt so guilty about letting her leave in that condition, especially in her condition. Even if I didn't help her for her, I should have helped her for the sake of her baby."

Max looks uncomfortable. Or should I say, more uncomfortable? He clears his throat before continuing. "So, she asked me to help her."

"Did you take her to the hospital?"

"No, um, that wasn't what she wanted. She told me she would explain everything, if I could just pick her up in a few hours."

"Pick her up? Where?"

"Um, Synder's Lake. By the gazebo."

"That's on the opposite side from where they found the car."

"She didn't say so at the time, but I've since figured out she ditched her car and then walked around to meet me."

I don't like where this is going. Not one little bit. "So then what?"

Max exhales, staring at the mug between his hands. He won't look at me, and I can't look away from him. "I picked her up and brought her to the B&B. She stayed there for a few days until I found another one for her about three hours away."

I feel as if he's punched me in the gut and stepped on my trachea all at the same time. I can't speak.

"Sadie." He finally looks up, those big blue eyes pleading with me. "Sadie, please say something."

I swallow, trying to find my voice. "What did you tell the police when they asked then? Certainly you knew I was under suspicion of killing Jenna. "

"Well, I knew you didn't do it. I wasn't concerned." He's so matter-of-fact. I'm livid. I jump up, slamming my hands down on the table. My hot coffee splashes onto my hand, and in some deep, recessed part of my brain, I register pain.

"You knew where she was all this time? Why didn't you say anything?"

He shrugs. "She asked me not to."

"Are you freakin' kidding me? She asked you not to? That's the best you can do?" I finally pull my hand back. I stomp over to the counter, grab a towel, and wipe up my mess on the table. A pink hue is spreading over the back of my hand. Great. Just what I need right now. Running the hand under cool water, I try to gain some composure.

Max is now standing behind me. I am so angry. Rage like I've never felt sears through my veins.

"Sadie, I thought I was helping you," he says quietly.

"Helping me? HELPING ME? You have got to be kidding me right now. HELPING ME? I thought my sister was dead and it was all my fault. I thought that she committed suicide, killing herself and her baby, and that I was the only one who could have stopped it. I have been laid off from my summer job because the customers thought I was a murderess. And I felt so guilty that I didn't—wouldn't—defend myself. And in the middle of all of this, my dad dies. So you, Mr. Knight in Shining Armor, decide to take my sister out of the picture like some deus ex machina."

"A what?"

"A deus ex machina. God by machine. It's a Latin term in literature for when they need a character to disappear, the gods swoop down from nowhere and cart the character away."

"I thought you taught American history?"

"It doesn't mean that I don't remember my literature from when I was in high school. Sister Mary Catherine was a very good teacher." Then I remember what brought this conversation up in the first place, and I am able to refocus my anger. "Dammit, Max, what the hell were you thinking?"

He shrugs again. So help me God, if he shrugs one more time, I am going to really lose it. "I thought it would help you. I mean, it's obvious that you two don't get along, and that you don't like her. She was always barging in on you, and it really seemed to upset you. I thought it was like a two-birds-with-one-stone thing."

"What do you mean by that?"

"Helping her leave town would help her, which she obviously needed, and it would help you by getting her out of your hair."

"So that was her plan all along? To leave town? Why? Why was she leaving and why was it such a rush?"

Max takes a step closer to me, but I hold up my hand to halt him. I want him nowhere near me. Max betrayed me. With my sister.

How has this happened to me? Again.

Obviously, it wasn't the same sort of betrayal, but it was still a betrayal. You know, maybe I had the right idea with swearing off love. I thought I was doing it so that I wouldn't hurt the other person. It turns out, I need to worry more about myself getting hurt.

And why, for someone with clairvoyance, do I keep getting blindsided by these things?

I want Max out now, but I have so many more questions for him. "Go sit down."

He does. I take a deep breath and sit back down as well. I can do this. It's like my first day teaching, facing that first class. I can't let him know how shaken I am on the inside. No, I need to fake it until I make it.

"So, you hid and harbored Jenna for a week. Did you get all warm and cozy with her?"

"Let's just say, I found out more about her than I ever wanted to."

"What was the plan again? I'm a little confused about this whole thing." My hands are folded on the table, my left hand still smarting from the burn. My back is ramrod straight. Slouching down in his chair, Max refuses to meet my eyes. I wait for him to start.

"I thought if I helped Jenna leave town, which is what she wanted, it would make your life better."

"So that's it?"

"Yeah, that's it." He looks up. I can tell by the look on his face that it is so not it. I cannot deal with any more deception.

"What? What else is there? What aren't you telling me?"

"I think you need to talk to your sister."

"She's the last person I want to talk to. I mean, after you of course."

Quietly he says, "I was just trying to help."

"You need to leave." My voice is eerily steady.

"Sadie, don't—"

"No, Max, you need to leave right now." I glance up at the clock. It's quarter after six. The fact that we're sitting together early in the morning finally pushes me over the edge. I snap, all steadiness gone. "Oh my God. You came here last night, expecting sex! You've been lying to me all this time! You *helped* my sister disappear! You withheld that knowledge. All that time, I was in agony because I thought I was responsible—oh my God! And then you kissed me! You spent the night in my bed! What the hell is wrong with you?"

"Sadie—"

"No, Max. I'm done. You're done. I ... you ... please leave. Now."

Without saying a word, he gets up and goes into the bedroom, where his shoes sit innocuously by the side of my bed. My bed! I can't believe I let him stay here! I almost slept with him. I guess I can be thankful that something stopped me and I didn't. That little instinct of mine saved me this time. Too bad it hasn't helped me more. I guess it did tell me not to get involved with Max. I should have listened.

Max walks with the slumped posture of a defeated man. I can't even believe he did this. He helped Jenna disappear. He kept her hidden all week. He brought her back to my dad's funeral.

"Wait! Before you go ..."

Max stops and turns expectantly, hope in his eyes.

"Why the funeral? Why did you bring her back for that?"

His shoulders sag again. "Sadie, I know you're angry, but you have to know I thought I was helping. I just wanted to help. I figured they would realize there was no crime and that she took off."

"So why the funeral?"

"You need to talk to Jenna to find that out. Let's just say I came into possession of knowledge that changed the picture."

"What? What did you find out?"

"You need to hear it from Jenna. It's not my place to say. I brought her back to make things right. You said you couldn't believe she wouldn't be there for it. I wanted to make things right. I hope you can believe me and forgive me."

Make things right

"Max, I don't know if I'll ever be able to do either." I pull open the door for him to leave.

"Sadie, please. You have to believe me."

"How? How can I? You knew I had major trust issues. You know what Rob did to me."

"But I thought you broke up with him. Isn't that what you said that morning at the B&B?"

"That's not the point. He still betrayed me. *With my sister.* Just like you did."

"I didn't mean to betray you. I was trying to help."

"Help? You thought this was helping? Bringing her back in the middle of the funeral. She knocked over my father's casket for Christ's sake! And then you come here, and try to sleep with me! What did you think I would do when I found out that you were harboring my sister?"

Max opens and closes his mouth, unable to say anything in his own defense. "You need to go, Max."

He steps past me and keeps going without looking back. He only stops walking when he realizes Fitzy is walking toward him.

Awesome.

CHAPTER FORTY-ONE

I hold the door open for Fitzy who enters without saying a word. It's revolving doors around here. One guy out, one guy in. Too bad that neither one is the guy for me.

"Did I come at a bad time?"

I sigh and head back into the kitchen. As much as I love my house, at this moment, it irks me that I have to walk from the front door, through the living room and dining room, before I can get into my kitchen. I need some coffee. My hand has had more than my mouth has. I look down and there's an angry red blotch on the back of my hand. It hurts something wicked. I grab a bag of peas out of the freezer and put it on the burn.

Sitting back down at the table, I take a sip of my coffee which is now cold. I don't care. I don't feel like heating it up. It's going to be another hot day. Fitzy looks at the cup left behind by Max.

"Is this seat taken?"

"Not anymore." And with that, I put my head down on the table.

"Everything all right?" Fitzy is fussing around. He clears the mug away and I hear him put it in the sink. I sort of expect him to start rooting around in the fridge like he did that first day, but instead he sits down.

"Peachy."

"Regretting your walk of shame?"

I lift my head. "For your information, I'm in my own home. I didn't have to do the walk of shame. And, not that's it any of your business, but nothing happened. Although I did find out some interesting information about Max and Jenna."

"I'm glad you brought that up. It's why I'm here."

That makes me sit up. "Yes, I know, Max helped Jenna leave town and kept her hidden."

"That's what he told you?"

I do not like his tone. Not at all. "Yes. Is there more I need to know?" I ask cautiously. In all honesty, I'm not sure that I want to know any more. I tell Fitzy that.

His face is totally shut down, and he's in business mode. Oh, this is not good. "Fitz, just spit it out and tell me what you need to. I don't know that things can get that much worse, but lay it on me."

"Sadie, things can get worse. And they're about to."

Great.

"I wanted to come here and tell you before you find out any other way. You have to try and stay calm though."

"When someone says that, it means they're going to tell you something so bad that there's no possible way you can remain calm."

A little smile spreads on his face. "Pretty much."

I take the bag of peas off my hand, examining my burn for a minute. It just feels numb right now. I wish I could put a bag of frozen peas on my brain and heart. Life would be a lot easier. "Okay, go."

He inhales slightly before beginning. "We brought Jenna in last night to find out what happened." I nod, encouraging him to go on. "She confirmed your story about slashing her wrists in your bathroom. She also confirmed that she was not trying to kill herself, but to do something that would force you to help her. So, you called that one."

"Yeah, being right is little consolation right now."

"She then said that when she left Max was still outside, and she convinced him to help her. She had him

~239~

meet her at the lake. In the meantime, she went home, grabbed some things, left her phone, and drove her car into the lake. She walked around and met up with Max. He took her to some bed and breakfast and put her up there for a few days."

"That's what he told me. I thought nothing was missing from her apartment?"

"I'll, um, get to that in a minute. Apparently, she had a small cache of money that she was able to take. I think her plan was to start over."

"Okay, all this I know. I mean, I'm surprised that she had some money set aside. She's never been that responsible, but maybe impending motherhood had changed her."

"No, it hadn't."

"Why do you say that? Did she have the baby? Did she lose the baby? Did she tell you what happened? Max wouldn't elaborate and told me I need to talk to Jenna."

"That's why I'm here. I don't want you to find this out from Jenna. I think you really would kill her if you could."

I sort of want to throw up when he says this. I know it's bad, but I can't imagine how much worse it can be than what she's already done.

"What is it then, Fitzy? Why can't you leave me alone? Why can't everybody just leave me alone?"

"I'm going to answer the first question now, but hold onto the other questions and ask me those again later."

I look at him expectantly. His face is all business but his green eyes betray a concern. The knot in my stomach tightens sharply.

"I'm here because there's information that you need to know. And when you find out, there's a high probability that you may go ballistic. And if you need to hit something, I want you to hit me. I promise, I'm okay with it. I don't want you going after Jenna."

"It's that bad?" I can't imagine what could possibly be any worse than what she's already done.

"It is. It took all my restraint not to hit her myself. So, I know you're going to want to, so hit me instead." He takes one more breath and then begins.

"Jenna needed to leave town. That's why she came to you. She thought you would help her, especially if she threatened her own life. She was quite upset when you didn't respond as she had hoped."

"But then Max, ever the knight in shining armor, came to her rescue."

"Yeah. He helped her get out of town. And I think that might have been the end of it, except Max discovered why Jenna needed to leave town so abruptly."

"And why exactly was that?"

"She was scheduled to have an ultrasound. Bernice and George Henderson were supposed to meet her there. That was when someone first got concerned that something had happened to her."

"Yeah, I'm fairly familiar with what happened next."

"The what, yes. The why, no. Jenna couldn't show up at that ultrasound with Bernice and George."

"Why not?"

Fitzy swallows. "Because Jenna wasn't pregnant."

Now I know why they call them bombshells. I can't even form words.

"It turns out, the whole pregnancy was a fabrication. She was never pregnant, and certainly never pregnant by Robin Henderson."

My mouth is dry and my tongue feels about ten times too large for my mouth. I try to swallow. "Wha ... what? I don't understand." My hands are gripping my mug, knuckles white.

"She faked the whole pregnancy. It turns out, which we sort of suspected, and this should make you feel better, Jenna and Robin did not have an affair. They weren't engaged. It was all big fat lie."

"What do you mean?"

"Jenna and Robin weren't together. Apparently, after you broke up with him that night, he went to a bar on his way home. Jenna was there and was too inebriated to drive. He was trying to be the nice guy in giving her a ride home. Jenna asked Rob what he was doing alone in a bar. I guess he confided in her that he had bought an engagement ring for you but chickened out on proposing, and then, for whatever reason, you ended things. She asked to see the ring, and he showed it to her. He was driving her home at that point. She, apparently, was bothered about at how upset Robin was over you, and she tried to seduce him."

"By whipping it out of his pants?"

"I guess. He got caught in the moment, and car met tree. Jenna said she needed to come up with a cover story for what happened, so she slipped the ring on her finger, and you know the rest."

Silence fills the room as I'm in shock. "You mean it was all a lie?"

"All of it. Robin didn't have an affair with your sister. Apparently she's in some financial trouble. She thought she could get money out of Rob's parents if they thought she was having his baby. The stash she had in her apartment was actually Rob's money."

"His rainy day fund." I always thought it was stupid that he kept a pile of cash around for emergencies.

"She had been allowed to take some mementos from his house. Apparently, that's one of the things she took. And, when she left her place, she packed regular clothes, not her maternity ones. It took us a while to realize that."

"She wasn't pregnant."

"No, because she and Rob were never together. She was planning on selling the ring."

"He ... didn't propose?"

"No, the ring was for you."

"But ... why?"

"Why what?"

"Why didn't he propose to me?"

~242~

"Didn't you break up with him?"

"Well, yeah, but ..."

"What would you have done if he proposed?"

"I'd probably have said yes." I think about it. If he had popped the question before the bat dive-bombed us, I would have said yes. We might even be married now. And while we'd be together, I think in some ways, I'd be more alone than I am now. I would have married Rob, and it would have been terrible.

"So is there any comfort in knowing he wasn't unfaithful?"

I think about it. I've had so many trust issues since then. And those trust issues contributed n to my erratic behavior, which led Max to help Jenna. Oh my God, how did this get so messed up? I sit there, unable to move. My limbs feel heavy and my brain is moving like a tilt-a-whirl. I can't move. I can't do anything.

It was all a lie.

CHAPTER FORTY-TWO

I know why Fitzy offered to let me hit him. I have never felt anything like I do in this moment. It was all a lie.

The web of lies spun by my sister has turned my life upside down. I'm immobile in my kitchen chair for a while. Fitzy finally leaves. I think he may have said something to me, but I didn't hear him. Eventually I get up, take a shower, and go back to bed. I repeat this pattern, shower optional, for about three days. I text people in response, just so they know I'm alive. I don't want to talk to anyone. I don't want to do anything. And so I don't.

On the fourth day, I actually make it to the shower. After I blow dry my hair, I dress in denim shorts and a blue tank top with a cream-colored crocheted tank over it. It doesn't matter what I look like on the outside. Nothing will touch how black I feel on the inside. I slide my feet into my sandals, grab my purse and keys, and head over to Mom's. I don't think she'll be able to relate to my feelings on this, but I know she'll be feeling equally bad, just for different reasons.

I'm not wrong. Her eyes are all puffy, and she's aged about ten years since I saw her at the funeral. The funeral. God, how can all this be happening at one time? She pulls me into her arms, and finally the tears start to flow. Hot and angry and seemingly endless.

"How could she, Mom? How could she do this to me?"

"I don't know. I'm so ashamed."

I can't even imagine what it must feel like to be the parent of someone who does something like this. Immediately, the Hendersons pop into my head. "Oh God, Mom! What about the Hendersons? This is going to kill them. They thought they were going to have a little piece of Rob forever. It's like they're going to lose him all over again!"

"Oh, those poor people! I don't even know what to say. And now that it's come out that Rob and Jenna weren't together, it was her acting so, so, so crudely that caused the accident. She's responsible for his death."

And while in theory, she is to blame (Rob a little too—he could have pulled over before, well, you know), I know the real cause. Me. Out of all the lies, one truth remains. I'm responsible for Rob's death. If I hadn't insisted on the romantic weekend. If I hadn't lost the baby and grown distant. If I hadn't freaked out on him about the bat, he never would have been in that car with Jenna. Then, the feeling that I would never speak to him again. Yup, it was me. I caused it.

I truly hated the thought that he had been seeing my sister, but in many ways it made his death easier to process. Believing he cheated on me kept me from questioning my decision to end our relationship, and it enabled me not to spend too much time mourning Rob. I am a truly terrible person.

"Where is she?"

"Um, she's in a treatment facility."

"A treatment facility? What do you mean?"

"She went away to some sort of rehab place or something. She's obviously not stable. There's something very wrong with her, and she's hoping to be able to get her life figured out."

"You know I'm done with her, right?"

Mom lets out a sigh. "I know you are, and you have every right to be. I wish it weren't so, but I understand. I don't know what to do about her. This is near unforgiveable. It's going to take a lot of work to get any sort of trust or relationship back. And that's a hard pill to swallow when it's your own child."

"Mom, there's something I need to tell you." I fill her in about the miscarriage and how Rob and I were not meant for each other. It feels good to come clean with her.

"Sadie, I have something for you. Jenna gave me a letter for you. I know you're done with her, but please, for me, just read it. You never know, it may give you the closure you're looking for."

I don't want to read it. I crumple it up and then quickly unfold it again, all three pages. The sight of the loose-leaf paper brings me back to our childhood, when it was Jenna and me against the world. She owes me this explanation. Her handwriting is no better than when we were kids. I walk out to the back yard to read the letter by myself. I sit on top of the picnic table in the farthest corner of the yard.

Dear Sadie,

I know you hate me. You've made that abundantly clear. Don't worry, I hate myself too. I know what I did was terrible. It's inexcusable. I wish I knew why I acted like this. Actually, I know why I started hating you. And I'm starting to see that it had nothing to do with you. When I was 12, something happened. I had been out in the woods with David McHale. I was amazed that a 15-year-old would be interested in me. So when he suggested he give me my first kiss, I thought it would be so romantic. Turns out he wanted more, and he took it. When I came home that day, you were so busy talking on the phone that you didn't even stop to say hello. You didn't notice that I was different. For a while after, I was in shock, not knowing how to process what had happened to me. How I had been violated.

So I kept it hidden. Almost as a badge of honor of how I was stronger than you. But then, you were there. Still perfect. Still pure. And I was jealous of you. Of that thing you had that had been stolen from me. The jealousy and pain consumed me until I was jealous of everything about you. Of your looks, your hair, your brains, your sense of humor. Jealous of how close you were with Dad. Jealous of how proud Mom is of you. With me, I've always felt that I was an afterthought. The 'woops' that just kept on woopsing. That I deserved what happened to me.

I know I've been a terrible sister. If I had me for a sister, I wouldn't want one either. I've taken every chance I had to beat you. To prove that I'm better. To make myself better. But I've known all along, and I suspect that everyone else knows too, you were always, and will always be the better person.

Damn, I wish I could be like you, but I'm not. I'm not kind or selfless. I'm not giving. I want back what was taken from me. I want everything I don't have. I want it all for me, and you stood in my way. So I took every chance I had to take things from you. In all this time, I never thought about doing the things in my life that would make me happy. I only thought about doing the things what would make you unhappy. It's no way to live, and no wonder I ended up where I am. Sometimes I think maybe I would be better off not being here, but I'm too selfish to even do that.

When the car crashed, I panicked. I knew it was my fault. When it first started, Rob kept telling me to stop. I wouldn't listen. I wanted to be exciting and daring and do things that my goody-two-shoes sister wouldn't do. I thought if people thought Rob and I were together, they would be less mad at me for the accident. The ring was in my pocket. He gave it to me to see, and I pocketed it. I'm not going to lie, I was planning on stealing it. I needed the money, so I was going to sell the ring. It was an ugly ring. Well not ugly, but certainly not you.

I think that might be one reason why I started doing what I did to Rob. I knew that you and he weren't right for each other. I mean, he didn't even realize you only wear silver! And, he was asking my advice about you. If he really knew you, he would have known to talk to Therese, not me, about you. He should have known that we weren't close. I sort of rationalized that I was doing you a favor. I do a lot of rationalizing.

Because people thought we were engaged, I got to go through Rob's stuff. I found his journal and of course, kept it. I was shocked to learn about the miscarriage. I guess that's what gave me the idea for the pregnancy thing. I wanted to be successful at the one thing you had failed at. That thought consumed me, and I didn't think the rest through. Plus, I thought I would get some more money, like benefits or something. When the Hendersons got involved, I didn't know what to do. If Max hadn't come along that night and helped me out, I don't know what I would have done. I know I need to make amends to them as well.

I know you won't believe it, but I'm trying to work on becoming a decent human being. I'm trying to be better. I'm also thinking about what I want in life. It has nothing to do with you. I need to have a life separate from you for a while, so I can figure out who I am, other than Sadie's sister. I know that won't be hard for you to stay away from me, but it will be hard for me not to want to be in your life. I am consumed with envy because I want to be you. I know it's not healthy, and I'm working on it.

I don't know if you'll ever be able to forgive me, but I hope someday you will. My door will always be open for you.

Sadie, I'm sorry you lost the baby. You would and will make a great mother. I'm sorry for the lying and cheating and deception. I'm sorry for not being your sister.

Jenna

CHAPTER FORTY-THREE

What am I supposed to do with this? I mean, it's obvious that Jenna has significant problems. She was raped. Violated. At such a young age. I wonder if she ever told my parents. It would explain why my mom is so protective and excusing of her. But that was such a long time ago. She's turned my life upside down. She's responsible for Rob's death. She's broken his parents' hearts for a second time. What do I do?

Before I can come up with an answer, because, let's face it, it might take me months to come up with an answer, I'm interrupted. Saved by the irritating cop.

"Hey."

"Hey."

Fitzy sits down on the picnic table with me. We're sitting on the top of the table, feet on the bench, elbows resting on our knees. I can see the birdfeeder in the neighbor's yard and am riveted by the comings and goings there. The day is hot and humid already, and I know I won't be able to stay out here for as long as I want.

"You're mom said I'd find you out here."

"Yeah, trying to solve all the world's problems. You know, the usual. What are you doing here?"

"Trying to make sure you're okay."

"Oh, yeah. Peachy-freakin'-keen."

"I've been worried about you."

I look over. Fitzy must have come from working out or something. He's in hunter green gym shorts and a heather gray t-shirt that's not nearly fitted enough. It's odd to see him out of his detective duty dress shirt and pants. "Why?"

"Because I care about you, Sadie. I don't like seeing you hurt."

"Then you picked a bad year to become reacquainted with me, since that's how it's been all year. I don't see it improving, either."

"It's only July. There's still time."

"Tomorrow's August first. Not that much time. I go back to school in a few weeks. My house isn't where I want it to be, and I've lost my handyman."

"Trouble in paradise?" He gives me a little nudge with his shoulder.

"There is no paradise. I can't be with Max. He's too intense. I mean, so intense he deceived me. I mean, I rationally can understand why he thought it was a good thing, but to me it's still deception. I have trust issues. Especially after Rob, but now everything's all mixed and muddled, and I don't know what to think. And so here I sit, trying to solve the world's problems. I think they'd be easier to solve than my own."

"Isn't the news that Rob didn't cheat on you a good thing?"

"Of course it is. But it doesn't change the fact that I am now insecure about that. And it doesn't change the fact that I'm just as responsible for his death as my sister is."

Fitzy starts laughing. "That's a good one."

I give him a quick jab with my shoulder. "Don't laugh, I'm being serious."

He tries to pull his face into an expression resembling seriousness. He's almost successful. "Okay, tell me how you killed Rob."

I sigh before beginning. At least he already knows about the visions and stuff. So I tell him. About how the last few times I had those premonitions, people ended up dying.

"Sadie, you can't think you kill people."

"How am I supposed to think anything else? I make a comment about someone dying, or about never speaking to them again, and—WHAM—they're dead. If that's not my fault, then whose is it?"

"It's the universe. You can no more control peoples' lives and deaths than you can control the wind. You have a gift. A clairvoyance. Actually, I think you may also have a claircongnizance."

"What the hell is claricog ... whatever you said?"

"Claircognizance. It's the ability to know something without prior knowledge, memory, or experience. You just know it and it is. You can know things without trying. Like an unexplained insight."

"What's clairvoyance then?"

"That's the ability to see something. A vision. Like seeing a number or a flash of something."

"That happens too."

"Really? Actual visions? Can you explain one?"

I think back. I've had two regarding Fitzy in the past few weeks. "The day you were at my house and they found Jenna's car."

"Yeah, what about it?"

"When you stepped out to take the call about the car, I had a vision. I was sitting in my kitchen, not facing the window. In my head, I could see you, in a specific spot on my driveway, talking on the phone and kicking rocks around. When I looked out the window, that's exactly what you were doing."

"Oh, wow, I was in one of your visions?" I think he's proud of it.

"More than one," I mumble. Unfortunately, we're sitting awfully close together, and he has good hearing.

"More than one? What was the other?"

I don't want to tell him about my dream. On the other hand, maybe talking about it will help me work it out. So I tell him. I tell him about the wedding and my dad, his shirtless appearance and the matching tattoos. Then I tell him about the groom and my dad's message, and finally waking up at the instant my dad passed away. "So I knew when it happened, and just waited for the phone call."

"That's so weird."

"Gee, thanks. Every girl likes to be called weird."

"No, I mean how it happens. It's cool."

"No, it's not. Not when people start to look at you funny when you say a poor sixteen year-old is going to wind up getting himself killed only to have it happen the next day. Plus, that dream, I don't know what to make of it."

"What do you mean by that? Seems like your dad was making sure you would be okay when he left, and he wanted you to know he's always going to be with you, even though he's not with you."

"Sadly, I completely understand that sentence. What I mean is the whole wedding thing. It seemed to me in the dream that you were not the right choice, and that Max was."

"Was Max even in your dream?"

"Yes. No. I don't know. I never actually saw his face."

"So you don't know it was Max."

"No, but I thought it could be. Now, it's abundantly clear to me that Max is not the right choice. I wonder if I was so reticent about getting involved with him because I somehow knew he wasn't right. And if it's not right, I'd be settling again, just like with Rob."

"And your dad told you ...?"

"To do the right thing." And then it dawns on me. In the dream, mostly naked Fitzy is the one that told me it could be right. I turn and look at Fitzy.

"Are you the right thing?"

"I can't tell you that, Sadie. You have to feel it."

I close my eyes and search deep within. We're sitting in the exact same spot where we'd been seventeen years ago. I let my mind go, and suddenly I know. Without a doubt. Because it just is.

I open my eyes and look at him. I can still see the boy I fell in love with when I was nine. "You're supposed to be Jacob."

A small smile dances across his lips. His lips look heavenly and sinful all at the same time. "What's that supposed to mean?"

"In the book, *Twilight*. Bella has to choose between Edward and Jacob. On paper, Jacob is the better choice, since being with him won't result in her death, most likely. But she chooses Edward, even though he's a vampire."

"And I'm Jacob?"

"Yeah, I mean, I thought you were. I thought you were the super hot and ripped best friend who's a comfort, and would be a great partner, but for some reason, *it's* not there. Maybe I had it all wrong ..." I trail off.

"At least I'm not a vampire."

"No, you're a werewolf."

"Well, now you're simply being ridiculous. Everyone knows that the werewolf gets the girl. It's why shifters are so popular."

"A, are we even having this conversation, and B, how do you know about shifters?"

"Michele reads a lot of that stuff. Sometimes, especially on stakeouts, things get boring. I've read some of the books on her Kindle. I mean, out of desperation, of course."

"Of course. Anything good?"

"I think Michele's favorite was *A Shift in the Water* by Patricia D. Eddy. I'm currently reading *Into the Light* by Tami Lund. It's pretty steamy."

"I'll have to look into them." I smile at him. "You know, this is where we sat at my graduation party."

"I know." His smile, those lips, are clouding my brain.

"I don't want to fall again."

"I promise I'm going to catch you."

"I know you will."

And with that, I close the miniscule distance between us. This kiss is sweet but quickly turns hungry. I don't know that I will ever get enough of this man. I know that my thoughts won't harm him, and my visions won't kill him. I'm not scared that he's going to cheat. I know that Jenna will not come between us. I know that this is not settling. I know that this is meant to be.

It's the right thing.

EPILOGUE

"Sadie, you need to get a move on. People will be here soon."

"I can't get up. I'm spent."

"You have to. Now."

Hauling myself up, I look at Fitzy. Somehow, he's managed to shower and get his pants on. He hasn't put his shirt on yet, and his hair is still wet. Damn, what a fine looking man. "This is all your fault you know. I'm going to be late because of you."

"How is this my fault?"

"If you hadn't ravaged me senseless, I'd have been showered and dressed already."

"Technically, then, it's your fault for being so damn irresistible." He leans over, gives me a quick kiss, and says, "I'll go put the food out. You, get in the shower."

I smack his firm rear end as he turns and leaves. "You know, you're sexy when you're bossy!"

"Sadie, don't distract me again. Get up!"

I haul myself out of bed and dash into the bathroom. People are supposed to be here around seven, and it's almost six-thirty. A quick dash through the shower and I'm ready to get dressed.

We're closing out the year with a vintage-themed party to go with my house. If you had asked me five months ago if I'd be pouring myself into an authentic 1960s-era rose-copper strapless dress that hugs my curves like a second skin, I'd have called you crazy. I know I'm mixing eras as I roll back the front sections of my hair into victory rolls like a 1940s pin-up model. But I don't care. Gold peep-toe slingbacks and a large flower behind my ear complete the look. I turn and look at my body in the mirror. Not too shabby.

Being with Fitzy has some advantages. I mean, besides the obvious. He works really hard to keep fit and has even gotten me into it as well. I like that we're working out together, but I like the way my body looks and feels even more. The best part of tonight is that I'm wearing this fitted dress with no Spanx!

In late fall, my dad's estate was settled. Not much changed, except the house was fully in my mom's name. Brady and Tina got their share, and we haven't heard from them since. They came up with some cock-and-bull excuse as to why they couldn't see Mom on Christmas. I don't expect to hear from them again until the money runs out. I got a nice little chunk of cash. I spent some of it finishing up the house. Max was kind enough to recommend some reliable people to me. I still feel bad about how things ended. I told him that I was over what he did with Jenna, and to some extent, I am. I didn't want to get into the whole thinking I was going to kill him and claircognizance thing. It sounds too weird, even for me. The rest of the money, I put into savings. I stopped tutoring, at least for this year. It turns out having an attentive and active boyfriend means you have a lot less free time in the evenings. Who knew?

Jenna is living with my mom. She is going to all sorts of support groups and working with a counselor. I think she is considering going back to school to become a counselor herself. The Hendersons filed a civil suit against her for wrongful death. Rather than drag things out, she offered them her entire inheritance. She gave up her apartment and is working fulltime in another clothing store. I rarely see her with new clothes or things, so I think she must owe the Hendersons a lot more. I haven't asked. We have a tenuous peace. I don't know that I can or will ever trust her again. Part of me understands what happened now. Part of my heart breaks for what my sister went through all alone. But another part of me is having trouble forgiving. I'm working on it. I can be in the same room with her, at least for the sake of Mom. I didn't invite her tonight. I'm not letting myself feel guilty about it. We're not there yet. Maybe someday, but not yet.

The doorbell rings, and Fitzy answers it. He's dashing in a white shirt and skinny, rat-pack era tie. Hell, that man is dashing in everything and nothing. Focus.

Therese and Andy are the first ones in, followed closely by Michele and Officer Richards, who does actually have a first name—Ben. And no, not like in The Running Man. Don't ask him that. He hates it. Michele and Ben make a weirdly cute couple. She smiles all the time and is actually nice. Two more couples from Fitzy's work, and two more from mine, make up our little fête.

The dining room table hosts a bevy of appetizers and finger foods. Each couple has added a dish or two, and the table is at capacity. Andy is already in the kitchen, working as a self-appointed bartender for the evening. I think he loves it, and he makes some mean martinis.

The night is going well, and everyone is raving about the house. I am very proud of it. But mostly, I'm happy. Despite all the events of this year, even finding gray eyebrow hairs, I'm happy. I have a job I like, teaching a subject I love. I have a house that I refurbished with my own two hands (and a little help from my friends). I'm surrounded by good friends and the man I love. I wish my dad could be here to see this, but I sort of know he is. Don't ask me how, I just know.

About ten 'til midnight, Fitzy grabs me by the waist as I'm coming out of the bathroom. He pulls me into the bedroom and kisses me long and hard. If not for the din coming from the other side of the house, I think I would have forgotten that we had a crowd of company.

"Have I told you how incredibly sexy you look?" he growls as he's nibbling on my neck and his hand is reaching up my hemline.

"Not in the last ten minutes."

His mouth starts moving down to my neckline, which is low. "Fitzy, stop. We have guests." I start to push him away but his tongue is doing something wonderful, not to mention what's going on beneath my skirt, and I lose strength in my arms. Okay, they won't miss us for a few minutes.

"I guess you're right. We should go out and tell our guests the news." He pulls back from me, leaving me feeling alone and far away.

"Aww, why'd you stop? And what news?"

"The news that I asked you to marry me and you said yes."

"What?"

In the blink of an eye, Fitzy is down on one knee. He produces a small, velvet box, which contains an Asscher-cut ring with a halo of diamonds surrounding the main stone. A delicate fleur-de-lis swirls up each side to the stones. It is the ring I saw in my dream. It is perfect. It is me.

"Are you ready to do the right thing?"

"Yes, yes! A hundred times yes!"

He slides the ring onto my left hand and pulls me into a deep, desirous kiss. "Now can we tell them the news?"

Fitzy takes my hand and leads me out. Our friends are standing there, all with champagne. They erupt in a cheer as soon as we exit. Fitzy raises our hands, like a victorious boxer. I can't help but smile.

"Oh, we have to call my mom and tell her!"

"She knows." Fitzy pulls me in and holds onto me tight. "I told her I was going to marry you and asked her permission."

"When? How long have you been planning this? Is that why we had to have a party?"

"No, we had to have a party to celebrate this wonderful year."

"This year was terrible."

"Not all of it."

I kiss him. "You're right. Not all of it."

"I asked your mom that day we sat on the picnic table, before I went out to talk to you."

"The picnic table? But that was before I even knew we belonged together."

"You're not the only one who knows things."

On the TV, the ball drops. Our guest pair up, kissing in the New Year. Hugs are passed around freely. Therese is already planning my wedding. I'll wait until tomorrow to tell her my dress will be gold, my roses will be pale pink, and my dad will be walking me toward the man I love, if only in my very full heart.

THE END

ACKNOWLEDGMENTS

Michele Vagianelis, my best friend and sounding board, you make all of this possible. Thank you for your brilliance.

I saw a Facebook meme recently that said, "Behind every successful woman is a tribe of other successful women who have her back." I have found this to be 100 percent true. My beta team is the best: Becky Monson, Jayne Denker, Celia Kennedy, Tracy Krimmer, Aven Ellis, Cahren Morris, and Heidi Simon. Thank you for all your insight, feedback, and suggestions. My online writing groups, the Writing Wenches and ChickLitChatHQ continue to give me the strength, encouragement, and wisdom to make this possible.

Becky Monson once again put together a beautiful cover for me. This time it wasn't nearly as painful. Oh, Becky—I'm still waiting for those cookies.

Wendy Nagel, thank you for being my friend and making me stretch to write a better book. Together, we got this (and there is a masseuse in our future).

Thank you Karen Pirozzi for being my editor extraordinaire. I'm trying to reduce your red-pen carpal tunnel. I really am.

My family continues to be my strength and my rock. Mom, Dad, Patrick, Jake, and Sophia, you make this all possible and worthwhile.

And to my fans, thank you. I never, ever imagined that my words would inspire, touch, or help anyone. Thank you for your support. I hope you enjoy this.

ABOUT THE AUTHOR

Telling stories of resilient women, Kathryn Biel hails from upstate New York and is a spouse and mother of two wonderful and energetic kids. In between being Chief Home Officer and Director of Child Development of the Biel household, she works as a school-based physical therapist. She attended Boston University and received her Doctorate in Physical Therapy from The Sage Colleges. After years of writing countless letters of medical necessity for wheelchairs, finding increasingly creative ways to encourage the government and insurance companies to fund her clients' needs, and writing entertaining annual Christmas letters, she decided to take a shot at writing the kind of novel that she likes to read. Her musings and rants can be found on her personal blog, Biel Blather. She is the author of *Good Intentions* (2013), *Hold Her Down* (2014), *I'm Still Here* (2014), and *Jump, Jive, and Wail* (2015).

If you've enjoyed this book, please help the author out by leaving a review on Amazon and Goodreads. A few minutes of your time makes a huge difference to an indie author!

Connect with Kathryn:
Amazon Author Central:
http://www.booklinker.net/mylinks.php
Blog: http://kathrynbiel.blogspot.com
Facebook: https://www.facebook.com/kathrynrbiel
Twitter: https://twitter.com/KRBiel
Goodreads: http://bit.ly/KRBgoodreads
E-mail: kathrynbiel@outlook.com

43967677R00161

Made in the USA
Charleston, SC
10 July 2015